"Who are you?"

"What the—" He swung ar̶o̶u̶n̶d̶ ̶a̶s̶ ̶s̶h̶e̶ ̶a̶p̶p̶r̶o̶a̶c̶h̶e̶d̶, his hand reaching instinctively for his sword hilt.

"Up here." A pair of brown leather boots, swiftly followed by a faded and old-fashioned green kirtle, launched themselves out of one of the sycamore trees lining the side of the road, plummeting downward through the foliage before landing neatly on the gravel in front of him.

Quickly, Ben removed his hand from his sword hilt, simultaneously impressed by the jump and annoyed at himself for having been caught off guard. Whoever the woman was, she would have made an excellent spy. Judging by the thick branch she was clutching in one hand, half hidden behind her skirts, she wasn't particularly pleased to see him there, either. If the ferocity of her expression was anything to go by, she wouldn't have any qualms about clubbing him with the stick.

"I asked you a question." She jutted her chin out when he didn't immediately answer. "Who are you?"

"Sir Bennet Thorne at your service, my lady."

Author Note

I never intended to write a Tudor-set story. To be honest, the whole era makes me think of gloomy corridors, danger, betrayal and really bad royal husbands—definitely not the stuff of romance. But then I went to see *Six* with my ten-year-old daughter and she showed an interest in history! We watched documentaries about Henry VIII together! And I started to wonder if maybe I'd been a little hasty. So I decided to embrace the gloomy corridors and danger and write something a little different from my usual romantic comedies: a mystery romance with a reclusive heroine and a hero with absolutely nothing in common with Henry!

I also included a cameo from the teenage Elizabeth I as a tribute to one of my favorite books as a child, Jean Plaidy's *The Young Elizabeth*. It's out of print now, but it was so evocative that it left me with an abiding interest in and love of history.

My daughter would still have preferred me to write about Anne Boleyn, but hopefully this will do when she's older.

A Wedding to Protect Her Fortune

———

JENNI FLETCHER

ISBN-13: 978-1-335-59616-1

Recycling programs for this product may not exist in your area.

A Wedding to Protect Her Fortune

Copyright © 2024 by Jenni Fletcher

For questions and comments about the quality of this book, please contact us at CustomerService@Harlequin.com.

TM and ® are trademarks of Harlequin Enterprises ULC.

Harlequin Enterprises ULC
22 Adelaide St. West, 41st Floor
Toronto, Ontario M5H 4E3, Canada
www.Harlequin.com

Printed in U.S.A.

Jenni Fletcher was born in the north of Scotland and now lives in Yorkshire with her husband and two children. She wanted to be a writer as a child but became distracted by reading instead, finally getting past her first paragraph thirty years later. She's had more jobs than she can remember but has finally found one she loves. She can be contacted on Twitter, @jenniauthor, or via her Facebook author page.

Books by Jenni Fletcher

Harlequin Historical

Cinderella's Deal with the Colonel
"Secrets of the Queen's Lady"
in *Tudor Christmas Tidings*
"The Christmas Runaway"
in *Snow-Kissed Proposals*
A Marriage Made in Secret

Regency Belles of Bath

An Unconventional Countess
Unexpectedly Wed to the Officer
The Duke's Runaway Bride
The Shopgirl's Forbidden Love

Highland Alliances

The Highlander's Tactical Marriage

Sons of Sigurd

Redeeming Her Viking Warrior

Secrets of a Victorian Household

Miss Amelia's Mistletoe Marquess

Visit the Author Profile page
at Harlequin.com for more titles.

For Dave and Rosie

Chapter One

Somerset, England, 1546

So this was Cariscombe Hall… Sir Bennet Thorne drew rein halfway along the narrow dirt road and considered the house before him. Meanwhile, the house, with its thick stone walls, squat corner towers and narrow arrow loops, seemed to consider him back.

It was old, probably a couple of centuries older than his own house, Draycote Manor, but built to last. Strong. Defensible. Uncomfortable. Unfashionable. A hulking grey relic of a past era buried deep in the forest like an outlaw trying to hide from the outside world. He was surprised that none of its previous owners had thought to tear the place down and replace it with something newer and grander, to add a few windows at least, though he had to admit the building had its own kind of charm. There was something indomitable and defiant about all of those turrets and buttresses, a resolute quality that appealed to him.

Strangely enough, he liked it.

Stranger still was the fact that this was the first time he'd ever seen the hall up close. Despite being born and raised on—then finally inheriting—a neighbouring estate, he knew almost as little about Cariscombe as he did the surface of the moon. Its recently deceased owner, Robert Flemming, had been a near recluse, friendly enough on the few occasions they'd met in town or at court, but always with a certain reserve. There had never been any entertainments or invitations to visit.

In that regard, nothing had changed. Ben wasn't visiting today either. He was only there as a favour, bearing a message he didn't understand, but that he ought to make haste and deliver. The sender had told him it was urgent, a matter of the utmost importance, even if it was hard to see why. Besides, he had his own home to get back to and he'd delayed that visit for long enough.

He set his jaw, about to ride on when a woman's voice floated out of thin air.

'Who are you?'

'What the—?' He swung round in his saddle, one hand reaching instinctively for his sword hilt, the other gripping his reins as his mare gave a startled whinny.

'Up here.' A pair of brown leather boots, swiftly followed by a faded and old-fashioned green kirtle, launched themselves out of one of the sycamore trees lining the side of the road, plummeting downwards through the foliage before landing neatly on the gravel in front of him.

Hastily, he removed his hand from his sword hilt, simultaneously impressed by the jump and annoyed at himself for having been caught off guard so completely. Whoever the woman was, she would have made an excellent spy. He hadn't noticed a single flicker of movement, nor heard so much as a twig snap, though she'd obviously been watching him the whole time he'd been staring at the house. Judging by the thick branch she was clutching in one hand, half hidden behind her skirts, she wasn't particularly pleased to see him there either. If the ferocity of her expression was anything to go by, she wouldn't have any qualms about clubbing him with it, if necessary.

'I asked you a question.' She jutted her chin out when he didn't immediately answer. 'Who are you?'

'Sir Bennet Thorne, at your service, lady.' He lifted his round-brimmed cap and bowed in the saddle, though he kept his eyes fixed on hers, too intrigued to look away. She had a distinctively feline appearance, with a pretty, heart-shaped face, accentuated by a widow's peak in the centre of her forehead. Her large hazel-green eyes were half obscured by the cloud of russet-red hair worn in loose disarray over her shoulders. Unwed then, though she was clearly of an age for marriage, eighteen or nineteen perhaps, despite the unladylike addition of several leaves and twigs in her hair.

'I've never heard of you.' Her tone suggested she didn't want to now either.

'I'm a friend.' He held his hands up, palms outward. 'I'm here to speak with Mistress Flemming.'

'Why? What do you want with my mother?'

'Mother?' He couldn't keep the surprise from his voice. 'You mean you're Annis?'

'Yes.' She nodded jerkily, as if she were unsure about the wisdom of admitting her identity. 'What of it?'

'You're not what I expected.'

'What did you expect?'

He lifted his shoulders, already regretting the comment. In truth, Annis Flemming was as much of a mystery as the house she lived in, for all that she was only five or six years younger than him and they'd grown up on neighbouring estates. He'd always been led to believe that she was sickly, far too sickly for guests. Her own father had told him so, and yet the fiery-looking woman standing before him now seemed perfectly, even robustly healthy. Capable of climbing trees and jumping out of them, in fact, but then some people grew out of childhood maladies. Perhaps she'd been a late bloomer or he'd simply misunderstood Robert Flemming's words. Only somehow, he didn't think so...

'Forgive me, lady. I spoke out of turn.' He gestured towards the south, deciding to change the subject before her scowl deepened any further. 'We're neighbours. I own Draycote Manor. I'm rarely there these days, but I knew your father a little. I was grieved to hear of his passing.'

'Thank you.' Her belligerent expression wavered, almost seeming to relent before hardening again. 'Is that all you came to say? Because if it is, I can share your condolences with my mother. There's no need for you to ride any further.'

Ben lifted an eyebrow, taken aback by her brusqueness. Robert Flemming had always been the epitome of civility and good manners. Clearly his daughter hadn't followed his example. Now that he knew who she was, however, he could see the physical resemblance. Her russet curls and the widow's peak ought to have given her identity away.

'That's not all.' He put his hat back on, deciding he'd tarried long enough, particularly in such hostile company. 'I also have a message for her.'

'From?'

'Another friend.'

'What friend?'

'One who prefers not to give their name.'

'I don't like mysteries.' Her eyes flashed and then narrowed. 'Give me the message and I'll pass it on.'

'Unfortunately, I promised to deliver it in person. I gave my word.' He dropped his gaze to her skirts. 'Stick or no stick.'

She stiffened, a crimson flush spreading up her neck and over her cheeks, bringing out the red in her hair until she almost seemed to glow like a beacon in front of him.

'A stick may be no match for a sword, but it could still hurt.' She brought the makeshift weapon out from behind her legs, her knuckles clenched tight around it.

Ben lifted an eyebrow, looking her up and down and then up again, faintly unnerved by her combative demeanour. Some degree of suspicion was natural, he could even admire her refusal to back down, but she struck him as overly defiant. What was she so afraid of?

'I'm not going to fight you, lady.'

'Then that gives me the advantage, don't you think?'

'Not if I ride around you.' He sighed as she immediately reached a hand out to grasp his bridle. 'All right, we'll do this your way. Give me some way to prove myself.'

'You say that you knew my father.' There was a note of challenge in her voice. 'Tell me something about him.'

'Very well. You look like him. You *don't* sound like him. He was a courtier, but he left court when he married your mother and retired here. As far as I know, he left home only a handful of times afterwards, usually when he was summoned by the King. How am I doing?'

'You could have learnt all of that from gossip. Tell me something personal.'

'Personal?' He rubbed a hand over his chin, admiring the tumble of russet curls over her shoulders as she tossed her head. Personal wasn't so easy. Robert Flemming hadn't exactly been a man for sharing confidences. Their few conversations had mostly been on subjects like the weather and livestock, although every so often a more intimate detail had crept in...

'Well?' She was already tapping her foot.

'I know!' He clicked his fingers triumphantly. 'I remember him telling me that you were born during a thunderstorm. It was a particularly wet year and nobody could travel. He said the roads were like rivers and there wasn't a single dry day until you were six months old. *And...*' he went on, warming to his theme '...for your eighth birthday, he had a chess set made from jet and amber. He said the two of you played every day.'

'Yes.' The suspicious light in her eyes dimmed, chased away by a sudden profound sadness. 'We did. Every evening until he died.' She dropped his bridle abruptly, twisting her face to one side. 'You can go. My mother's in the house, probably in the kitchens at this time of day.'

'Thank you.' He took up his reins again. 'May I escort you back there?'

'No.' Her voice was rough, as if she were struggling to speak at all.

'Well then...' He hesitated, reluctant to leave now that she looked and sounded so mournful. Apparently his talent for making women unhappy was stronger than ever. He'd spent barely five minutes with this one and already she seemed close to tears, which meant the kindest thing he could probably do was to leave her alone... 'It's been an honour to meet you at last, Annis Flemming.'

She made a dismissive sound and stepped aside, the branch still held tightly in her hand. She didn't wish him a good day.

Something was going to happen. Annis threw the stick aside and watched as the man dismounted and walked up to the intricately carved oak door of Cariscombe, though not before throwing one last look in her direction. Instinctively, she stepped sideways, concealing herself behind a tree. Men were trouble. That was what her mother had always taught her, although this one didn't seem like it. He'd said he was a friend and neighbour, but she'd never seen him before. She would have remembered. He was bigger and broader than any man she'd ever met, built like a bear with chestnut hair, a brooding expression and eyes so dark they were almost black. Definitely memorable. Most of the time, she gave little thought to her appearance, but something about him had made her acutely conscious of her tangled hair and ragged outdoor apparel.

Annoyingly, however, he'd been just as forthcoming as her mother, which was to say not at all, as if he were another part of the conspiracy of silence that hung over Cariscombe. It had been a month now since her father had collapsed suddenly one afternoon. She felt as though she'd been walking around in a fog the whole time, surrounded by dangers that everyone else could see, but that no one would talk about or explain, no matter how often or vociferously she asked. As if she were still a child in need of protection instead of an heiress who owned both the manor house and almost a hundred acres of land to the north.

Her mother was frightened, that much was obvious, and strange things had started to happen, too—first in the stables, where she'd noticed the grooms looking at her with half-hostile, half-fearful expressions, then in the house itself. A couple of days ago, the servants had started gathering in corners, whispering furtively together before leaving, usually at night and without any explanation, until only a handful remained. The last time she'd counted, there were only six people left in the hall altogether, herself and her mother included.

And now another strange thing was happening: this stranger's sudden arrival when visitors had always been so few and far between, bearing a message from a 'friend'. What friend?

She peered out from behind the tree, making sure it was safe to come out, before making her way along the dirt track that ran parallel to the road and through a gate into the apple and plum orchard at the side of the house. What had he called himself? Sir Bennet Thorne... If only she knew what his message was, but there was no point in trying to listen at doors. Margery, her mother's devoted attendant, would be standing guard as always, making sure that *she* was kept in ignorance.

Absently, she plucked a damson from a branch and sat down on the grass to suck out the juices. Perhaps she ought to have been more welcoming to Sir Bennet. If she'd been polite and flattered him then he might have given her a hint as to the contents of his message, but her nerves were strung too tight for good manners. And she wouldn't have known how to begin anyway. She hadn't met enough men in her life to know how to cajole them, and as for flirting... no doubt she would have made an even bigger fool of herself than she had by threatening to club him with a stick.

She winced at the memory and tossed the soggy damson stone aside, licking her fingers as she looked back at the hall. It was her home, the place where she'd woken every morning, eaten every meal, learnt every lesson, played every game and then gone to bed again for the past eighteen and a half years. She might have felt restless and frustrated there on occasion, wondering what lay beyond the village that marked the far edge of her travels, but she loved it, every archway and arrow slit and doorway. It was more than a house; it was her whole world, all that she needed. Until a month ago, she'd considered herself fortunate and happy.

Now, however, she was increasingly aware that her world, the one she'd always thought so safe and comfortable, was collapsing, beset by forces from outside. Her father's death had changed everything in ways she didn't understand but that seemed irreversible and inexorable. If she stared at the hall long and hard enough, she thought she might actually be able to see the turrets crumbling...

The sound of hoofbeats jolted her back to the present. Sir Bennet was already leaving, it seemed, mounting his horse, turning his back and riding away. Whatever his message had been, it hadn't taken long to deliver. What did that mean?

She pushed herself to her feet and gave her body a small shake, trying to rid herself of the dread that now plagued her every waking moment, but it was no use. The hollow, ominous feeling in her chest wouldn't be shaken away. Something was *definitely* going to happen. She could sense the tension in the air, as if an invisible rope was being slowly coiled and tightened, noose-like, around Cariscombe Hall and everyone inside. Unfortunately, she had no idea who was wielding the rope or what she could possibly do to stop it.

Worse than that, she had the horrible feeling that it was already too late.

Chapter Two

It began with a shout. No, *shouts*. Not just one voice or two, but many, all raised together until they became indistinguishable, like a wave of noise rolling towards the house. Annis turned onto her back, rolled her shoulders and slowly opened her eyelids, her sleep-fogged brain needing a few moments to comprehend that the sounds were real and not part of some dream, but then the banging started and she knew the moment she'd feared had arrived. The front door was already creaking and groaning as if it were under assault from a battering ram. Gradually, in the midst of all the shouting, one word became distinct.

Witch.

Her stomach lurched as she sprang upright, tore her bed curtains apart and hurtled across to the narrow slit in her wall that passed for a window. She clamped a hand over her mouth to stifle a scream at the sight below. There were a dozen men at least, illuminated by torchlight, wielding pitchforks, spikes and even spades, all hammering against the front door, calling for her mother to show herself. To her horror, they were all wearing masks.

'Annis!' Margery flung open the door of her bedchamber suddenly, her normally stern features contorted with fear. 'Get away from there!'

'Who are they?' Annis didn't move, not deliberately disobeying, just unable to move her legs. Her feet seemed frozen to the spot, her blood running cold with horror, as if she were being slowly encased in ice. 'Are they from the village? What's happening?'

Margery didn't answer, only flung a hand out and grabbed hold of Annis's wrist instead, hauling her roughly out of the room, along the upstairs gallery and down the stairs.

'Tell me!' Annis dug her heels in as they reached the corridor that divided the hall from the solar, the lack of reply frightening her more than anything. Her mother's attendant was usually full of words. Reprimands and lectures mostly, but at that moment she wanted to hear them. She wanted anything that would drown out the sounds of banging and angry voices. It seemed to be coming from several directions at once now, as if the mob had surrounded the house. 'What do they want with my mother?'

'There's no time to explain.' Margery finally let go of her wrist and began rummaging in a chest, thrusting a cloak and pair of leather boots into her arms. 'Here. Put these on.'

'Why?' She obeyed out of habit. Panic clawed at her throat, making her voice shake along with the rest of her. 'Margery, I don't understand! Why do I have to wear these?'

'Because you need to get away from here.' Her mother appeared at that moment, emerging from around the screen that led into the great hall. She was walking slowly, her long golden hair hanging loose around her shoulders and her hands clasped in front of her, looking as beautiful and serene as ever, as if she were completely oblivious to the mob of men outside, baying for blood. *Her* blood. 'You need to go out through the tunnel and run to Draycote Manor.'

'The tunnel?' Annis gave a shocked start. To her memory, the tunnel had never been used. The only reason she knew it existed was because she'd overheard her parents talking about it once, when they hadn't realised she was close enough to overhear, and then begged and pleaded with her father to show her. It was a secret passage that led from a trapdoor in the solar to another in the stables. Not far, but enough to escape.

'Once you reach the stables, go out through the back door and then head for the forest.' Her mother's voice held a new urgency. 'Run down to the ford over the river. Then, when you've crossed that, go up the hill to where the trees are thinner and you'll find a track. Follow it south and it should take you straight to Draycote Manor. It's almost three miles, but you can do it. When you arrive, ask for Sir Bennet Thorne.'

'The man who came here today?'

'Yes. How did you...' A surprised expression passed swiftly over her mother's face. 'Never mind. Tell him I ought to have listened and then ask him to take you to Isolde.'

'Who? No!' Annis protested as the shouts rose in volume again. 'I'm not leaving you, not with them!'

'You *have* to.' Her mother placed a hand on either side of her face, cradling her cheeks the way she'd done when Annis was a small child. 'You must.'

'But—'

'This mob has been coming for me for a long time. Your father held them off for as long as he could, but now he's gone, I can't hide any more.' She smiled softly. 'And I certainly can't run.'

'Then we'll find a way to reason with them.' Annis shook her head desperately, hot tears burning her eyes and scorching their way down her cheeks. 'Please, let me stay and help you.'

'You can't reason with men like this.' Her mother moved closer, pressing their foreheads together. 'And the only way you can help me is to leave. Be strong for me. Be brave. Save yourself.'

'At least tell me why they're here, why they're calling you…' her voice cracked '…a witch?'

'It must be because of my past.' Her mother's expression was anguished. 'I should have told you about my life before I came here. I should have told you everything, but I was trying to protect you. I thought that if you didn't know then maybe you would be safer…' She dropped her hands again. 'It's too late now, but whatever happens, I'm no witch. I did my best for you. I tried to protect you. I love you.' She took a step backwards as a loud thud on the front door seemed to reverberate throughout the whole house, shaking the foundations like an earthquake. 'Now go. Run to Draycote Manor and promise me you won't stop until you get there.'

'But I can't—'

'Yes, you can. Promise me.'

'I promise.' Annis gave a strangled sob, reaching for one last embrace, but it was already too late. She caught one final glimpse of her mother's face, filled with love and pale with tension, before she disappeared back round the screen to the hall.

'Come! Do what she says.' Margery pulled Annis into the solar and then dropped into a crouch, sweeping aside the rushes scattered over the floor and tugging at a metal handle attached to one of the flagstones beneath. It gave way with a loud creak. 'We don't have much time.'

'What about you and the other servants?' Annis turned pleading eyes towards her.

'The others have all gone, and the mob isn't calling for me.' Margery's face took on a look of grim resolve. 'But they won't get past me easily either.' Her expression softened as she caught Annis's eye. 'I'm an old woman. You have your whole life ahead of you. Just remember, whatever you might hear later, whatever people might say, your mother is innocent. She always was. Remember that.'

'I will.'

'Good girl. Now go. Run. Don't stop, don't look round and don't come back, no matter what.' She thrust a lantern into her hands. 'Blow this out when you reach the stables.'

A rush of cold air hit Annis full in the face, turning her tears to ice, as she staggered down a set of steps into a narrow tunnel and the trapdoor closed with an ominous thud behind her. Instinctively, she took a deep breath, trying to calm herself, then gagged as the taste of stale, dank air filled her mouth. For a moment, she thought about not going anywhere, about waiting and listening and then bursting out of her hiding place when the time was right to help her mother, but she'd made a promise. And maybe if she hurried then she could reach Draycote Manor in time to gather some men to come back and dispel the mob. It was three miles, but if she ran the whole way, there might still be a chance to stop this, whatever *this* was.

Spurred on by the thought, she pressed her cloak to her mouth, bent over and hurried forward, her pulse pounding as she ran towards the second trapdoor at the far end of the tunnel. She braced her hands against the wood, listening for a few seconds before pushing upwards. For one horrible, heart-stopping moment, the door didn't move, as if something heavy had been placed on top, before the wood gave way with a high-pitched creak.

She tensed, blew out the lantern and waited for something to happen. There were shuffling sounds all around her as the horses shifted positions and flicked their ears in their sleep, but thankfully nobody else seemed to have heard her.

She waited a few more seconds, giving her eyes a chance to adapt to the darkness, and then hauled herself out, closing and covering the trapdoor behind her with straw before creeping towards the back door of the stables. It was late summer, nearly autumn, but the clear skies meant that when the temperature dropped it felt almost like winter. She had no idea what time it was, but the moon was high and full, bathing the world in an eerie silver glow. She could see the forest ahead of her. If she crept around the edge of the stables and ran swiftly across the lawn, she could be in the trees in less than a minute. Then all she had to do was run down to the river, over the ford, up the hill and head south...

She hitched her night-rail up around her knees, gathered her courage and sprinted headlong across the grass, reaching the forest just as the scent of smoke hit her nostrils. She heard wood splinter and a loud, wicked cheer filled the air. Instinctively, she spun around, starting back a few steps before remembering her promise. She couldn't go back, no matter what, no matter how badly she wanted to fight and scream and rail at their attackers.

Reluctantly, she turned round again, pressing one hand against her chest as she ran, trying to shield herself from a pain she could sense coming for her, but that she couldn't bear to confront just yet.

* * *

'Has he stopped crying yet?' Ben tore his gaze away from the fireplace as his mother appeared in the parlour doorway.

'He's asleep.'

'Finally.' He sagged forward, pressing his elbows against his knees and pushing his hands through his hair, as if the heaviness in his heart was actually dragging him over. 'That was a disaster.'

'He needs time to get used to you, that's all.'

'He doesn't even remember who I am.'

'And whose fault is that?' His mother groaned as she lowered herself onto the settle beside him. 'It's been almost a year since your last visit.'

'I know, but it's not easy to get away. I need permission from the King to leave Hatfield House at all.'

'Then maybe you should ask permission to leave for good and come home. You've served the King for almost five years now. I don't see why teaching somebody else's son is so much more important than teaching your own.'

'Edward isn't just *somebody else's* son, Mother. He's a prince.' Ben threw a cautious glance towards the door, making sure nobody else was around to overhear. 'You should be more careful about what you say.'

'Pah! I trust our servants.' His mother made a disparaging sound. 'Besides, I'm an old woman. What would the King do to me? Put me on a scaffold like his wives?'

'Two of his wives and yes, perhaps.' Ben sat up straight again, keeping his voice low. 'Think what you like about Henry, but for pity's sake, don't say it out loud. The King grows more paranoid every day and no one is safe any more. What if George were to repeat such words in company? We could all be sent to the Tower.'

His mother pursed her lips, though for once she didn't argue. Hopefully that meant he was getting his message across.

'George was frightened of me today,' he murmured, turning his face back to the fire.

'It's not personal. You're just bigger and taller than most men. He probably thought you were a giant from one of the stories I tell him. Don't worry,' his mother chuckled at his horrified expression, 'I always make the giants the heroes.'

'How comforting.' Ben rolled his eyes. 'He looks like Eleanor.'

There was a momentary pause before she answered. 'Yes. It's in his eyes.'

'His expressions, too. She used to look at me in the exact same way, as if she couldn't wait to get away from me.'

'It's not the same. She was a milksop.'

'She was a good person, Mother. She was just unhappy.' He glanced up at the oil portrait hanging over the fireplace. He'd left it there so that George would remember what his mother looked like, though in retrospect he wished he'd commissioned something smaller. Even two years after her death, his wife's blank stare seemed to strike a fresh dagger into the already gaping wound in his soul, as if she were rejecting him all over again.

'And what did she have to be unhappy about?' his mother retorted. 'Any sensible woman would have been grateful to have a young, handsome husband with a fine estate.'

'But *she* wasn't.' He clenched his jaw at the memory. As arranged marriages went, theirs had been doomed from the start. It might have made sense on parchment—Eleanor had been a rich ward, raised in the home of a family friend, and had brought both money and connections to the marriage—

but the reality had been a nightmare. She'd never been happy about anything. He couldn't remember ever seeing her smile, not when they'd met, not on their wedding day, not even when George had been born. Nothing had ever seemed to please her, *especially* not him. Her son—*their* son—seemed to have inherited that from her as well.

'George reminds me of you, too.' His mother's tone was defiant, as if she knew what he was thinking. 'He's a fine archer.'

'Really?' That made him feel slightly better.

'Yes. He can show you himself tomorrow. You have almost three weeks to get reacquainted with each other.' She placed a hand on his knee, using it to push herself to her feet. 'Now it's time for my bed. It's good to have you home again, Ben, even if it's only for a while, and things with George will improve, you'll see.'

'I hope so.' He reached a hand out, steadying her as she wobbled. 'Is it your back?'

'My hip. That's one thing that isn't improving. I'm getting old.'

'You should hire a maid to look after George.'

'He's my grandson. A maid won't care for him like I do.'

'Then hire someone to help you.'

'Pah. What the boy really needs is a father at home and a new mother.' She gave him a pointed look. 'Maybe a few siblings too.'

'So you always tell me...' He sighed and tipped his head back against the settle. There was no point trying to explain why none of those things were ever going to happen. His mother would never understand his feelings about either marriage *or* Draycote Manor. The truth was, he felt homesick every moment he was away. He missed the house, the gardens, the park, even the forest around it with an almost visceral pain. He missed his son even more. But his love for his home was now inextricably bound up with his conflicted feelings about Eleanor, which made coming home both a pleasure he yearned for and a gut-wrenching pain. He'd left for a reason, because he'd failed her as a husband, and now...now his conscience wouldn't permit him to come back. It *definitely* wouldn't let him marry again, even if he could bring himself to believe that he could make a different woman happy. Just the memory of Eleanor's melancholy expression was enough to put him off the idea for ever. Some men were simply made for solitude, not companionship.

'I'm only telling you the truth.' His mother tapped his shoulder none too gently.

'Maybe, but we've been over this.' He lifted an eyebrow. 'Several times. At length.'

'That doesn't mean the subject is closed. You're still a young man and not all women are milksops.'

'I know that.'

'So?'

'So has it never occurred to you that maybe I'm just not suited to marriage or fatherhood? Perhaps Eleanor was right about me.'

'*Right* about you?' His mother's expression sharpened. 'What do you mean? What did she say?'

'Nothing. I just meant—' He stopped, turning his head and frowning at the sound of knocking on the front door. Not gentle, polite knocking either, but a heavy, almost frantic pounding.

'Who on earth can that be?' His mother's mouth dropped open. 'What time is it?'

'Too late for visitors.' Ben sprang to his feet, reaching for a candle. 'Wait here while I go and see.'

'Do we open up?' Ellis, his steward, was waiting beside the door when he entered the hall, surrounded by a cluster of servants, roused from their pallet beds by the commotion.

'Not yet.' He put the candle aside on a table and went to the door, raising his voice over the now incessant pounding. 'Who is it?'

'Open up! *Please!*' a female voice called back. 'Help me!'

He paused, one hand on the drawbar. It could be a trick, robbers using the ploy of a damsel in distress to trick them into opening up. On the other hand, there was something familiar about the voice, something that made him think of fierce hazel eyes and soft-looking russet curls. Although surely that was just his imagination playing tricks, the result of too much time spent thinking about her after their meeting, for almost the entire distance between Cariscombe and Draycote Manor, in fact... It *couldn't* be her...could it?

'Annis?' he asked quietly.

'Yes!'

He didn't hesitate any longer, hoisting the bar, twisting the door handle and then bracing himself as she toppled straight through the gap into his arms.

'Help me!' She clutched at his chest, her face tear-stained and wild-looking. The defiant, poised young woman with a stick he'd met earlier that day was gone, replaced by a distraught-looking girl covered in scratches and dressed in a white cambric night-rail.

'What is it? What's happened?' He pulled off his doublet and wrapped it around her shoulders, trying to ignore the press of her uncorseted body against his chest as he looked past her into the night. The moon was full and bright, illuminating the parkland around the house. But as far as he could tell, she was alone. Alone in a night-rail. *What the hell?*

'My mother...' she was panting so heavily she could hardly get the words out '...she told me to run...to use the secret tunnel...to come here...'

He looked back at her, feeling a fresh jolt of surprise. 'You've come all this way by yourself in the dark?'

'Yes.' She seemed to be getting her breath back now. 'There was a mob... They had torches and weapons. They called her...' her voice faltered again '...they called her...'

'What?' He wrapped his fingers around her upper arms, holding her steady.

'A witch.' She looked straight into his eyes, her face twisting with pain. 'They called her a witch.'

He sucked in a breath, holding onto her gaze for a few horrified seconds before squeezing her arms. 'Stay here. I'll go.'

'Not without me!' She clutched at his chest again, digging her fingertips into the linen of his shirt, her eyes large and pleading. 'I have to come with you.'

'No. It's too dangerous.'

'She's my mother!'

'That's why you can't come. She wouldn't want it.' Gently, he extricated her hands from his shirt. He wasn't about to tell her the truth—that if a mob really had come to accuse her mother of witchcraft, then the chances of him reaching Cariscombe in time were small, though he'd do his damnedest anyway. More than that, there were sights that she ought not to see, ones that she might never be able to forget. Besides, judging by the violent way her hands were trembling, she was in no fit state to go anywhere.

'Do you know where the mob came from?' he asked her urgently. 'Did you recognise anyone?'

'No.' Her whole body was shaking violently now, as if she were cold, though her cheeks were a livid shade of scarlet. 'They wore masks.'

'Masks?' He frowned, beckoning to his steward. 'Take her to my mother while I gather the men, then bolt the doors and don't let anyone else into the house until we return. *Anyone.* I don't care if the King himself comes to the door.' He turned his face grimly in the direction of Cariscombe, a shiver of unease snaking down his spine at the sight of a faint orange glow on the horizon. 'Keep her safe.'

Chapter Three

Annis paced up and down the oak-panelled parlour, wishing that she'd insisted on going back to Cariscombe with Sir Bennet. Then she would have known what was happening and not be trapped in this nightmare state of uncertainty and panic. Despite getting her breath back, she couldn't seem to breathe properly. Her head was pounding so hard it felt like a hundred small fists were hammering against the inside of her skull. Where was he? What was taking so long? She must have marched up and down the room at least a hundred times by now. Her feet were probably covered in blisters, but movement was the only thing keeping her sane. At least if she kept moving then she was doing *something*!

'Why don't you go and lie down?' Sir Bennet's mother, Lady Joan, suggested for at least the dozenth time since she'd arrived. 'I told you, we've prepared a bedchamber for you.'

'No.' Annis shook her head vehemently. 'I'd never be able to sleep, but you should go. I can wait by myself.'

'What kind of a hostess would I be then?' The older woman stretched her neck from side to side, arching her back as if she were trying to find a more comfortable sitting position. 'We'll wait together, only in mercy's name, girl, stop walking or you'll wear a path in the floor.'

'Oh…' Annis glanced over her shoulder as if she might be able to see one forming behind her. 'Sorry.'

'Hmph.' Lady Joan waved away her apology. 'It's understandable given the circumstances, but it won't help.'

Annis forced her feet to stop moving and crouched down in front of the fireplace, tugging Sir Bennet's doublet tighter around her shoulders. Lady Joan had offered her a long shawl, but she preferred to keep this. She had no idea what had happened to her own cloak. Presumably she'd dropped it at some point during her frantic run through the forest, but she'd been too hot from exertion and terror to notice. She hadn't given a thought to what she'd been wearing when she'd arrived, although on reflection she supposed she must have looked somewhat wild. Completely scandalous, in fact. She'd flung herself into Sir Bennet's arms wearing nothing more than a cambric night-rail.

'How long do you think it's been?' she asked, dragging her mind away from the memory. 'It seems like an eternity. Do you think that's a good or bad sign?'

'I don't think anything.' Lady Joan touched a hand to her shoulder. 'Not yet, and neither should you.'

'I shouldn't have left her. She told me to, but I should have stayed and fought.'

'You would have made it even worse for her if you had.' Lady Joan clucked her tongue, contradicting her sternly. 'She wanted you to leave. Any good mother would have. Trust me, you did the right thing. I'm just surprised that you could run such a distance.'

'It's not so far. Only three miles.'

'Aye, but for someone so ill…'

'*Ill?*' Annis twisted her face away from the flames in surprise. 'Who told you I was ill?'

'Your father.' Lady Joan gave her a long, evaluating look. 'I came across him in the village on occasion. He said that your condition was the reason he could never entertain guests, because it was too great a risk. Tonight is the first time I've set eyes on you since you were a baby. What was that? Eighteen years ago?'

'Yes.' Annis dropped her gaze evasively. It wasn't her place to contradict her father, even if what he'd said had been a blatant lie. It didn't make any sense either. She couldn't remember the last time she'd been ill. Even the sweating sickness that had ravaged the local area two years before had passed her by, though both of her parents had been bedridden for weeks. So why on earth would he have spread such a story about her?

'Well, I'm glad to meet you now, though naturally I wish the circumstances were different.' Lady Joan went on. 'It always struck me as odd that I didn't know what my own neighbour's daughter looked like, but then I haven't set eyes on your mother for a good fifteen years either. I thought perhaps the pair of you had a similar ailment?'

'No. She didn't—*doesn't*—like to leave home, that's all.' Annis lifted a fist to her mouth, chewing on her thumbnail. 'Do you think that's why they accused her of witchcraft?'

'No.' Lady Joan sounded definite. 'She always had a reputation for keeping to herself, but nobody ever minded before. Whatever's behind this must have happened recently or I would have heard rumours. Something to do with your father's death perhaps? It was very sudden, was it not?'

'Yes. He was perfectly well in the morning. Then he started coughing up blood during the afternoon and by nightfall... Why?' Annis whipped her head round again, belatedly grasping the implication. 'What are you suggesting?'

'Nothing.'

'My mother loved my father! She would never have hurt him!'

'Peace, child, I'm not saying otherwise, but you have to admit, your father's death could be used against her, especially considering how quickly it happened.' Lady Joan's expression turned faintly accusing. 'Not to mention the speed with which he was buried. I would have come to the funeral had I known anything about it. He and my husband were good friends once.'

Annis compressed her lips, unable to offer an explanation. Her mother had insisted on the funeral being just the two of them and Margery, even though her father had had family still living, a sister and nephew, albeit estranged. The whole thing had taken place in near secrecy, which, now that Lady Joan mentioned it, was undeniably odd.

Thankfully, she was saved from making any comment by the tread of rapid footsteps in the gallery outside.

'That sounds like Ben.' Lady Joan stood up hurriedly.

'Have you found her? What's happened?' Annis flew across the room, almost colliding with Sir Bennet in the doorway. He looked even bigger and more bear-like than she remembered, and almost as wretched as she felt—filthy, exhausted and with his brow smeared with dirt, soot and sweat.

'We found her.' He met her gaze sombrely. 'I'm sorry.'

'What?' She inhaled sharply, her body seeming to give one violent tremor before going completely numb. Meanwhile, there was a ringing sound in her ears, as if she'd just taken a heavy blow to her head. 'Did they…was she…' She had to force the words past her lips. 'Because they thought she was a witch?'

'I don't know exactly what happened. The place was deserted when we arrived, but...' A muscle clenched in his jaw as he touched a hand to just below his rib cage. 'It was a sword wound. Here.'

Annis staggered backwards, wrapping her arms around her own chest. 'I don't understand. Why would anyone hurt her? Why would anyone accuse her of witchcraft? What did she ever do to anyone?'

'I don't know. Come. Sit.' Sir Bennet took hold of her elbow, steering her towards the settle and then crouching in front of her. 'Have you had any rest?'

'She refused to sleep.' His mother poured a cup of ale and thrust it into Annis's hand. 'She's been pacing up and down the whole time.'

'There wasn't even a trial,' she murmured, wincing as she caught the scent of smoke on his clothes. 'Did it look like she suffered?'

'No.' He shook his head. 'There wasn't much blood. Whatever happened, it was quick.' He gave her a long look before turning to his mother. 'Have there been any rumours in the area about Cariscombe or witchcraft in recent weeks?'

'None that I've heard.' Lady Joan frowned. 'I asked the servants and none of them had heard anything either.'

'Then it doesn't make sense. A mob can be whipped up quickly, but surely there would have been some indication of bad feeling beforehand? Mobs don't usually stop to put on masks either.'

'Margery!' Annis gasped suddenly, clutching at Ben's arm.

'Who?'

'My mother's attendant. She was completely devoted to her. She said that the mob would have to get through her if they—' She stopped and gulped. 'Did you find her, too?'

'I'm afraid not. We didn't see anyone else.'

She gulped again, harder this time. Maybe Margery had been hiding, or maybe... She dropped her chin, unable to finish the thought, staring down into the swirling amber liquid in her cup. She wanted to drink, to soothe the ache in her throat, but she couldn't seem to lift her arm. All of her limbs felt too heavy, as if she'd been drugged. She had a feeling she wouldn't be able to pace another step if she tried.

'I'm sorry.' Sir Bennet touched his fingers gently against hers. 'Truly.'

'Thank you.' She nodded, pressing her lips together until she felt able to speak again. 'Did you bring my mother back with you?'

'No. We took her into the house for now, but my men will go back early in the morning to fetch her.'

'You took her into Cariscombe?' She jerked her head up again. 'You mean, the mob didn't burn it down?'

'Half of it is, yes, but we managed to put the fire out and save the other half.'

'Oh...' She felt a small, very small, sense of relief. That was something. At least some part of her world was still standing.

'Annis...' Sir Bennet cleared his throat. 'Earlier you said that your mother sent you here. Did she give you any specific message for me?'

'Yes. She said to tell you, she ought to have listened.' She stiffened at the words. 'Wait, did you *know* she was in danger?'

'Not like this.' His brows snapped together. 'I would never have left Cariscombe today otherwise.'

'Oh…no.' She felt a twinge of guilt for the question. 'Sorry.'

'Was there anything else?' His voice sounded harder now. 'Anything about what she wanted me to do?'

'She said to ask you to take me to Isolde, but I don't know anyone called Isolde. Do you?'

'Just one.' He bowed his head for a moment before standing up. 'In that case, we have to leave.'

'What?' She stared at him in confusion. 'But I can't go anywhere. I can't leave her.'

'She'll be properly tended to.' He turned to his mother. 'Will you make the arrangements?'

'*I* have to make the arrangements!' Annis leapt to her feet in protest, flinging her arms out and spilling ale across the flagstones. 'She's my mother! I have to do it!'

'I'm sorry, but that's not possible. Ellis?' Ben called out, waiting until his steward appeared in the doorway. 'I'll need two horses and enough provisions for a week. Blankets too. We have to leave for London as soon as possible.'

'But you only just came home!' Lady Joan objected, her voice sharp.

'I know, but it can't be helped. Mistress Flemming entrusted her daughter to me and I intend to take care of her.'

'Mistress Flemming? What did Mistress Flemming ever do for us?'

'*Mother!*'

'It doesn't matter.' Annis stepped between them. 'I'm not running away, not again!'

'You have to, at least for a while.' Sir Bennet's tone was inflexible.

'I don't *have* to do anything.' She planted her feet and pushed her face up to his in frustration. 'I'm going to stay here, find out who was behind this and then bring them to justice.'

'That might be easier said than done. We'll send word to the Justice of the Peace to investigate, but you said you didn't recognise anyone and there were no clues at the scene, none that we could find anyway. The absence of any rumours suggests this wasn't done by anyone local either. That means we have to assume whoever did this came from elsewhere and arranged it to look like a mob in case of witnesses.' He paused meaningfully. 'Your mother obviously had enemies.'

'I know that now! She told me her past was catching up with her, but that it was too late to explain.'

'That makes sense.' He looked thoughtful. 'When we spoke earlier today, she seemed to expect some kind of danger, only she didn't specify what. I got the impression that she was concerned for you.'

'Me?' Annis froze, a tendril of fear unfurling inside her as the words sank in. 'You mean, she thought her enemies might come for me too?'

'Perhaps. We're only assuming they came for your mother, but we don't know for certain. It's possible the accusation of witchcraft was just an excuse for the attack and she wasn't the only one they wanted. And if they're still searching for you…' He let the words hang in the air.

'But why would anyone want to hurt me?' Her voice appeared to have jumped up an octave. 'I don't know anyone! Besides, won't I be safe here with you?'

'Honestly, I don't know. I'll do everything I can to protect you, but until we know who we're dealing with and what they want, it's best to be cautious, especially since...'

'Especially since what?' She held onto his gaze as his voice trailed away.

'Especially since you're a wealthy woman. You own Cariscombe and all the land around it.' He grimaced. 'And greed can be a powerful motive.'

'That's monstrous!'

'Money can make men into monsters.' He quirked an eyebrow. 'Who stands to inherit if anything happens to you?'

'I'm not certain. My father had a sister, but they hadn't spoken in years.'

'Why not?'

'Something to do with my mother, but my parents wouldn't talk about it.'

'So she's your aunt. Do you know where she lives now?'

Annis racked her brains, trying to remember. Her father had only mentioned his sister once when she'd found an old portrait and asked about her. 'Taunton. She married a landowner called Hawksby.'

'Does she have any children?'

'Yes, one son at least. Oliver. I remember my father mentioning him.'

'A son.' Ben made a face. 'Which makes him your heir and gives him a motive. Maybe this is what your mother was afraid of.'

She gasped, hardly able to take in such a horrifying idea. 'But we've never even met! We've never had anything to do with each other. Surely he can't be behind this?'

'That's what the Justice of the Peace needs to find out.' His gaze turned even more sombre. 'I'm not saying it's what happened, but it's one possibility.'

Annis gaped at him, too shocked to speak for a few seconds before shaking her head. 'No, I'm still not leaving. Cariscombe is *my* home, my inheritance. If even one room is still standing then that's where I belong. I won't be chased away, no matter what the danger.'

'Forgive me, but yes, you will.' Sir Bennet moved a step closer towards her, his expression implacable suddenly. 'Your mother sent you to me and that makes me responsible for you. I'd rather you come with me willingly, but if not then I'll bind your wrists and take you anyway. I'd rather have that on my conscience than the alternative.'

'I'm not a child to be ordered about.' She squared up to him. 'I'm a grown woman and I can make my own decisions. I'll hire men to protect me, if necessary.'

'Men?' He looked sceptical. 'And how will you know which men to trust?'

'I don't know, but you have no right to tell me what to do!'

'Maybe not, but I want you to live.' He dropped his gaze, taking a step back again as she flinched. 'I'm sorry. I don't mean to threaten or scare you, but the situation may be more dangerous than you imagine. If your mother was right then there's more to this than we understand at the moment. Closer to London will be safer.'

'London?' she repeated shakily. 'I've never even gone beyond the village.'

'I know.' His voice softened. 'But you have a friend there. I can't tell you more about who they are just yet, but I promise it will all make sense soon.'

'I doubt it. Nothing makes sense any more.' She narrowed her gaze accusingly. 'And how do I know I can trust *you*? How do I know you weren't involved somehow?

Maybe it's not a coincidence that you arrived on the very same day this happened.'

'Hush, girl!' Lady Joan stepped forward. 'How dare you!'

'No, she's right to be suspicious.' Sir Bennet lifted a hand, blocking his mother's path, before locking eyes with Annis again. 'You can trust me because I have no motive to hurt you. And because your mother told you to. And because your parents, for whatever reason, raised you out of sight in a forest, and you need to trust someone.'

Annis gulped, her mind whirling. He was right. To all intents and purposes, she was completely alone in the world. And according to her mother, the world wasn't kind to women on their own, whether they were heiresses or not. All of which meant that she needed to control her emotions and try to think clearly. If only it were that easy! Especially when the fog surrounding her seemed thicker than ever. But Sir Bennet was also right about one other thing: her mother, who trusted no man except her father, *had* trusted him. That would have to be good enough.

'Very well. I'll come with you on one condition.' She drew in a deep breath and then released it slowly. 'Promise me that it's not for ever. Promise me that I'll be able to come home again.'

'I promise. Once I'm confident it's safe for you to return, I'll do everything in my power to bring you home.'

'Then I'll trust you.'

'Thank you.' He turned back to Lady Joan. 'She'll need some men's clothing to wear on the journey and something to wear when we arrive.'

'Men's clothing?' Annis watched in confusion as Lady

Joan gave one last sniff of protest and then marched purposely away.

'Yes. If it's just going to be the two of us, it'll be safer for you to be dressed like a boy.'

She stiffened. 'Why will it just be us?'

'Because if we travel in a large group we'll attract attention, and if anyone's searching for you they're more likely to hear about it and follow. If my men were soldiers, it might be different, but we don't know who we're dealing with, or how well armed they are. This way, we should avoid notice. Then, by the time they give up searching the immediate area, it should be too late for them to catch up.' He frowned, as if he were thinking his plan through. 'Fortunately, only a few people know I've returned so nobody will connect the two of us.'

'Oh...' Annis bit her tongue. She'd never been alone in the company of any man except her father before. It didn't seem like something either of her parents would approve of—but, then again, what choice did she have?

'You're not running away.' Sir Bennet put his hands on her shoulders, his grip warm and firm, misreading the reason behind her reluctance. 'And neither am I. We're simply removing ourselves to a safe distance so that we can work out the best way to act next. Trust me, I want to find out who did this too.'

'Why?' She tipped her head back, looking up at him. 'Why do you care?'

'Because this shouldn't have happened.' His dark gaze intensified. 'And because I met your mother once. It was at a village fair before you were born. She gave me a roasted apple and smiled at me. It was such a kind smile. I always remembered that. What happened to her tonight was wicked and wrong and whoever did this shouldn't get away with it.'

'Clothes for the journey.' His mother came back into the hall at that moment, her arms full of garments. 'A warm cloak, too, as well as a gown for when you arrive. It's one of Eleanor's old ones, a little old fashioned now, but it's well made. You'll need to lift the hem a bit, but the rest should fit.'

'Thank you, mother.' Sir Bennet strode past her towards the door. 'I need to wash my face and change my clothes too, then we'll leave.'

'In the middle of the night?' Lady Joan objected. 'Why not wait until morning and say goodbye to George?'

'We can't.' He paused in the doorway, a pained expression crossing his face. 'You'll have to make up some excuse. Tell him I was called away on urgent business, but that I'll come back again soon.'

'Surely a few hours won't make that much difference?'

'Maybe not, but I don't want to find out.' A muscle flexed in his jaw. 'If anyone comes to the house tomorrow, asking questions, tell them you were asleep all night and you didn't see or hear anything. As for Annis...' his dark gaze flickered back towards her '...you've never seen her before in your life.'

Chapter Four

He'd had no choice, Ben told himself, straining his eyes and ears for any signs of pursuit, as he and Annis rode east along the road that led through the forest. He'd spent the hours since dawn trying to decide whether or not he was doing the right thing by taking her away from Somerset. It might be what her mother had wanted, but whether the person they were going to find would feel the same way was another matter. As far as he could tell, however, Isolde was the only one left in the world with any close connection to Annis, even if Annis herself appeared to have no idea Isolde existed. And just to complicate matters, he'd given his word not to speak about her. No, he had no idea whether or not he was doing the right thing. All he knew was that he'd had no choice. If Annis was in danger then he was honour-bound to protect her and this was the best way.

He was just relieved that she'd seen sense and finally agreed to accompany him. He really hadn't wanted to compel her, even for her own safety, and it would probably have meant bringing more men along to help. At least this way they stood a chance of escaping in secret. Judging by the confident way she'd mounted her palfrey she was a competent rider, which, considering the length of the journey ahead—a hundred and fifty miles at least—was another element in their favour. He only wished he'd had a little more time at Draycote before having to leave again, just a couple of days to remind George who he was and hopefully start to build some kind of relationship with him. Now if his son felt anything about his sudden departure, it would probably be relief. He'd probably dismiss Ben's whole brief visit as a bad dream.

But there was no point dwelling upon it now, he told himself, pushing that particularly depressing thought to the back of his mind and focusing on the danger at hand. Neither he nor Annis had spoken since they'd left Draycote Manor, riding as fast as they'd dared through the forest to put as much distance between themselves and Cariscombe as quickly as possible. He'd stayed ahead to avoid looking at her, trying to give her time and privacy to grieve, though he was also reluctant to talk about what had happened himself. The sight of her mother's bloodied body wasn't one he thought he was going to forget in a hurry.

Now that the sky was beginning to lighten in earnest, however, as the summer sun burned away the grey mist shrouding the tops of the trees, he tugged on his reins, slowing his horse to a trot alongside her.

'Thirsty?' He pulled a wineskin from the side of his saddle bag and held it out.

'No.' Her voice was flat and weary.

'Hungry then? I have some rye bread.' He drew his brows together, alarmed by how pale and pinched her face looked. Her eyes were swollen and there were blotches on both of her cheeks, as if she'd been crying while they rode. He felt a stab of regret. Maybe giving her privacy had been a mistake after all.

'No.'

'It might make you feel better?'

'It won't.' She gave a brittle laugh. 'Usually, I'm ravenous in the mornings, but now...' She placed a hand over her stomach, her expression queasy. 'I couldn't swallow a thing.'

'That's understandable.' He gave a sympathetic nod before tucking the wineskin away again. 'Just tell me if you change your mind.'

'I will. Thank you.'

'And we should—'

'My mother had nothing to do with my father's death!' She interrupted him suddenly, the words erupting out of her in a voice thick with emotion.

'I never thought she did.' He turned his head again in surprise. 'What makes you say that?'

'Your mother suggested that might have been the reason she was attacked, why the mob called her a witch, too, because my father's death was so sudden, but she would *never* have hurt him. She loved him deeply. She cried for a week after he died. She was so lost, I was afraid she might hurt herself too. It was all she could do to stand up at the funeral. I think that's why she didn't invite other people, because she couldn't bear to see anyone else, let alone talk to them.'

'That makes sense.'

'And maybe...' Her voice faltered. 'Maybe part of her hoped that if we kept it quiet then other people might not know he was gone. Because when she stopped crying, she was afraid. I'd never seen her that way before.' She tightened her fingers around her reins. 'If only she'd told me what her fears were! If only she'd confided in me, I could have helped.'

'Maybe she hoped her fears were unfounded,' he suggested. 'Or maybe she didn't know how to tell you.'

'I still had a right to know!' She rounded on him again, her gaze fierce. 'She ought to have told me.'

'Yes,' he agreed. 'She ought to have.'

'What was the message you gave her yesterday?'

He grimaced. As glad as he was to see some of her former spirit returning, he'd hoped to avoid that particular question. *'He knows...'* That was it, the extent of the message he'd been asked to give her mother, though who 'he' was and what he knew, he had no idea. Given what had happened, however, he could only presume that Oliver Hawksby was involved somehow.

He cleared his throat. 'I'm afraid I still can't tell you. It was private.'

'What does that matter now?'

'It might matter to the sender.'

'Is that who you're taking me to?'

'Yes.'

'This Isolde person?'

'Yes.'

'In London?'

'Not London itself. Hatfield House. It's about twenty miles to the north.'

'Hatfield House.' She repeated the words slowly, as if they might tell her something more. 'Is that their home?'

'In a manner of speaking. It doesn't belong to them, but it's where they live.'

'What do they do there?'

'I'm afraid...'

'You can't tell me that either.' She finished for him, tipping her head back with a frustrated sound. *'Argh!* I hate this feeling! It makes me feel like I didn't know my mother at all, but I did! I loved her and she loved me. I *did* know her, I just didn't know *everything* about her.'

Ben threw her a sympathetic look—he was seized with an unexpected yet instinctive urge to wrap an arm around her shoulders and offer comfort. She was right. It wasn't fair that he knew something about her mother she didn't, and he knew precious little, but none of this was his business to tell. Only he wanted to at least *try* and make her feel better...

'The message was a warning,' he said before he could stop himself, 'although I didn't realise that until I saw her reaction. She seemed panicked, so I suggested that she might want to get away from Cariscombe for a while. I even invited her to Draycote Manor, but she refused.'

'Is that why she said she ought to have listened to you?'

'I think so. It wasn't a very long conversation.'

'I see.' She caught her bottom lip between her teeth, her expression thoughtful.

Ben averted his gaze quickly, turning his face up to the sky. It had been navy with streaks of orange and pink when they'd ridden away from Draycote Manor, like puddles in the sky. Now it was more light than dark. It was time to be getting off the road and onto one of the old, little-known tracks through the forest so they wouldn't run the risk of being spotted.

'This way.' He gestured towards the side of the road. 'We'll have to make our way through the trees from now on.'

'Through the trees?' She looked startled. 'But I thought you said we needed to travel as quickly as possible?'

'We do. We'll just have to do it on foot for a while. Then we'll rest and ride again once it gets dark.'

'Won't the horses mind all the undergrowth?'

'They're used to it.' He jerked his head towards her palfrey. 'Yours is called Berengaria, by the way.'

She blinked and then wrinkled her nose. 'That's the strangest name for a horse I've ever heard.'

'I know. My own horse was too tired after the journey from London so we're both riding my mother's palfreys. She likes to name them after queens. Berengaria was Richard the Lionheart's wife.'

'I've never heard of her.'

'She never set foot in England.'

'Well, in that case I'm calling this girl Berry for short.' Annis leaned forward, stroking her mount's mane. 'What's yours called? Matilda? Isabel?'

'Emma.'

'There was never a Queen Emma!'

'According to my mother, there was. She was married to Ethelred the Second and then later to Canute.'

'So she was a queen twice?'

'Apparently so. Damn.' He stiffened at the faint sound of hooves coming from around a bend up ahead.

'What?' Annis looked from him to the road in confusion. 'What is it?'

'Someone's coming.' He threw another glance into the trees, but there was no time to hide. If whoever was coming were to see them disappear into the woods, it would only provoke their suspicions. Far better to brazen it out.

'I don't hear anything.'

'Trust me.' He gestured to her hat. 'Tuck your hair away. Some strands have come loose.'

'Only a few.'

'It's still noticeable. You're supposed to be a boy, remember? So keep your head down and, if anyone asks, you're my servant, Thomas, and we're travelling to market in Yeovil.' He gave her a sharp look, willing her to understand how perilous their position was. 'If we're going to make it to Hatfield safely, you need to trust me.'

'All right, but don't you think you're overreacting a little? We don't even know for sure if we're being followed and whoever *that* might be is coming from ahead of us, not behind,' Annis answered sceptically, tucking the strands of hair away and tugging the brim of her hat lower—a mere second before a cart rolled into view ahead of them.

'Well met,' the driver called out, raising a hand in greeting.

'Good morning.' Ben slapped a broad smile onto his face, acknowledging the man with a wave. 'A fine one it is, too.'

'Aye, but we could do with some rain!'

'Not today. We're on our way to Yeovil.'

'Then safe travels, my friend!'

'There, that wasn't so bad,' Annis whispered once the cart had gone past.

'*That* was a mistake.' Ben pulled on his reins, dismounting the moment they were round the bend and the cart was out of sight, pulling his horse towards the line of trees. 'Hurry. We need to get off the road before anyone else comes.'

They made their way into the forest, not far enough away to lose sight of the road, but enough not to be seen if they didn't want to be, though it wasn't easy. It was so dark, it seemed as though night had fallen again, and so cold that he was aware of goosebumps rising on his skin.

'Here.' He reached for Annis's bridle. 'I'll take your horse.'

'I can manage.' She waved his hand away, pushing a branch out of her face at the same time. 'I'm your man-servant, remember?'

He took one look at the stubborn set of her jaw and nodded. 'As you wish.'

'Why was it a mistake for that man to see us?' She spoke again after a few minutes of walking, a nervous edge to her voice now. 'He looked like a farmer.'

'He probably was, and he's most likely harmless, but if he meets anyone else on the road and they ask him who he's seen this morning…'

'Oh.' Her face clouded. 'I see.'

'Hopefully you're right and I'm being over-cautious. In fact, I probably am. The chances of him—' He halted abruptly, the words barely out of his mouth before he heard the thud of more hoofbeats back on the road.

'Don't move.' He caught hold of her arm, but she'd already frozen. Thankfully, the trees were thick, but he still caught a fleeting glimpse of a group of riders, at least half a dozen men, passing by at a determined gallop.

'Do you think they're looking for me?' Annis took a step closer.

He gave a grunt of assent, suddenly very aware of her proximity, not to mention the fact that his fingers were still curled around her upper arm. 'It seems too much of a coincidence otherwise.'

'Maybe they heard what happened at Cariscombe and want to help?' Her face was ashen. 'Rumours travel fast, don't they?'

'They can,' he answered dubiously. Although he couldn't think of any other land owners who lived close enough to hear rumours *that* quickly. Besides the fact that they were riding in the wrong direction...

'Or maybe they were part of the mob and they want to do to me what they did to my mother.' Her voice wobbled. 'Maybe that's a hunting party.'

Ben clenched his jaw. He'd hoped that he'd been overstating the danger, but he suspected a hunting party was exactly what they were, which made Annis their quarry. And they were still several days' ride from Hatfield House and safety.

'Sir Bennet?' There was a definite tremor in her voice this time.

'If they are, then we won't let them catch us.' He tried to sound reassuring. 'Come, we need to keep moving.' He didn't add that, at that precise moment, moving was the only thing they *could* do.

Chapter Five

They carried on in silence. There seemed to be some kind of track through the forest, but it was so wild and over-grown it obviously wasn't used very often. It made the journey hard going, as they forged a path over fallen branches and around brambles that scratched at their faces and tore at their clothes. But at least physical exertion kept Annis's darker thoughts and fears at bay. Back on the road, she'd managed to convince herself that Sir Bennet was overstating the danger, taking her away from Cariscombe when there was really no need, but the sight of the riders had chilled her to her core. It was horrible enough to know that she was being hunted; she didn't want to think about what would happen if they found her.

Now, without being able to see the sun overhead, she had no idea what the hour was or how much time had passed before they reached a small, sunlit clearing beside a trickling brook. In other circumstances, she might have found it quite idyllic. The whole forest seemed different here, the trees thinner and fewer, so that golden rays of sunshine spilled through the canopy and bathed the scene in a lustrous golden glow. For the first time since the attack, she felt her overwrought nerves begin to calm a little.

'How do you know about this place?' she asked Sir Bennet as he tethered their palfreys to a tree.

'I've travelled back and forth to London a great deal. Not many people know about these old tracks, but sometimes the weather makes the road too rutted to use, so it helps to know other ways around. Here.' He pulled a blanket from his pack and laid it down on a mass of pine needles between some tree roots. 'You need to get some sleep. I'll stand guard.'

Annis looked at the blanket with trepidation. Briefly, she considered refusing, too afraid to close her eyes. Awake, she could keep her memories of the night before at bay through sheer force of will, but asleep she wouldn't be able to control the images that might flit through her brain. On the other hand, her head felt heavy, she was swaying on her feet, and her eyelids were already drooping, as if there were actual weights pulling down on her lashes. No, there was no point in refusing. It wouldn't be long before she collapsed otherwise.

'Just for a little while,' she agreed, stretching herself out on the floor. 'An hour at the most. Then it's your turn.'

'Good idea.' He handed her another blanket before sitting down on a fallen tree trunk.

'Mmm? What was that?' She sprang up with a jolt a mere second after her head hit the ground.

'My apologies.' Oddly enough, Sir Bennet was standing on the opposite side of the clearing now. How had he moved so quickly? 'I just startled a bird and it woke you. Do you feel any better?'

'But I didn't... I haven't...' She rubbed her hands over her face. 'Have I been asleep?'

'For about two hours.'

'*Two?*' She gaped at him. 'But you were supposed to wake me after an hour!'

He lifted a shoulder, one corner of his mouth tugging slightly, *very* slightly, upwards. 'I changed my mind.'

'Well, now it's your turn.' She scrambled to her feet with an effort, her head still feeling much too heavy on her shoulders. 'I insist.'

'Very well, but not for long, and only on condition you take this.' He pulled a scabbard from his saddlebag and held it out across his palms. 'You need to be able to defend yourself.'

'I don't know... I've never used one before.' Annis looked at the leather hilt of the dagger protruding from one end of the scabbard, then up at him again soberly. He was much taller than she was. To be fair, most people were, but him in particular. When they stood face to face, like now, the very top of her head only reached as high as his chin. Which had absolutely nothing to do with her taking his dagger, she realised...

'Hopefully you won't have to use it today either.' He sounded sympathetic, as if he understood her reluctance. 'But you ought to have some kind of weapon, just in case.'

'I suppose so,' she conceded, lifting the scabbard from his hands and sliding it onto her belt.

'Thank you. Now wake me if you hear anything.'

'I will,' she promised, stretching her arms wide and yawning in a manner that would have earned her a vigorous scolding at home, as Sir Bennet lay down on the blanket. She felt marginally better after her nap, but she still didn't dare to sit down in case she fell asleep again. What kind of guard would she be then?

Slowly, she walked in a large circle around the clearing, rubbing her hand along each of the tree trunks, a feat that took approximately one minute. Next, she went to the horses, tapping her foot impatiently as she fed them each a handful of oats from her saddlebag. Another minute.

She glanced over her shoulder at Sir Bennet. He was lying on his side, eyelids closed, as if he'd fallen straight asleep, too. What now? Maybe she could explore the forest a little—she wouldn't go far. It would be all too easy to get lost amongst the trees, especially if she wandered too far away from the clearing, but surely she could take a careful look around. It was better than letting her thoughts wander back to her mother and Cariscombe.

Mind made up, she made her way back towards the brook, splashing cold water over her face and neck to wake herself up, before tying a scarf to a tree branch to mark the spot. Then she turned on her heel, following the winding path of the water so it would be easy to find her way back again. It all looked so pretty and peaceful, it was almost impossible to believe the horror of the night before had actually happened—even harder to believe there could be any danger close by.

No sooner had the thought crossed her mind than she heard voices and caught a glimpse of movement through the trees up ahead, a group of men standing around while their horses drank from the brook. Obviously she'd come closer to the road than she'd intended.

Quickly, she dropped into a crouch, concealing herself in the undergrowth, heaving a sigh of relief that she'd spied them first. It was the same group of men who'd ridden by earlier, she realised, eight of them in total, all in plain clothes except for one at the front who was more finely dressed than the others.

She screwed her eyes up, wishing she could get a closer view. If these men were connected to her mother's death then she ought to find out as much as she could about them, to discover *some* clue about their identities at least. But there was only one way to do it…

Carefully, she slid forward onto her hands and knees and crawled closer, her nerves prickling with every movement, horribly aware that the tiniest snap of a twig might give her away. Just a little bit closer… *There*. She stopped, holding her breath as she studied the men. Most of them were strangers, but the one in finer clothes looked vaguely familiar, around her own age, with flaxen-coloured hair and a short beard, although she couldn't place his face.

As she watched, he turned his head, looking straight towards her before saying something to one of the others. The words were muffled, drowned out by the heavy thud of her own heartbeat, although their meaning was clear as he lifted a hand and pointed. For one terrible moment, she thought that she'd been spotted and they were all about to charge into the woodland towards her, but then he shook his head, mounted his horse and they all rode on again.

The moment the sound of hooves faded, Annis sagged forward, lying flat on the ground for a few seconds to catch her breath before leaping up again, spinning about and charging back to the clearing.

'Wake up!' She flung herself on top of Sir Bennet, grabbing hold of his shoulders to shake him awake, before toppling backwards with a startled cry as he jolted upright. For a moment, she had no idea what was happening. The world span, everything seemed to happen in a heartbeat, as he whipped a dagger out of his sleeve and pressed it against her throat, his black eyes glittering.

'Sir Bennet!' she squeaked. He was so close, all she could see was his face, though he looked like a completely different man, fierce and dangerous and *still* holding a knife to her throat…

'Forgive me.' He sucked in a breath as recognition lit his eyes, yanking the knife away and tucking it back inside his sleeve as quickly as it had appeared. 'I thought you were—' He sounded almost as shaken as she felt. 'Are you all right?'

'Yes,' she croaked, pressing a hand to her neck protectively. 'I just saw the men from before. They were resting their horses where the brook crosses the road.'

'The road?' His brows snapped together. 'What were you doing over there?'

'I was trying to stay awake by looking around.'

'That was reckless. You put yourself in danger.'

'Says the man who just held a knife to my throat.' She gave him an arch look. 'Anyway, they've gone now. They rode back west.'

'Did you see their faces?'

'Yes. There was something familiar about one of them, although I don't think I've seen him before.'

Sir Bennet rubbed a hand over his jaw, blowing air between his teeth at the same time. 'Well, whoever they are, now that we're fairly certain they're searching for us, we can't risk re-joining the road, even at night, but we can't travel like this all the way to Hatfield House. It would take weeks.'

'Maybe we could stay here for a while?' she suggested, gesturing around the clearing. As camps went, it was quite pleasant. 'Just until they give up. They can't search for ever.'

'You mean live in the forest?' His lips curved briefly

before a new tension entered his face. 'I doubt they'll give up. And if they bring dogs...' He let the sentence trail away.

'Oh.' She caught her lip between her bottom teeth. They were lucky the riders hadn't brought dogs so far. If they had then she would have been discovered for certain. 'So what should we do?'

'We'll lead the horses though the brook for a while. Hopefully that should be enough to lose our scent. Then we'll leave the woods on the other side and travel east across country until we can join a different road to London. It's still dangerous, but not quite as risky. They won't be expecting it.'

'Brook, east, different road.' She nodded decisively, feigning a bravery she wasn't remotely close to feeling. 'All right, then.'

'And you'd better keep that.' He dropped his gaze to the dagger at her belt. 'Make sure that people can see it. Let them know you're not defenceless. Even when you're not being hunted, the roads can still be dangerous for travellers.'

'How dangerous?' She heard the waver in her own voice. Presumably he was talking about robbers and outlaws, as if they weren't surrounded by enough threats already...

'Don't worry.' He put a hand on her shoulder. 'I've made the journey dozens of times. We just need to keep our wits about us, that's all.'

'I can do that.'

'Good.' His fingers squeezed gently. 'Then we'll be at Hatfield House in no time.'

They trudged onwards. Then they trudged some more. And after that... More trudging. Annis spent most of the afternoon trying to decide which was worse, the trudging or the constant fear of pursuit, but at long last they reached the edge of the forest, emerging onto a hillside that sloped steeply downwards into a grassy valley—or what appeared to be a formerly grassy valley. There hadn't been any rain for several weeks and the landscape was more yellow than green.

'We'll stay here for the night,' Sir Bennet said, his dark gaze searching the horizon, presumably for any sign of riders in the distance, though thankfully there was nobody there.

'Night?' Annis looked up at the sky in surprise. She'd lost all sense of time in the forest, but now he mentioned it the sun was a lot closer to the horizon than she'd expected.

'It'll be dark in another hour.'

'Oh.' She looked around, feeling disoriented and slightly underwhelmed. Apparently their camp for the night was to be a patch of dirt beside an old fallen tree. 'Can we risk a fire?' she asked hopefully.

'A small one. I'll see to it in a moment.' He removed the packs from their horses and dumped them onto the ground. 'Take a seat. You must be tired.'

'I could say the same for you. I can help.'

'As you wish. You can gather some branches for the fire while I go and catch dinner.'

'Wait. What?' She felt a stab of panic. 'You're leaving me alone?'

'Not for long. I won't be far away, I promise, but you need to eat.' He fixed her with a stern look. 'And don't tell me you're not hungry.'

'I wasn't going to.' She shook her head, actually surprised by how hungry she felt. Or at least by how her stomach felt. Her brain might not want to eat, but apparently her body had other ideas.

'Good. Because you're going to need all the energy you can get.'

She watched as he disappeared back into the trees and then set to work, gathering twigs and small branches and depositing them into a heap beside the log, keeping a wary eye on her surroundings the whole while. Now that it was twilight, the forest looked different, less like a refuge and more intimidating. All of the branches that had provided welcoming safety and shelter during the day now seemed like spindly arms reaching out towards her. There were strange sounds too, creaks and cracks and the eerie rustle of the wind through the leaves. For a moment, it sounded as if the entire forest was sighing.

She gave a nervous shiver and placed all of the branches into a pile, arranging the smaller twigs and some dried leaves in the centre, then building a ring of stones around it, before sitting back on her haunches and looking around at their makeshift campsite. She'd never slept outside before, never slept anywhere except for her own bed in her own bedchamber... The thought caused a sharp pang in her chest, so strong she almost doubled over. This time yesterday, that was where she'd been, kissing her mother goodnight and retiring to bed in blissful ignorance of the danger already gathering against them. This time just over a month ago both of her parents had still been alive, and she could never have conceived of the horror ahead. That was how little time it had taken for her whole life to fall apart.

She brushed a hand across her cheek, wiping away a tear, just as Sir Bennet pushed his way back through the undergrowth, throwing a rabbit onto the ground in front of her.

'Dinner.'

'That was quick.' She blinked the remaining moisture from her eyes and gestured towards her pile of firewood, relieved by the distraction. 'What do you think? I would have lit it, but I didn't know where you keep the tinderbox.'

'Ah. I should have thought of that.' He reached into his jerkin and pulled one out. 'You've done a good job.'

'You sound surprised.'

'Forgive me, I didn't mean it that way.' He gave her an apologetic look as he crouched down, pulling out a flint and striking it against the fire steel. 'I just don't know many ladies who could build a campfire so quickly. Play the lute or embroider a cushion, yes—build a fire, no.'

'My mother taught me a lot of practical skills. She thought that women ought to be able to live independently.' She tipped her head to one side, struck by a sudden idea. 'Maybe she was preparing me in case something like this ever happened.'

He lifted his head, regarding her thoughtfully for a few seconds while sparks caught the wood. 'Maybe she was.'

An owl hooted suddenly and they both jumped. Sir Bennet was on his feet in an instant, hunched protectively in front of her, knife in hand.

'False alarm.' Annis laughed nervously. 'Fortunately I'm getting used to you doing that.'

'Sorry.'

'At least you were on my side this time.' She took his place by the fire, carefully feeding bigger twigs into the burgeoning flames. 'Sir Bennet... Can I ask you a few questions? They're not about who you're taking me to, I promise.'

'Aren't you tired?'

'Exhausted, but I still have questions.'

'Why do I get the feeling I'm going to regret this?' He sat down and reached for the rabbit. 'All right, but let's make dinner first.'

'One question.' Ben propped his shoulders against the fallen tree trunk after they'd finished eating and he'd raked over the dying embers of the fire. As much as he appreciated the warmth, he hadn't dared risk letting it burn all night. Not while there were riders out there hunting for them. '*Just* one. Then you need to get some rest.'

'*One?*' Annis gave a snort. She was lying on the opposite side of the fire, already wrapped in a blanket. 'I need ten at least.'

'Three.'

'Seven.'

'Five. That's your final offer.'

'Oh, all right.' She rolled onto her side, propping herself up on one elbow. 'What did your mother mean when she said you'd only just got home?'

'Ah.' He frowned at the reminder. 'When we first met at Cariscombe, I was on my way to Draycote Manor for a visit. Usually I live elsewhere, as part of Prince Edward's household. It moves around, but most of the time he's at Hatfield House.'

Her jaw dropped. 'But that's where you said we're going!'

'It is, although Edward is away at present. That's why I was able to come home.' He paused briefly, wondering how much to reveal. 'The person I'm taking you to serves Lady Elizabeth, the King's daughter. She lives at Hatfield House, too. The King believes it's a healthier environment than London for his children.'

'The King's daughter...' Annis let out a long whistle. 'How long will it take for us to get there?'

'Usually about four days of hard riding. Travelling this way, probably a week, maybe longer.'

'So I have time to ask a lot more questions?'

'You do, although I may not answer all of them.'

'We'll see about that.' She gave him a pointed look. 'And that last one doesn't count, by the way. So what do you do at Hatfield House?'

'I teach the Prince archery.'

'Are you any good?'

He permitted himself a swift grin. 'The King only wants the best for his son.'

'And you're the best?'

'One of them.'

'That's reassuring to know. Who's George?'

He stiffened, aware of a muscle twitching in his jaw. 'You've had your five questions.'

'Have I?'

'That's six.'

'Just one more?'

'Seven.'

'*Please.* Who's George?'

He gave a small sigh. 'My son.'

'You're married?' She gave a jolt, as if she were genuinely surprised.

'No—I was, but she died two years ago.'

'Oh...' She nodded with a look of understanding. 'You mean from the sweating sickness? It was terrible. So many people died. Both my parents were sick for a long time.'

'My wife wasn't. It took less than a day.'

'How terrible. I'm sorry. What's your son like?'

'Five years old with curly hair and blue eyes. He acts like he has no idea who I am.' Ben stretched his legs out, not sure why he'd added that last part.

Her eyes widened. 'Why?'

'I took the position at court shortly after he was born and I've spent most of his childhood away. Now my mother thinks I ought to give it up and return home.'

'So why don't you?'

'For a start, because it's not so easy to say no to the King. And because I can't go home, not permanently.' He had no idea why he was telling her this either...

'Why not?'

'Because I made a promise to myself after my wife died. Never to marry again and never to return home, not to live anyway.'

'Why on earth would you make a promise like that?' She looked horrified. 'I don't know what I would do if someone told me I couldn't go back to Cariscombe.'

He lifted a shoulder. 'It's just how it is. I visit occasionally to see George and my mother, but that's all.'

'I see.' She bit down on her bottom lip, as if she really didn't. 'In that case, I'm sorry for making you leave so soon after you got back. Without saying goodbye to your son either.'

'It couldn't be helped.' He rubbed a hand over his jaw. 'Now that's definitely enough questions. You've had more than five.'

'Just one more. Have I put him in danger?' She sounded anxious suddenly. 'Everything happened so quickly last night that it never occurred to me, but if people found out that you'd helped me, could I be putting him at risk? Your mother, too?'

'No, I don't think so. Besides, there was no alternative. I couldn't just abandon you.'

'Some men might have.'

'Some men might have,' he conceded. 'Now go to sleep. I'll wake you when it's your turn to watch.'

'I could watch first, if you like?'

He narrowed his eyes, noticing the fearful look in hers. 'It won't help to put it off. You'll have to sleep eventually.'

A half-embarrassed, half-guilty expression flickered across her face. 'I'm just afraid of dreaming. I don't want to remember. *Or* think.'

'I know, but I'll be here.' He held onto her gaze, trying to reassure her. 'Now close your eyes. That's an order, Mistress Flemming.'

'Annis.' She sighed as she lay down. 'You can call me Annis. Since it seems like we're going to be travelling together for a while.'

'In that case, my friends call me Ben.'

'Ben.' She lifted a hand to cup her cheek as she laid her head on the blanket. 'Goodnight.'

Chapter Six

The next few days seemed to drag on for ever. There were no more signs of pursuit, though Annis had a sneaking suspicion that time had stopped and the pair of them were destined to wander through identical scenery—up and down hills, through rounded valleys and along dusty tracks—for the rest of their lives, or at least until they finally collapsed from exhaustion. They ate and slept only when they needed to and the rest of the time they kept moving.

Fortunately, Ben seemed to know where they were, but she'd never imagined that anywhere could be so far away or that her body could feel so wretched. Every part of her ached, especially her thighs, which were sore and chafed from so many hours in the saddle. They were lucky in one regard with the dry weather, which allowed them to camp outside rather than risk sleeping in taverns where they might attract notice. But the blazing sunshine was relentless and the heat oppressive. Her cheeks felt permanently flushed and she was horribly aware of sweat pouring between her shoulder blades as they rode, making her clothes stick to her back. No doubt she smelled terrible too.

At the same time, she was aware that their situation, as hard as it was, could also have been a great deal worse. She never noticed Ben watching her—and whenever *she* looked, his gaze was always focused intently on the road—and yet somehow he seemed to know whenever she was hungry or tired or upset or simply reaching the end of her tether. Always giving her the biggest portion of food, letting her sleep first and for the longest amount of time.

Meanwhile, her mind struggled to come to terms with the attack on her mother. During the day, her emotions swung wildly between anger and grief about what had happened and trepidation about what was to come, while at night she was plagued by nightmares, waking up with her heart pounding so hard she thought it was going to burst straight out of her chest. Each time she awoke it was to find Ben crouched by her side with an understanding expression, ready to talk or fetch her a wineskin. One time, she'd been so upset that she'd simply flung her arms around him, needing comfort. He'd stiffened at the contact, his body going so rigid that for one mortifying moment she'd thought he'd been going to push her away. But then he'd wrapped his arms around her instead, holding her close and letting her sob on his shoulder for as long as she'd needed, which, as it turned out, had been a considerably long time.

The following morning, they hadn't discussed what had happened, eating a small breakfast of dried meat and bread before mounting their palfreys and carrying on with the journey, but she'd found herself looking at him differently. She'd rarely been so close to a man who wasn't her father before and she'd certainly never embraced one, and yet embracing Ben had felt strangely comforting, as if they shared some kind of affinity. For a few minutes she'd felt safe, as if everything was really going to be all right. More than that, he'd stirred a whole new confusing feeling inside her, one she didn't have a name for, but that for some reason caused goosebumps to break out on her skin whenever she thought of it.

After four solid days of riding, they decided they were far enough away from Cariscombe to safely stop at a village to buy some provisions, but as they drew closer she found her nose twitching, noticing a strange, foul smell on the air. There was something wrong with the scene before them, too. The village was too quiet, the streets empty, as if it were completely deserted.

'What's that smell?' She covered her nose with her hand.

'A plague pit.' Ben drew rein with a sharp tug. 'We can't stop here.'

Annis gasped, feeling a chill despite the blistering heat of the midday sun, struck with a combination of horror and pity. She'd heard rumours about the sweating sickness being particularly bad again that year. No wonder there was nobody out on the streets. Any survivors were probably cowering inside their homes, afraid to come out. They definitely wouldn't want visitors.

'Those poor people. Isn't there anything we can do to help?' She felt her eyes well with tears, unable to drag them away from the deserted streets.

'Unfortunately not. I wish there was.' He reached for her bridle, turning them both around. 'Are you all right?'

'No.' She sniffed, feeling exhausted and homesick all of a sudden. 'You know, I used to wonder sometimes what was out here, in the world beyond Cariscombe, but now I wish I could go back... I miss my mother. Although I'm very grateful for your help.'

'You don't have to explain.' His tone was gentle and

kind. 'You've had a great deal to cope with in a short space of time.'

She sniffed again, drawing her brows together thoughtfully. Maybe it was the mention of plague, but she was suddenly struck by a memory that had been dancing around the back of her mind for days.

'When we met, you thought I was sickly, didn't you?' she asked slowly. 'Your mother said the same, too.'

'Yes.' He seemed surprised by the question.

'Because that's what my father told you?'

'Yes.'

'What did he say exactly?'

'Just that you'd never been strong and were prone to illness.'

'Which was why he couldn't invite people to our house...' she murmured. 'But I'm never ill. *Never.* So I don't understand why he would tell people that.' She swung towards Ben enquiringly, lifting a hand to her forehead to shield her eyes from the bright midday sun. 'Do you think it's odd that I've hardly met anyone from outside my own house? I mean, I've never known any different so it seems normal to me, but *is* it odd?'

He gave her a sidelong look, as if he were afraid of saying the wrong thing. 'It's a little...unusual.'

'And I've never travelled anywhere. No further than the village, and that was only a few times a year. Is that odd, too?'

Another pause. 'For a lady of your station, I suppose so.'

'My mother said she didn't tell me about her past because she was trying to protect me, but from what? There must have been a reason my parents thought it safer to hide me away and tell everyone I was sickly. I just wish I knew what it was.'

'I've no idea, although given that you're an heiress, it was unlikely you could have stayed hidden for ever, especially once you came of age for marriage.' Ben lifted an eyebrow. 'Forgive me for asking, but why aren't you married already?'

'Because my mother advised against it. She warned me that marriage was a prison for most women and it was much safer to keep my fortune and independence.'

'A prison?' A strange, half-startled, half-guilty expression passed over his face.

'Yes. She never said so in front of my father, of course, although I don't think she was referring to him either. They were very happy together.'

'But didn't your father want to arrange a marriage for you?'

'No. He just said that if I ever wanted a match then he'd select some appropriate suitors and I could choose between them.'

'You could *choose*?' He sounded amazed.

'Yes, not that I ever cared to.' She started to pull her shoulders back and then slouched again. 'But then Father died and Mother seemed so frightened, I thought that maybe she'd changed her mind and was planning a marriage for me, after all. When I saw you approaching Cariscombe that first day, I was afraid that was why you were there.'

'You mean, you thought I was a suitor?' There was a sharp edge to his voice suddenly.

'Only at first. That's part of the reason I was so unwelcoming, but then you mentioned your message and…well,

I suppose I wasn't much more welcoming then either, but I was anxious.'

'I must have made a bad first impression on you.'

'It wasn't that.' She was taken aback by the bitter way he spoke, as if he were genuinely offended. 'It's just hard to be told you have a choice and then for it to be taken away.'

'Mmm.' He twisted his face away, his expression brooding.

'What about your marriage?' She decided to change the subject. 'Was it a love match?'

'No.' He still sounded tense. 'My parents arranged it with her parents.'

'How odd. I mean, I've heard it's the custom, but it's such a strange idea, having to spend the rest of your life with someone you haven't even chosen for yourself. What if you don't get along? What are you supposed to do then?'

He didn't answer, his expression unreadable.

'*Did* you get along?' she persisted.

There was a long pause before he finally spoke again. 'The first time I saw her, I thought I was the luckiest man alive.'

'Oh… You must have loved her very deeply.'

He made a sound like a grunt. 'I felt guilty for not being with her when she died, for not…'

She averted her eyes as his voice trailed away, the note of pain obvious. He sounded utterly heartbroken. That explained why he couldn't go back to live at Draycote Manor. Clearly it hurt too much to live in the place he'd shared with his beloved wife. For a moment, she wondered what it would be like, to be loved so deeply…

'I'm sorry.' The words didn't seem sufficient somehow.

'So am I.' He threw a swift glance over his shoulder before digging his knees into his palfrey's sides. 'Come on, we need to get as far away from here as possible.'

'Yes.' She watched him go, feeling a pang of something like wistfulness.

They rode hard, galloping as far and as fast as the horses could manage, past a couple of farms and a windmill, all of them seemingly deserted, though he wasn't just trying to outrun the plague, Ben realised. He was trying to outrun Annis's questions too. He didn't think he'd ever met anyone quite so inquisitive. It was no wonder, given the circumstances of her sheltered upbringing, but Eleanor was the last person in the world he wanted to talk about. The plague pit was just another reminder of how completely he'd failed her. As for marriage, that was definitely a subject best avoided.

'We'll stop here for a while.' He finally drew rein to give the horses some rest.

'Thank goodness.' Annis slid out of her saddle with a weary groan, pressing her hands against the small of her back. 'Do you remember the sycamore tree where we first met? I fell out of it once when I was twelve years old. This feels like that all over again.'

'Sorry.' Ben winced, feeling a pang of guilt at having pushed her so hard. He ought to have remembered she wasn't accustomed to riding so far. 'Here. Have something to eat.'

'Thank you.' Her fingers brushed lightly against his as she took the chunk of bread he offered her. 'How much further is it to Hatfield House now?'

'Only another couple of days, but the land is flatter from now on.' He frowned, surprised to find his hand tingling where she'd touched him. Quickly, he flexed his fingers, trying to shake the feeling away.

'That's a relief.' She stretched her body from side to side, wriggling her hips in a way that made his pulse quicken uncomfortably. 'So what will happen when we get there? Will you take me straight to this Isolde?'

'Yes.' He shifted his gaze away, tipping his head back to watch a flock of birds circling overhead.

'Do you think she will help me find out who killed my mother?'

'Hopefully the Justice of the Peace will do that, but as for Isolde, I don't know,' he answered hesitantly. He didn't want to discourage her, but she needed to be prepared. 'To be honest, I don't know how she'll react to any of this. I'm certain she'll want justice, but whether she'll be able to do anything about it is another matter.'

'I see. Well, whether she can or not, I'll find the truth out somehow. I won't give up, not ever.'

'Annis...' Ben clenched his jaw. It seemed she wasn't going to be discouraged no matter what he said, and apparently he couldn't bring himself to be any sterner with her anyway. 'Look, I still have a couple of weeks left before the Prince returns to Hatfield House, and I want to spend some more time with George. Once you're safe, I'll go back to Somerset and see what I can find out.'

'Really?' Her face lit up. 'You'd do that for me?'

'I will. I'll just need to rest the horses for a day or so and get some supplies first.' He inclined his head. 'I might need a bit of sleep, too.'

'Wait...' Her expression clouded again. 'What if it's dangerous?'

'I'll be careful, don't worry.'

'But I *will* worry. I don't want you getting hurt because you were trying to help me.'

'Then I won't get hurt.'

'It's not funny.' She gave him a chiding look, and then relented. 'But I do appreciate the offer. Will you let me know what you discover?'

'Of course. As soon as I return, as long as I'm not needed at court.'

'Thank you.' She stretched again. 'Will you tell me about the court? And London? What's the city like?'

'Big. Crowded. Overwhelming.' He lifted his shoulders. 'That's what I thought the first time I saw it anyway. I was terrified. There were people everywhere and so many buildings, all pressed up against each other. I felt so small.'

'*You* felt small?' She made a show of tipping her head back to look up at him.

'I was only ten at the time,' he pointed out.

'What about the court?'

'It varies,' he answered tactfully. The mood at court was better than it had been a few months ago, but it was still tense. Menace lurked just below the surface of every conversation. A wise man kept his head down and his mouth firmly shut.

'That bad?' She gave a nervous laugh.

'It's complicated.' He rubbed his hands together, wondering how much to tell her about the ways of the court. Given her somewhat unusual upbringing, he probably ought to give her some warning about how to behave, just for her own safety. 'Did your parents tell you much about the King?'

'We talked about him sometimes. I remember my father

saying that he'd just married his sixth wife, and my mother saying she still felt sorry for the last one.'

Ben winced, feeling a moment's panic at her bluntness. 'That isn't something to say out loud.'

'Well, I wouldn't say it to the King, *obviously*.' She rolled her eyes. 'Although I felt sorry for Katherine Howard too. My father said she was found guilty of betraying the King with another man so he had her beheaded.'

'Because she committed treason. Adultery against the King.'

'My mother said she didn't blame her.' She shook her head. 'You know, she was only my age when she died. It seems so wrong, especially when the King is so much older.'

'Annis.' Ben put a hand to his forehead. 'It's not that I disagree, but the King doesn't tolerate criticism. Any criticism. Even his closest friends live in fear. A single wrong word can be dangerous and there are spies everywhere. So when we get to Hatfield House, you can't say such things to *anyone*.'

'What a horrible way to live. Very well. I'll keep my mouth closed.'

'Thank you.'

'*When* we get to Hatfield, that is. Until then...' She smiled mischievously. 'I doubt you would have wasted your time looking after me for the past week if your plan was to turn me in for treason.'

'Maybe I just like your company.' He couldn't resist smiling back, his hand tingling again as his gaze lingered on her face. It was all he could allow himself to do, but it was a good thing they were approaching Hatfield—he was finding it harder and harder to *stop* looking at her. Somehow she had the ability to look simultaneously incredibly messy and yet very desirable. She was also stubborn, inquisitive and clever, with a resilience he hadn't expected from somebody who'd never travelled before. He would have expected her to be shy and timid, but if she was frightened she wasn't showing it. She was unique, unlike any other woman he'd ever met before—*nothing* like Eleanor or the sophisticated ladies of the court. She was tougher, braver and ten times more attractive, with her wild bird's nest hair, guileless hazel eyes and the row of freckles, brought out by the sun, that now spread across her cheeks and over the bridge of her nose. And when she smiled, the combination of sparkling eyes and curving lips was captivating...

None of which he ought to be noticing, he reminded himself. No good could come of thinking about her in that way, not least for her. She deserved better, somebody who could make her happy. Only he seemed completely incapable of *not* noticing her. He was aware of every movement she made. She stirred feelings in him he thought he'd long since put aside.

'Do you feel that?' She interrupted his thoughts suddenly, tilting her head sideways.

'What?' He gave a jolt.

'The air. It's changed. There was no breeze a few moments ago.'

They both looked over their shoulders at the same moment. Sure enough, a large anvil-shaped cloud was drifting rapidly in their direction, as if it were trying to catch them unawares. There was a new tension in the air too, a sense of tumult building all around them. He would have detected it sooner if he hadn't been so preoccupied with staring at her.

'Come on.' He reached for his horse as a rumble of thunder sounded in the distance. 'We need to take shelter.'

'Maybe we could try to outrun it?' she suggested.

'It's too late and the horses are already tired. We have to take cover.'

He looked around, searching for somewhere they could shelter, but the land was flat and empty except for a few scraps of woodland. There wasn't a single building in sight either, although, considering their proximity to the plague village, it would be probably safer to take their chances with the storm.

'There isn't any low ground.' Annis echoed what he was thinking. 'We'll have to head for some trees. We can shelter amidst the smaller ones.'

'Good idea.' He pointed. 'There's a copse over there.'

They clutched at their reins, tugging the palfreys along the road towards the trees. It wasn't ideal, but at least there were no bodies of water close by, and with the wind building so quickly it was the best they could do. Both of their horses were skittish now, sensing the danger in the air, whinnying and flaring their nostrils as they reared onto their haunches and staggered sideways, protesting all the way.

'Give me your reins!' Ben called out as they reached the edge of the copse. 'I'll hold onto them. You shelter as best you can, but keep your eyes open. If lightning hits any of the trees, you need to be ready to run.'

'No! I'm not leaving you to manage two horses alone.' Annis shook her head, stubbornly holding onto her reins. 'If they panic, it'll be too much for one person to hold them and we can't afford to lose a horse.'

Briefly he thought about protesting and then changed his mind. She was right. If the horses bolted, they would be in really big trouble—and there was no time to protest anyway as lightning cracked overhead and the skies opened, spilling sheets of water over the landscape.

'It's like a waterfall!' Annis called out, lifting her voice above the sound of the deluge. The drops sounded more like hailstones, hitting the ground, bursting open and then splattering wide until the ground seemed to be covered with hundreds of tiny, fast-flowing streams. Meanwhile the wind was whipping through the trees, causing a high-pitched howling sound that seemed to echo all around them.

'Look out!' Annis called out suddenly, lifting her hands to his chest and pushing hard.

Ben staggered backwards, wrapping an arm instinctively around her waist as she flung herself against him, then stared in shock as a large branch fell to the ground where he'd just been standing.

'Thank you.' He let out a ragged breath, very aware of the pressure of her hands through the linen of his shirt, not to mention the feeling of her waist beneath his fingertips. All of their clothes were already soaked through, clinging to their bodies in ways that left little to the imagination. 'That would have hurt.'

'What next?' She tipped her head back, panting heavily as she looked up through the branches at the grey clouds above.

'What do you mean?' He frowned, finding it hard to think clearly all of a sudden.

'First a mob, then a fire, then being chased through a forest and now this! It's been disaster after disaster ever since we met.' She gave a high-pitched laugh. 'What's going to happen next?'

'I'm not sure I want to know.' He gave a grudging chuckle.

'I wouldn't blame you for abandoning me.' She made a sound that was part laugh, part sob. 'I seem to bring nothing but trouble.'

He watched as she dug her teeth into her bottom lip, as if she were trying to stop herself from crying properly. Her face was already wet, although whether that was from rain or tears, or a combination of both, he couldn't tell. The sight pierced his heart. And he was staring at her again, for longer than he ought to...

'I'm not going to abandon you.' He let go of her waist and lifted his hand to her chin without thinking, tilting it so that she was looking straight up at him. 'I swear, Annis, I won't abandon you. No matter what happens.'

'Thank you.' She whispered the words as her gaze latched onto his, her hazel eyes wide and compelling. He was aware that he ought to let go and step back from her, only for some reason he couldn't bring himself to do it. His whole body seemed frozen in place.

'Annis...' He heard her name emerge from his lips, though he had no idea why or what else he wanted to say. It took him a few seconds to realise that he was bending his head too, moving closer towards her as if drawn by some invisible yet completely irresistible force.

'Yes?' Her own lips parted.

He gave a start as lightning cracked overhead, bringing him back to his senses.

'Nothing.' He dropped her chin abruptly. 'Forgive me.'

He moved away, turning his attention back to the storm while his heart pounded so hard he could feel it thumping against his ribcage. What the hell had just happened?

He'd almost kissed her! Almost taken advantage of a vulnerable young woman who'd just been through a terrible ordeal, who had absolutely no experience of men, who he was supposed to be protecting, and with whom he had no possible future! A few seconds ago, she'd been crying, or close to tears at least. Only a scoundrel would kiss her under such circumstances.

He gritted his teeth, battling a combination of desire, frustration and guilt as thunder rolled and the rain continued to pour down in sheets. The sooner he got her safely to Hatfield House, the better for them both.

Chapter Seven

'There it is…' Ben pointed at a magnificent, red stone building in the distance. It had large gables at each end, a square tower in the centre and was surrounded by an expanse of immaculately tended gardens. 'Hatfield House.'

'Truly?' Annis looked from him to the house and then back again, her expression disbelieving.

'Truly.' He quirked an eyebrow in bemusement. 'Don't you believe me?'

'Of course, but…' She gave her head a small shake. 'I suppose I'd just started to believe we were going to be riding for ever.'

'I know what you mean.' He smiled and then looked away again quickly. Now they were nearing the end of their journey, he felt conflicted, torn between regret and relief. Regret because he suspected he was going to miss her when she was gone, relief because he'd fulfilled his duty to her mother and got her there safely. But it was high time to part ways. Her presence was becoming more and more disconcerting for his peace of mind. Not to mention the rest of him.

'You've done well for someone who hasn't left home before. I would never have guessed.' He cleared his throat awkwardly. 'How do you feel?'

'Like I could sleep for a week.'

'Then hopefully you'll be allowed to.' He gestured ahead. 'I'll ride as far as the river with you and then you can go the rest of the way by yourself. I'll keep watch and make sure you get safely inside, then I'll follow in a few hours. If we want people to believe you've made the journey alone then we can't risk being seen together.'

'But why do we want people to believe that I travelled here alone?'

'Because if we arrive together there'll be rumours. A man and a woman travelling in each other's company for over a week could cause quite a scandal.'

She looked surprised. 'But surely if we tell people it was an emergency they'll understand?'

'Unfortunately, the court doesn't work that way. Just the fact that you're supposed to have made the journey alone will damage your reputation, but with any luck your friend will defend you.' He gave a wry smile. 'The size of your fortune ought to help too.'

'Oh…' She frowned. 'But I can tell my *friend* the truth?'

'Yes. Given who she is, she should understand.'

'Right. Well, regardless, I ought to change my clothes first.' She plucked at her hose. 'I can't meet anyone dressed like a boy.'

'Good point. A bath wouldn't go amiss either.'

'What?' She jerked her head up with a splutter. 'Are you saying that I smell?'

'Yes. No! Sorry.' He made a face. 'Eleanor used to tell me I had as much charm as an ox. I meant that we both do. *Understandably*, since we've been on the road for so long.'

'Eleanor?' The curious light in her eyes was back. 'Was that your wife's name?'

'Yes,' he answered brusquely. 'We can take turns to bathe in the river.'

'But what if somebody sees us? You just said you wanted to avoid a scandal.'

'I'll stand guard.' He lifted a hand. 'And I'll keep my back turned, I promise.'

'Then you'll only be guarding me on one side.' She tutted and then sniffed at her sleeve. 'But I suppose it *is* necessary.'

They rode onwards, breaking away from the road after a furlong to make their way down a steep incline, towards a narrow river lined by rows of willow trees. It was a perfect place to bathe. Even if there were people close by, it was unlikely that anyone would be able to see them through the foliage.

'Here.' Ben reached into his pack as they dismounted, pulling out a bundle of women's clothes. 'These are for you.'

'Thank you.' Annis kicked off her boots and headed down to the riverbank at once, calling back over her shoulder, 'Although I'm going to miss wearing hose. They're so much more comfortable than a kirtle.'

Ben harrumphed and turned around, folding his arms as he looked from side to side. He couldn't help thinking that he was going to miss her wearing hose too, especially in the rain...

'It's freezing!' she shouted after a few minutes, her voice higher pitched than usual.

'Try not to think about it,' he called back, chuckling at her indignant tone. 'Just do it quickly. The sooner you put your head under the water, the sooner you can pull it out again.'

There was a splash followed by a shriek.

'That was terrible advice!' She sounded as if her teeth

were chattering. 'How long to get rid of the smell, do you think?'

'You don't smell that bad!'

'You're only saying that because you smell the same. They're probably wondering what the stink is all the way from Hatfield House!'

'Probably.' He laughed and then sobered again at the sound of splashing, his imagination sparking with visions of her naked body, her small breasts streaming with drop-lets of water, making her wet and slick and shiny. What harm would it do to take a quick peek?

He stiffened, surprised by his own wandering thoughts, keeping his gaze fixed on the road. Since when had he started thinking about her body, naked or otherwise? Sud-denly he wished she would hurry up and get out of the river so that *he* could get in. A cold bath was just what he needed. The colder, the better. Preferably with a layer of ice.

'Oh, no!' she exclaimed behind him.

'What?' He felt a jolt of panic, only just stopping him-self from turning around. 'What's the matter?'

'I forgot to bring something to dry myself with. Do you have a cloth I can use?'

'Just a moment.' He went back to his horse for a blanket, then walked backwards, holding it out behind him. 'We'll have to make do with this.'

'Look out!' Her hand pressed against the small of his back. 'You're about to trip over a root.'

He grunted, the touch of her fingers causing a feeling like fire beneath his skin. He really, *really* needed to get in that river.

'Phew, that's better.' There were sounds of rustling and rubbing. 'Your turn.' She came to stand in front of him, wrapped in the blanket, a pair of slender ankles poking out underneath. 'I'll get dressed behind that tree while you bathe.'

He grunted again. At that moment, it was the only sound he seemed capable of.

Annis peered out from the side of the tree trunk as Ben strode down to the river, casting garments aside as he went. First his shirt and undershirt, revealing powerfully corded muscles across his back and shoulders, then his belt, then his...

She gasped and whirled about, feeling alarmingly short of breath as she opened up her bundle of clothes and set to work dressing. Lady Joan had provided a linen shift as well as a plain, respectable-looking blue kirtle with a matching partlet and hood. They were slightly worn and badly crumpled, but any dress was more respectable than what she'd been wearing for the past week.

She pulled on the shift, then risked another peek around the tree trunk on the pretence of assuring herself Ben hadn't slipped and fallen in some way. She'd never seen a naked man before. Or partially naked, since the lower half of his body was now submerged in the river. Or it had been a moment ago.

She gave a small squeak as he took a step backwards and a pair of buttocks emerged from the water, whipping her head round so fast she felt slightly dizzy. She'd definitely never seen *those* before. She wondered what the front view would be like, but she could hardly look without running the risk of him catching her and, besides, it would be wrong. Scandalous. Immoral... She oughtn't to have peeked at all, especially when he'd kept his own face averted from her. His privacy was no less important than hers... Meanwhile, there seemed to be a small bird in her chest, beating its wings frantically against her ribcage, just as it had during the storm, when she'd flung herself against him and he'd looked at her in a way that had made her forget all the dangers surrounding them and want to—

'Have you finished dressing?' His voice almost made her jump out of her skin.

'Not quite.' She wrenched the kirtle over her head, warmth rushing through her as she peeped round the tree again, but he was still facing in the opposite direction, giving her a fresh opportunity to admire the view. Which was very firm and...tight. Well-muscled seemed the best description. Probably from so many hours in the saddle. She felt a spark of something low down in her stomach, like kindling catching alight.

'Ready!' she declared, diving back behind the tree as he started to turn, almost tripping over as her foot caught in the kirtle. Oof! She clutched at the trunk to steady herself. She'd completely forgotten Lady Joan's advice about adjusting the hem! Ben's wife had obviously been quite a bit taller than she was.

'Annis?' His voice was significantly closer now.

'I'm all right.' She strove to sound calm. 'I just stumbled, that's all.'

'Ah. I need the blanket.'

'Oh...yes, of course.' She plucked it off the branch where she'd hung it to dry and held it out to one side.

'Thank you.' Their hands touched as he took it, causing a hot shiver to ripple up her arm and then spread outwards through her body.

'So...' She pursed her lips, tugging at her laces as she listened to the sound of him dressing on the other side of the tree. 'I don't suppose you're ready to tell me a little more about my *friend* Isolde?'

'Actually, I am.' His voice was muffled, as if he were rubbing the cloth over his head. 'Since you'll need to ask for her.'

'I will?'

'Yes. Her full name is Lady Isolde Downing.' There was a brief pause. 'You're certain your mother never mentioned her to you before the night of the attack?'

'Not that I remember.'

'So you've never heard the name before?' he pressed.

'I've already told you, never.'

There was another, longer pause this time. 'In that case, your meeting might come as a bit of a shock for both of you at first, but she ought to be able to explain everything.'

'About my mother?'

'I think so. It was she who sent me with the message for your mother.' He came round the side of the tree then, dressed in clean clothes and pushing a coil of damp hair away from his forehead. 'Hopefully, all of this will make sense soon. Trust me.'

'I do trust you.' She noticed the swell of his forearm through his damp shirt and quickly lifted her gaze, trying very hard to look like a person who would never even dream of peeking at a naked man. 'But what if the guards won't let me in?'

'They will. Just tell them they'll have Lady Isolde to answer to otherwise.' His lips quirked. 'You'll see what I mean when you meet her.'

She blinked. When he smiled like that, he looked younger and more handsome. How was it she'd never noticed how handsome he was before? 'So this is goodbye?'

'I'm afraid so.' His gaze sobered again as he pushed a

hand through his hair, making it look even more tousled. 'I doubt that we'll get another chance to talk before I leave for Somerset again after I've rested my horse. The King doesn't like men near his daughter's household, not unless they're sixty years old anyway.'

'I see.' She studied his face, suddenly noticing how tired he looked. There were purple shadows around his eyes that looked like bruises—and no wonder. Now that she thought of it, he'd been on guard almost constantly for the past week and a half, barely sleeping while he'd taken care of her. It must have been exhausting, and yet he hadn't complained or raised his voice even once.

'In that case, you'd better take this.' She held out the dagger he'd given her on their first day together. 'I probably shouldn't go inside armed.'

'Good point.' His lips quirked as he slid it onto his own belt. 'I'm glad it wasn't needed.'

'So am I.' Impulsively, she took a step forward, holding a hand out. 'Thank you for keeping me alive.'

Something flared in the depths of his eyes as he looked down at her hand for a long moment and then folded his own around it. Somehow the movement pulled her even closer towards him, close enough that she could feel the warmth of his body emanating through his damp shirt.

'And thank you for everything else too,' she went on, talking quickly so he wouldn't notice how much his proximity affected her. 'For making me feel better.'

'Feel better?' He quirked an eyebrow.

'Yes. After everything that happened, you stopped me from despairing. You made me want to keep going.' She sucked in a deep breath, aware of heat flooding her cheeks. 'So thank you.'

'You're welcome.' His voice sounded gravelly. 'It was my honour. Goodbye, Annis.'

She swallowed, struck with a sense of the world speeding up and then slowing down again, giving her a heightened awareness of everything about that moment—the feeling of his fingers against hers, the shimmering golden glow of the riverbank, the cloudless sky, the light breeze stirring the willow branches around them, the sound of the river trickling in the background—most of all, the tingling sensation that seemed to fill every nerve ending... She had the strangest sensation of tumbling headlong into the depths of his dark eyes. They looked like warm pools... Without thinking, she raised herself up on her tiptoes and pressed her lips against his, before spinning around again, grasping her horse's bridle and walking away—with only one brief stumble.

Chapter Eight

Annis held tight to the bridle, chest heaving and cheeks blazing as something quivered inside her. Her heart had skipped so many beats it was amazing she was even still upright. Had she really just kissed Ben? She hadn't intended to. She'd acted purely on impulse, because actually saying goodbye to him had been too difficult, but what must he think of her now? He hadn't flinched away, though that was possibly only because he'd been so shocked. His lips had been soft and chilled from the river, and yet somehow they'd sent a fresh bolt of heat straight to her core, sending her temperature soaring even higher. She felt red hot.

Feverishly, she pressed a hand to her forehead, trying to establish some order over her scattered thoughts. She *ought* to be feeling happy—relieved!—that they'd arrived at Hatfield House without being caught. And yet walking away from Ben made her heart ache, as if she were losing someone else dear to her.

Part of her wanted to turn around and go back, to run away from whoever or whatever was inside the house, but she had no choice except to keep going. She and Ben could hardly keep roaming the countryside for ever, and besides, he had other, more important responsibilities: a position at court, an estate, a son. He'd been kind to her. More than that, he'd saved her life, but she'd taken advantage of his kindness for long enough. He'd said it was his duty to protect her and he had, but now that duty was discharged, he was probably glad to be rid of her. He'd probably forget about her completely in a few days.

She threw a quick glance over her shoulder as she re-mounted Berengaria and spurred her in the direction of the house. Was Ben watching her progress? Probably, although there was no sign of him. The only signs of life she could see were a herd of cows being driven by two men to her right and a pair of carts, laden with sacks, being driven by packhorses to her left. To all intents and purposes, Ben was already out of her life.

Her heart plummeted before she hoisted it determinedly up again. On second thoughts, going on alone was for the best. She and Ben had been thrown together by necessity, that was all; now it was time to move on. After all, *she* had responsibilities, too; a house to get back to, a fortune to protect and a mob to bring to justice. She couldn't afford to get distracted, especially not by a man, and *definitely* not when she had absolutely no intention or desire to get married. That would be the same as throwing her independence away! She liked Ben, she felt grateful to him, she might even have enjoyed watching him bathe, but it wasn't as if she had any deeper feelings for him. It was only sentiment that made her wonder otherwise, made her think that if anyone could change her mind about marriage then it would be him. He didn't *seem* like the kind of man who would make marriage a prison...

She brought herself up with a jolt. Had she forgotten her mother's advice so quickly? No, separation was the best thing for both of them, no matter how much she might delude herself into thinking she missed Ben already.

'What do you want?' A guard hailed her as she approached. There were two of them, standing on either side of the gatehouse, both regarding her with a combination of amusement, curiosity and suspicion. No doubt she made a curious picture. A young woman in old-fashioned, crumpled clothes approaching the home of the heirs to the throne as if she belonged there, too. They probably thought that she was some kind of madwoman. After the past few weeks she felt a bit like one, but she'd come this far...

'My name is Annis Flemming.' She stopped in front of the guard who'd spoken, lifting her chin with resolve. 'I'm here to see Lady Isolde Downing.'

'Lady Downing?' For some reason, the name wiped all amusement from his face. 'What do you want with her?'

'It's private business.' She pushed her chin even higher. 'For her ears only.'

'Is she expecting you?'

'No...' she admitted. 'But she'll want to see me.'

The guard moved a step closer, dropping his voice conspiratorially. 'The thing is, she's not the kind of lady whose time you'd want to waste.'

'I'm not. She'll *want* to see me,' Annis repeated more firmly, remembering what Ben had told her. 'Imagine what will happen if you *don't* tell her I'm here and she finds out later.'

'There's no need for threats.' The guard exchanged a faintly nervous glance with his companion. 'Annis Flemming, you said?'

'Yes. From Cariscombe. Thank you.'

'On your head be it.' He stepped aside as she dismounted

and handed the other guard Berengaria's reins. Then he ushered her through the gatehouse, along a gravel path and into the house through a large double door. 'Wait here.'

Annis nodded, too dumbfounded to speak. She'd never seen such a magnificent hall in her entire life. After a week and a half of travel in the open air, it felt like years since she'd been under a roof, and this one was spectacular: high and vaulted, with a plasterwork ceiling covered in fleur-de-lis and Tudor roses. Meanwhile, the rest of the hall was equally impressive, with a minstrel's gallery at one end and a wide fireplace in one wall, with a selection of elaborately carved oak chairs around it. She was tempted to sit down in one and make herself comfortable, but it felt presumptuous somehow. Lady Isolde might think so, too, and she wanted to make a good first impression. If the guards' behaviour was anything to go by, she was frightening enough...but who was she? And how on earth had her mother known her?

At last, she heard rapid footsteps approaching and wrenched her shoulders back, trying to look as calm and ladylike as possible. Unfortunately, it wasn't enough. One look at the other woman and she couldn't help uttering a small scream of shock. Her mother was standing on the opposite side of the room, her gaze cold and accusing.

'Mother?' She staggered backwards, clutching at the back of one of the chairs for support. She needed to touch something solid, to reassure herself that she hadn't just toppled headlong into a dream. Either that or she was looking at some kind of apparition.

'Don't be foolish.'

Annis blinked. The woman's voice was strikingly different to her mother's. It was harder, sharper and a great deal less loving. A few seconds of closer inspection revealed other differences, too. The oval face, high pointed cheekbones and wide blue eyes were the same, but the woman's skin was perfectly smooth and unwrinkled, while her hair was golden where there had been grey strands before. It was the mother from her childhood, looking more stunningly beautiful than ever, but how?

'I don't understand.' The room seemed to be spinning. 'Who are you?'

'You know my name.' The woman came to stand in front of her, dismissing the relieved-looking guard with a flick of her wrist. 'You asked for me.'

'I was told to, but…' She couldn't stop staring. 'You look so much like her.'

'I know.'

'Are you her sister?'

'Not *hers*.' The woman clucked her tongue, looking around. 'Where is she?'

'Who?'

'Our mother, who do you think?'

'*Our* mother?' The spinning sensation was getting faster. 'But how… You mean, you're *my* sister?'

'Yes!' The woman rolled her eyes impatiently. 'For pity's sake, that ought to be obvious to anyone with a brain. Now where is she?'

'She's…' Annis put a hand to her throat. It felt very tight suddenly. 'She's…'

'What?' Panic flashed across the other woman's face as she lunged forward abruptly, grabbing hold of her arm. 'What's happened to her?'

'Ow!' Annis cried out. She tried to wrench herself free as the woman's fingernails dug into her skin, but the grip was too strong, sending a spasm of pain up her arm to her shoulder.

'Tell me what's happened!'

'They called her a witch!' Her voice returned with a vengeance.

'A witch?' The woman's hand fell away as her face blanched. 'Is she...'

'Yes.' Annis nodded miserably, rubbing at her wrist. 'There was a mob. They came at night with pitchforks and—'

'Shh!' the woman hissed. 'Keep your voice down!'

'I'm sorry. I didn't mean...' Annis's voice trailed away as the woman took a few steps backward. For a moment, she thought she was simply going to walk away and abandon her, but instead she seemed to shrink into herself, her arms curling around her waist as her shoulders slumped forward, until she was completely hunched over.

'You didn't know who I was?' Her voice was smaller now. 'She never told you about me?'

'No.' Annis shook her head, too tired and confused now to be tactful. 'I don't understand. How can I have a sister I never knew about? We can't be so far apart in age.'

'Nine years.' The woman straightened again suddenly, as if she'd merely crouched down to pick something up, the moment of weakness evaporating as quickly as it had arrived. 'You're eighteen, are you not? And we're not sisters. We're *half*-sisters. We have different fathers.' Her blue eyes, so uncannily like their mother's, narrowed. 'You must take after yours. I can't see anything of her in you.'

'I know. She was beautiful.' Annis swayed on her feet, beginning to wonder whether coming to Hatfield House had been a mistake after all. So much for having a friend here. There was nothing friendly about Lady Isolde! As for everything making sense finally, the opposite was true. The fog surrounding her was as thick as it had ever been. As a child she'd begged her mother to have another child, to give her a sibling to play with, and yet all that time she'd *had* a sister. A *half*-sister. Only her mother had never told her, had never so much as hinted. Now she felt as though all the nervous energy had just drained from her body, leaving her utterly exhausted and disoriented.

'Did she suffer?' The woman's voice sounded different again, as if she were in pain herself.

'I don't think so. She was stabbed, but… Sir Bennet thought it was quick.'

'Sir Bennet? He brought you here?'

'Yes. When we were attacked, Mother told me to run to Draycote Manor and ask for his aid. She said to ask him to bring me to you. She seemed to think I might be in danger, as well.'

'Is he here?'

'No. He thought it would be better for my reputation if we arrived separately.' She paused. 'He said that if anyone asked, I ought to say I travelled alone.'

The woman gave a sceptical snort. 'As if anyone will believe that.'

'He thought it was less scandalous than saying we travelled together.' She squared her shoulders. 'He'll return here later tonight.'

'And did he tell you what *I'm* supposed to do with you?'

'No. All he told me was that I'd be safe here and that you were a friend.' She laughed, though it sounded odd, echoing inside her head as if she were standing inside a cave. At that precise moment, she hardly cared what happened to her. It was all too much to take in.

The woman looked her up and down critically. 'Your clothes are a mess. You look like a peasant. *And* you're exhausted.' She made it sound like an accusation.

'Yes.' She laughed again.

'What's so funny?'

'Nothing. None of it. It's all terrible.' Annis pressed her palms to her cheeks. Dark shadows were creeping into the edges of her vision and black dots were dancing in front of her eyes. She was aware of sounding hysterical, but the laughter wouldn't stop. And it was better than crying. So she laughed, peals and peals of it racking her frame, until she could barely stand straight and all of her limbs were trembling. Her whole body seemed to be beyond her control. She wanted to keep on laughing, she wanted to sleep for a whole month, she wanted to be back on the road with Ben—

'Stop it!' Lady Isolde's voice was sharp and authoritative, that of someone used to giving orders and being obeyed. If she hadn't been at the end of her tether, Annis thought she might have obeyed, too.

'I will. Any moment now.' She tipped her head back as another peal burst out of her. It was the last thing she remembered before the world tipped, her knees buckled and she crumpled to the floor with a thud.

Chapter Nine

'Bennet Thorne! This is a surprise. We didn't expect you back for a few more weeks!' A man with gaunt cheeks, grey hair and a beard that stretched halfway down his stomach called out from a chair by the privy chamber fireplace.

Ben stopped and put his bag down with a smile. He'd waited until nightfall before making his way through the gates of Hatfield House and into the Prince's apartments, trying to be as unobtrusive as possible so that nobody would connect his early return with Annis's arrival. But it was impossible to avoid being seen completely. If it had been anyone else hailing him, he might have worried, but Richard Northam was a good friend and one of the few people in the household he trusted completely. He was also the Prince's physician and usually travelled everywhere with him, but at that moment he appeared to be taking his ease, sitting on a chair with one leg propped on a stool and a large goblet in his hand.

'Richard.' Ben put a hand on his shoulder. 'Some unexpected business brought me back early, but what causes *you* to still be here?'

'My knee. I managed to fall off my horse before we were even a quarter of the way to Hampton Court.' Richard tapped the leg in question and chuckled. 'Once everyone stopped laughing, they agreed that Lady Mary's physician could serve both her and Edward for a few weeks. Now you find me enjoying that rarest of all things, some peace and quiet. It's bliss. I may have to make a fool of myself more often.'

'Then I'm sorry to have disturbed you.' Ben tipped his head towards the door. 'Should I go?'

'You, my friend, are allowed to disturb me.' Richard spread his hands out magnanimously. 'Now pour yourself a drink, sit down and explain yourself. *What* unexpected business?'

He did as he was told, pouring a cup of wine from the jug on the table beside Richard before taking a seat opposite. He ought to have known that his friend would guess there was more to the story, and wouldn't be content until he found out what it was either. At almost sixty years old, the physician had keen eyes, a sharp tongue and an even sharper mind.

'Somebody needed my help.'

'*"Somebody"*? You'll need to give me more than that. A family member? A stranger you met on the road? A damsel in distress?'

'Actually...' Ben lifted his cup, bracing himself with a large mouthful of wine. 'The last one.'

'No!' Richard sat forward, eyes glinting with a look of avid interest. 'Now you absolutely must tell me more.'

'All right, but only because I know I can trust you to keep your mouth shut.' Ben threw a cautious glance around the room. 'When I left, Lady Isolde entrusted me with a message, a warning for her mother, though unfortunately it wasn't heeded.' An image of Cariscombe's burning turrets popped into his mind before he pushed it away. 'It's a long story, but the upshot was that I needed to bring her sister back here with me from Somerset. There was a good chance she would be in danger if she stayed.'

'Lady Isolde has a sister?' Richard lifted his eyebrows. 'I had no idea.'

'Half-sister.' He decided *not* to add that the two women had never met before. Instead, he turned his face in the direction of the Lady Elizabeth's apartments, wondering how their first meeting had gone. Lady Isolde was notoriously prickly and difficult to get along with, even for court—from what he'd heard, she made the King himself seem easy-going—but hopefully she'd soften a little for her sister.

Thinking about Annis made him realise how much he missed her already. Spending so much time together had made him wonder how different his life might have been if his parents had betrothed him to a woman like her and not Eleanor, somebody he could have cared for—theoretically maybe even loved. They'd only been apart for a few hours and yet he'd thought about her every minute, one memory in particular. He'd been so shocked by her kiss that, by the time he'd gathered his wits, she'd already been turning and walking away. Then it had taken all of his self-control not to run after her and do it again, only this time more thoroughly… His body stirred anew at the thought. How would she have reacted if he had? Would she have welcomed his embrace or had her kiss simply been a farewell gesture? Admittedly he was out of practice, but it hadn't *felt* like farewell… The way she'd looked at him had sent a surge of desire straight to his core. Eleanor had never looked at him like that, not once in four years of marriage.

'So what's the half-sister like?' Richard's voice jolted

him back to the present. 'As beautiful and terrifying as the delightful Lady Isolde?'

'Beautiful, yes. Terrifying? No.' Ben laughed. 'I'd say they're about as different as it's possible for two sisters to be. You would never guess they were related.'

'And you say that you travelled *all* the way from Somerset with her? *Just* you?'

'Yes. There was no choice. Like I said, she was in danger, although the official story is that she travelled alone.'

'I won't say a word.' Richard tapped the side of his nose. 'Still, it must have been interesting, being on the road with a beautiful young woman for...how long?'

'A week and a half.'

'Indeed? Now you're making me jealous, my friend.'

'It wasn't like that.' Ben tensed at the implication.

'I know. Most men I wouldn't trust for a day, but you're a man of honour. You wouldn't take advantage of a situation like that.' Richard swilled his cup gently. 'Only you've glanced at the door at least half a dozen times since we sat down. Do you like this woman?'

'I admire her.' Ben turned his face towards the fire, avoiding his friend's all too perceptive gaze. 'She's brave and resilient and determined, despite everything she's been through.'

'High praise indeed. Don't tell me you're finally smitten?'

'I'm simply wondering how she's getting along.'

'*Because* you like her?'

Ben clenched his brows, unable to deny it. 'It doesn't matter. I doubt I'll get a chance to speak with her again.'

'There are ways and means.' Richard waggled his eyebrows. 'For a determined enough suitor.'

'Not in this case. She doesn't want to marry.'

'Why not?'

'Her mother warned her against it, apparently. And even if she wasn't against marriage, *I* am, remember?'

'Pshaw.' Richard snorted. 'You need to move on, never mind what foolish promise you made to yourself. Some women like big, brooding men.'

'Thank you.' Ben laughed shortly. 'How would you like to injure your other leg too?'

'If it means I get to sit here longer then I don't mind at all. Just make it painless.' Richard grinned as he leaned backwards, regarding him keenly. 'You really do like this woman, don't you?'

'Maybe I do.' Ben pushed a hand through his hair. 'But, however I feel, I need to put it behind me and forget her. Even if I thought marrying again was a good idea, which I don't, I'd have to choose a widow, somebody who knows how to raise children, because I have no idea where to start.'

'Ah. Things didn't go well with your son then?'

'I didn't get much chance to see him. I was only home for a few hours before I had to come back again.' He took another mouthful of wine. 'But that's enough about me, tell me what's been happening here. Anything of interest?'

'More interesting than this? No.' Richard shook his head with a sigh. 'You know, one of these days, my friend, you ought to allow yourself to be happy.'

Footsteps.

Annis drew her brows together, dreaming of footsteps clattering back and forth across a wooden floor, getting louder, then fading away, then getting louder again, filling her head with noise, as if they were actually trying to wake her.

'Finally!' a woman's voice declared as she stirred, rolling her head from side to side. 'I was starting to think you were going to sleep all day.'

Slowly, she prised her eyelids open, trying to place the voice, although when she did she almost wished she hadn't. Her half-sister's tone was even more clipped and cold than before. As for her expression, it sent an actual chill down her spine. Whatever else she might be, Lady Isolde definitely wasn't a nurse.

'Where am I?' Annis heaved herself up to a sitting position, eyeing the room warily and feeling a sudden, intense pang of yearning for Cariscombe and her mother. This wasn't the high-ceilinged hall where she'd fainted. Instead she was lying on a pallet bed in a small, white-washed room with three other beds, a trio of coffers and a fireplace that was currently unlit. 'How did I get here?'

'I ordered one of the guards to carry you.' Isolde folded her arms and regarded her disapprovingly. 'You should have told me you were so tired.'

'I didn't realise I was, but it was such a long journey, I suppose everything caught up with me all at once.' She made a face. 'You didn't seem like you cared how I felt anyway.'

'Perhaps I was a little harsh, but it was a shock to see you.'

'For me, too, but at least *you* knew I existed. I thought you were some kind of apparition.'

'Well, that was hardly *my* fault.' Isolde shrugged before going over to the fire and coming back with a bowl. 'Here. You need to eat something. It's only mutton broth from the dinner table, but I've done my best to keep it warm.'

'Oh!' Annis grabbed at the bowl and spoon, falling on the broth ravenously.

'Good grief.' Isolde looked horrified. 'You eat like a savage.'

'I'm hungry.'

'I can see that.' Her half-sister's lips tightened. 'Why didn't Sir Bennet tell you who I was? He could have prepared you for our meeting. Obviously he gave you my name.'

'Yes.' Annis nodded between mouthfuls. 'But he said it wasn't his place to tell me any more than that.'

'Well, that's true. Although given the circumstances, it might have been useful.'

'Has he returned yet?' Annis twisted her head towards the window, as if she might be able to see him approaching the house. 'How long have I been asleep?'

'Almost eight hours. As for Sir Bennet, I have no idea.'

'But will you see him when he does?' She stopped eating mid-chew, studying her sister's face as a new idea occurred to her, one that brought with it a slightly queasy sensation. Were the two of them close? Was that why Isolde had sent him with the message for their mother? In which case, what would she say if she knew that Annis had kissed him? Would he tell her?

'I doubt it.' Isolde lifted a shoulder dismissively. 'Why?'

'I thought that perhaps the two of you…because you seem to trust him…and he's a widower and you're… I mean, I don't even know if you're married.'

'Oh, for pity's sake.' Isolde made a derisive sound. 'No, I'm not married. The only reason I asked him was because I needed to get a message to our mother and I'd heard that he was travelling to Somerset. He has a good reputation, too. He's not a man who spreads rumours.'

'So you won't seek him out once he returns?'

'No.' Her half-sister fixed her with a stern look. 'He did me a service, but he belongs to the Prince's household and, as such, he has nothing more to do with us. That's for *our* own good, not to mention his. The court has eyes and ears everywhere. Remember that.'

'That's what Sir Bennet said too,' Annis commented, lifting her spoon again. 'Something like it anyway.'

'Because he's an intelligent man.' Isolde lifted her hands, pressing her fingertips together. 'Now, as soon as you're rested, I need you to tell me everything about the attack on Cariscombe.'

'I will, only I want you to tell me about our mother too,' Annis answered between mouthfuls. 'When the mob came, she said it was too late to tell me about her past, but I want to know everything.'

Her half-sister's expression wavered briefly before she nodded and stood up. 'Very well. I'll tell you, but not yet. Right now there are people coming so don't say any more than you have to and let me answer any questions.'

The words were barely out of her mouth before the door opened and a lady with chestnut hair and a pretty, round face dotted with smallpox scars peered round the edge. 'Is it all right to come in and change my hood? Is she awake?'

'Just.' Isolde stepped to one side.

'Welcome to Hatfield House.' The woman rushed across the room and crouched down beside Annis's pallet bed, her expression filled with concern. 'You look a hundred times better now. You were so pale when they first brought you up, we were all worried. I'm Cecilia, by the way. I'm very sorry to hear of your mother's illness.'

Annis threw Isolde an interrogative look. She didn't bat

an eyelid, but something about her half-sister's expression told her not to correct the words.

'Thank you.' She managed a small smile. 'I do feel much better.'

'Good, because you can't stay here.' Another lady, this one with silver-blonde hair and cold grey eyes, appeared in the doorway. 'This room is small enough as it is.'

'What would you have me do, make her a bed of hay in the stables?' Isolde's voice hardened.

'Honestly? I don't care.'

'Peace.' Cecilia put a restraining hand on Isolde's arm and winked at Annis. 'Don't mind Lettice. She enjoys upsetting people.'

'*Lady* Lettice, thank you.' The blonde-haired lady tossed her head. 'All I'm saying is that this is *our* room and I don't see why we have to share it with yet another person, especially some *half-sister* Isolde has never even mentioned before.' Her eyes grew even colder. 'I'm not thrilled with the fact that she's been sent here because their mother is sick either. How do we know she won't make us all ill? There's the Lady Elizabeth's safety to consider.'

'Don't be so dramatic. She wouldn't have come if it were anything contagious, and Isolde is right, where else is she supposed to sleep tonight?' Cecilia took off her hood and quickly replaced it with another. '*I* say she can stay and that makes two against one. Now, come on, we have a masque to enjoy downstairs.' She smiled at Isolde. 'We'll be back in an hour or so.'

'We'll see about that!' Lady Lettice's expression was positively chilling as she stalked away, followed by Cecilia. 'She'll need permission to stay!'

'That's true,' Isolde admitted, making a rude gesture at Lady Lettice's departing back. 'We will need permission.'

'But I don't want to stay,' Annis protested. 'Not for long anyway. I only came because Sir Bennet convinced me it was the safest thing to do while the Justice of the Peace investigates the attack on Cariscombe, but he promised it was only temporary. He's going back to Somerset soon to find out what's happening, but as soon as he returns, hopefully with some answers, I intend to go home. One way or another, I'll get justice for Mother.'

'Don't be absurd.' Isolde looked sceptical. 'You're a woman. What do you think you can do?'

'I don't know, but I'm not going to let whoever killed her get away with it.'

'If you say so. In the meantime, I'll go and speak to Kat.'

'Who?'

'Kat Ashley, the Lady Elizabeth's governess. She's a good woman, extremely clever, but the biggest gossip you'll ever meet so, whatever you do, don't confide in her. I'll ask her permission for you to stay for a little while.'

'Princess Elizabeth?' Annis caught her breath, momentarily distracted. 'So it's true, she really lives here?'

'Hush!' Isolde turned her head sharply. 'We don't call her that. She's the *Lady* Elizabeth.'

'But she's the King's daughter, is she not?'

'Yes, but the title of princess is forbidden. The Lady Mary and Prince Edward also keep their households here on occasion, but they're both away at present. *Lady* Elizabeth is still here, however, probably causing mischief somewhere.' Her half-sister's face actually softened, looking almost tender for a moment. 'Hopefully you'll be able to meet her in the morning, but Kat will have a better idea of what the King might say.'

'The King?' Annis blinked. 'Why would I matter to the King?'

'Because you're staying in his daughter's household and he's not particularly fond of young women since his last wife. He thinks that matrons make better role models for his daughter.'

'*You're* a young woman.'

'Hardly. I'll be twenty-eight years this winter. In any case, for the time being you need to be on your best be-haviour. If you don't give Kat any reason to send you away then hopefully she'll put in a good word to the King.' She heaved a sigh. 'We'll just have to wait and see.'

'Thank you.' Annis smiled tentatively. 'I didn't mean to sound ungrateful when I said I wanted to go home. I honestly appreciate everything you're doing for me.'

'It's what Mother wanted me to do.' Isolde sniffed. 'So you tell me anyway.'

'Yes, but I know this must be hard for you. I've had some time to grieve for her, but you must still be in shock.'

Isolde flinched briefly before her face closed up again. 'There's no need to worry about me. I've been at court for more than ten years. I've seen five queens come and go. Trust me, I'm used to grieving and shocks.' She reached for the door. 'I won't be long, but if Lettice comes back while I'm away, pretend to be asleep.'

'That shouldn't be too hard.' Annis spread her arms out and yawned. 'Wait!' she called out as Isolde turned to go. '*Why* is it forbidden to call Lady Elizabeth a princess?'

'Because of her mother, Anne Boleyn. There are some people the King prefers to forget, and when a powerful man decides to get rid of a woman, he finds a way.' She gave her a meaningful look. 'And there's very little anyone, especially a woman, can do about it, let alone get justice.'

'Oh.' Annis felt a hollow sensation in her chest, like a gaping hole of disquiet.

'Quite.' Isolde's lip curled. 'Welcome to court.'

Chapter Ten

Annis slept fitfully. After giving Isolde an account of everything that had happened since her father's death, she was plagued by dreams again—not memories of Cariscombe for a change, but vivid scenes from the journey to London, only this time, it was a journey in which she was completely alone.

In one, she was riding across the open countryside with no idea where she was, being chased by invisible pursuers that she could hear but couldn't see. In another, she was lost in a forest, pushing her way through dense undergrowth that never seemed to change. In a third, she was standing in an empty village while thunder roared overhead. And there was no Ben to comfort her each time she awoke, clutching her sheets in a cold, shivery sweat. It was a relief when dawn finally came and she was able to get up and dressed, though since there wasn't yet any official decision about whether or not she could stay, she had to remain in the small bedchamber while the others went down to breakfast.

'Ah, there you are.' Isolde sounded impatient when she burst back into the room half an hour later, as if she'd spent half the morning searching for her. 'Kat says you can meet the Lady Elizabeth before her lessons.'

'That's a relief.' Annis stood up nervously. 'I'm ready when you are. How do I look?'

'Awful.' Her half-sister put her hands on her hips. 'You can't possibly wear that. It's too long and at least three years out of date.'

'Does that matter?'

'Of course it matters! What you wear reflects on me.' She narrowed her eyes. 'You'll have to borrow something. Fortunately, we're about the same size.' She flung open a coffer, rummaging inside for a few moments before thrusting a hooped skirt at her.

'Oh, no.' Annis shook her head in alarm. 'Mother said I didn't have to wear farthingales. She said they were far too constricting.'

'*Mother* lived in the middle of a forest where it didn't matter what anyone wore because there was nobody important to see. You could have wandered about wearing a sack and it wouldn't have mattered, but here at court you need to look respectable.' Isolde folded her arms with an intransigent expression. 'Now put it on.'

'But—'

'*Now!*'

'Oh, very well.' Reluctantly, Annis stripped down to her shift and stockings before hoisting the stiff fabric over her legs. It was, she reflected, a little like wearing a barrel.

'Now these...' Isolde handed her more garments.

She did as she was told, pulling on a dark green bodice and matching overskirt before slipping into a pair of red velvet shoes.

'Better.' Isolde scrutinised her. 'But your hair is a disgrace. It looks like you haven't brushed it in weeks. Sit.' She pointed imperiously at a footstool.

'How?' Annis held her arms out, looking down at her lower half. Thanks to the farthingale, her skirt stuck out by almost a foot. 'How am I supposed to bend?'

'It's perfectly easy. Just hold the front of your skirt down with your hands so that it doesn't come up.' Isolde waved a comb. 'Hurry! I don't have all day.'

'Urgh.' She bent her knees, lowering herself cautiously onto the edge of the stool. 'Actually, that wasn't so bad.'

'I know. Now don't move.'

'Ow!' Annis gave a startled shriek as Isolde dragged the comb through her hair.

'Don't be such a baby.'

'Don't be so rough!' She clamped a hand to her head. 'I'd like some hair left afterwards.'

'Oh, for pity's sake.' Isolde pushed her hand away, re-doubling her efforts before yanking a hood over the top. 'That will do. Now come on.'

'What should I say if anyone asks about Mother?' Annis hurried to keep up as Isolde led the way along an upstairs gallery towards the Lady Elizabeth's apartments. 'I can't tell the truth, can I?'

'Stay as close to it as possible, but no, you *absolutely* cannot tell anyone the truth about what happened.' Isolde lowered her voice to a hiss. 'If you're asked directly then stick to what we've agreed. Our mother is ailing and you travelled all the way to London by yourself. It's ridiculous, but it could, just about, be plausible.'

'Right.' She paused. 'When are you going to tell me about Mother's past?'

'When the time is right, which definitely isn't this morn-ing. Now remember, Lady Elizabeth is the daughter of the King and she expects to be treated accordingly, no matter that her mother isn't Queen any longer. So be courteous and respectful and speak only when spoken to.'

'Understood.'

'And don't look around so much. It makes you look provincial.'

'I can't help it. Everything's so interesting.'

'Honestly, anyone would think you'd never seen a house before.' Isolde made an exasperated sound as they entered a large oak-panelled chamber, crowded with ladies in sober yet fashionable looking dresses. All of them were wearing farthingales.

'Isolde!' A voice hailed them at once. 'There you are! Kat says your sister is here!'

Annis looked across the room to see a girl jump up from a cushion by the fireplace and come rushing towards them. She looked to be around twelve or thirteen years old, with long red-gold hair and dark eyes.

'Is this her?' The girl tipped her head back, studying her as if she were some kind of curiosity. Young as she was, she'd already perfected a regal manner.

Annis dipped into a deep curtsey, as deep as she could manage in a farthingale anyway, hardly daring to breathe under such direct scrutiny.

'Yes, my lady.' Isolde curtsied too. 'This is my half-sister, Annis Flemming.'

'Annis. I heard that you fainted when you arrived. How are you now?'

'Much better, thank you, Your Highness.'

'Ahem.' Isolde gave a small cough.

The girl lifted her eyes to the ceiling. 'What Isolde is trying to say is that you can't call me that. Not that *I* mind, of course, but there are rules.'

'Oh…' Annis flushed, mortified that she'd forgotten her instructions so quickly. 'I'm sorry, Your… That is, my lady.'

'Come, let us talk in private.' The girl gave her a shrewd look before hooking a hand through her arm, leading her away from the others and back out to the gallery.

'I have an older half-sister, too,' she whispered once they were out of earshot. 'She's ten years older than me and very different, just like you and Isolde, I think. Do you like her?'

'Isolde? I'm not sure.' To her surprise, Annis found herself answering honestly. 'She's quite intimidating.'

'It's just her manner. You'll get used to it. *I* like her anyway. If she's severe then it's because she's had to be.' Lady Elizabeth glanced behind them, an impish smile spreading over her face. 'Look at my ladies trying to pretend like they're not listening. They're worried about what we might be discussing.'

Annis peeked over her shoulder. Sure enough, the ladies were all following behind, like a gaggle of ducklings following their mother.

'I say that Annis should stay!' Lady Elizabeth called out abruptly, her expression suddenly regal again.

'We'll need your father's permission,' a tall, dark-haired woman interjected, coming along the gallery at that moment. She was a little older than the others, with a pleasant, intelligent face.

'This is Kat, my governess.' Lady Elizabeth grinned. 'She knows all the rules and how to break them, which in this case is easy. We'll simply get my stepmother to ask the King if you can stay. *She* can persuade him to do almost anything.'

'As you wish. Then I shall write to the Queen immediately.' Katharine bowed her head before smiling at Annis. 'You may stay until we receive an answer.'

'There you go.' Lady Elizabeth squeezed her arm. 'Now let's celebrate by taking a walk in the garden.'

'It's still misty and it's almost time for your lessons,' Kat scolded.

'But the mist is already clearing like it did yesterday and then it will be too hot later,' Lady Elizabeth protested. 'Far better for us to walk outside now in the cool, don't you think? The house looks so pretty in the mornings and Annis needs to learn her way around. She is our guest, after all.'

'Oh, very well,' Kat relented, smiling indulgently. 'But you must wear a cloak.'

Lady Elizabeth was right about the weather. By the time all of her ladies were dressed in capes and hoods, the mist had cleared, peeling away like a lacy white curtain to reveal a sky of pure cobalt blue dotted with only a few scraps of wispy cloud.

'There. Didn't I tell you?' she crowed as they went outside, linking arms with Kat and beaming affectionately as the rest of her ladies followed behind in a group. Just like ducklings again, Annis thought, admiring the easy way the former princess charmed and manipulated everyone around her.

She admired the intricate knot gardens behind Hatfield House too. The flowerbeds were an organised riot of colour, bursting with roses and framed by perfectly symmetrical layouts of lavender, thyme and marjoram. They made a stark contrast to the wilderness of the woods around Cariscombe, even if something about them felt a little too orderly and constrained... She tipped her head back, breathing in the many different scents as they made their way between carefully clipped hedges and along neatly trimmed avenues. It felt good to be back in the fresh air. After so long on the road, being surrounded by walls again felt strange.

They were making their way across a terrace when she caught sight of a familiar figure striding around the side of the house in the company of another man. Just a glimpse made her breath hitch and her heart leap so high she almost started coughing. There was no mistaking who it was, though his clothes were noticeably richer and finer than they'd been on the road. For the first time in their acquaintance, he looked like a courtier.

As if sensing her gaze, he turned his head, his eyes locking on hers with a suddenly arrested expression. For a moment, they each seemed to mirror the other's movements, their steps faltering as they simply stood and stared. Then he turned away, saying something to his companion before heading alone towards the far corner of the knot garden— sliding a sharp, significant glance towards her as he passed.

Annis looked around, wondering if anyone else had noticed their silent exchange, but the other ladies seemed engrossed in their conversations.

'Isolde?' She tugged gently at her half-sister's sleeve. 'Do you mind if I stay out here and walk for a while?'

'You *have* just been walking.' Her half-sister was to the point, as usual.

'I mean on my own. I'm not used to having so many people around me and the knot garden is so pretty.'

Isolde's face twisted as if she were about to refuse, before she sighed and waved a hand. 'Oh, very well, but don't be long.'

* * *

Ben paced restlessly up and down one of the narrow avenues that ran along the edge of the knot garden, hardly able to breathe with anticipation. Annis had definitely seen him, but whether she'd be able to get away from her sister and the other ladies was another matter. He was surprised by how desperately he hoped the answer was yes. He'd been restless and uneasy ever since his arrival at Hatfield House, unable to sleep properly despite his exhaustion. Now it occurred to him that it was because he'd been constantly on edge, wondering where Annis was and what she was doing.

He'd made discreet enquiries that morning, confirming for himself that she'd arrived and met Lady Isolde, but the blunt truth was that—after more than a week in each other's constant company—it felt strange *not* to be near her. More than that, it felt wrong. He *wanted* to be close to her, he realised. He missed her. He couldn't seem to go five minutes without thinking about her. And the fact that she'd looked as pleased to see him as he'd been to see her just now made his heart soar!

All of which explained why he'd done the worst, most completely out-of-character thing possible. It was utter madness.

He stopped pacing abruptly at the thought. What *had* he been thinking, impulsively beckoning to her when he ought simply to have given a brief nod and kept walking towards the stables? This was all Richard's fault for talking as if there was some hope of a future together! There *was* no hope, which meant that, now he'd effectively summoned her, he needed to get rid of her as quickly as possible. If they were seen meeting together in secret, it could provoke rumours, and rumours could be enough to destroy Annis's reputation and have her banished from Hatfield House for ever. Where would she go for safety then?

'Ben!'

He swung about just in time to see her come running round the end of a hedge, though for a moment he wondered if he'd summoned the wrong woman. He hadn't paid any attention to her clothes when he'd glimpsed her on the terrace, but now he saw she was dressed like a lady of the court in a green velvet gown that perfectly reflected the hazel hue of her eyes, with her wild hair confined by a fashionable French hood. It was a striking, somewhat heart-stopping, change to boys' clothes, and yet she was still definitely Annis, panting, breathless and smiling, as if she'd run up and down every avenue looking for him.

He felt a primitive, powerful urge to close the distance between them and sweep her up in his arms, to seize her lips and kiss her until they were both breathless. He actually felt himself sway forward before common sense kicked in and he stopped himself, clasping his arms behind his back and standing completely still, as if he were another one of the marble statues that ornamented the garden.

'Ben?' She almost skidded to a halt, repeating his name in a questioning tone as her smile faded and an embarrassed blush spread over her skin.

'Annis.' He bowed his head, hating the stern note in his voice, hating that he was the one responsible for making her face change. 'How are you?'

'Good.' She dropped her eyes and clasped her hands in front of her, as if she were making a sudden, supreme effort to be ladylike. 'Very well, thank you.'

'How was your meeting with Lady Isolde?'

'Terrible.' She peered up through her lashes, her expression faintly chiding. 'At first anyway, though things are a little better now. It would have helped if you'd given me a clue about who she was.'

'I know.' He grimaced. 'I'm sorry. I didn't know much to reveal.'

'I understand, and at least she didn't disown me.' She nudged the ground with the toe of her shoe. 'Lady Elizabeth has asked her governess to ask the Queen to ask the King for permission to let me stay here for a while.'

'I see.' He nodded slowly as he thought the words through. 'That's good.'

'But I still want to go home as soon as possible.' She slid her tongue between her lips. 'When are you leaving?'

'Soon.' He averted his gaze quickly. 'The day after tomorrow probably. I just need to give Emma and Berry some time to recover first.'

'Give them some oats from me.'

'I'll do that.'

They lapsed into silence, Ben curling his hands into fists to stop himself from reaching for her. The impulse to touch her was even stronger than it had been on the road, as if all his nerve endings were straining towards her. He clenched his teeth. This meeting was a mistake. He couldn't offer her marriage, even if that was something she wanted, which meant that he had to trample any impulses he might feel and get away from Hatfield House as quickly as possible. This time it *had* to be a proper goodbye, no matter how much it might pain him.

'I miss our campfires.' She blurted the words out suddenly and then looked surprised, as if she hadn't intended to say them.

'So do I,' he agreed.

'I *don't* miss riding,' she went on. 'Although I keep wondering where Berry is. It still feels odd to be out of a saddle.'

'For me too.'

'I've been worried about you.'

'You have?' The thought shouldn't have pleased him, but it did.

'Yes. I wanted to know whether you'd returned safely, but Isolde told me it was too dangerous to ask questions.'

'She's right.' He hesitated, knowing he ought to end the conversation, but unable to bring himself to do it quite yet. He wanted to keep talking, just for a little longer... 'So what do you think of Hatfield House?'

'It's very impressive. I never knew places like this existed. There are so many people here.'

'There are, most of them watching and listening.' He lifted his gaze towards the building. The windows sparkled back, seemingly empty, but who knew how many eyes might be watching them? That thought gave him the impetus to be blunt. 'That's why we can't meet again. It's far too risky. We shouldn't be meeting now, but...' He coughed. 'I wanted to make sure you were safe and content. I know that Lady Isolde has a reputation for being difficult.'

'She's not so bad. And yes, I'm safe.' Annis wrinkled her brow, her tone formal as she took a step back from him. 'In that case, I hope you have a good journey and an enjoyable time with your son. Please give my regards to your mother.'

'I will.'

'And when you get back, you'll come and tell me at once what you've discovered about Cariscombe?'

He opened his mouth to agree and then changed his mind. 'I'll send word to Lady Isolde.'

'Oh.' A look of disappointment mixed with hurt flitted across her face. 'Goodbye, then.'

He nodded, watching as the wind caught hold of her hair and blew a russet strand across her forehead. It took every ounce of self-control he possessed not to lift a hand and brush it aside. 'Goodbye, Annis.'

He tore his gaze away, his heart plummeting as she turned on her heel and walked in a dignified manner back around the corner of the hedge. There. It was done. If that didn't make her never want to see him again, nothing would.

Chapter Eleven

'What do you think of my new sleeves?' Lady Elizabeth grabbed hold of Annis's arm, hoisting her to her feet and marching her determinedly towards a window alcove in her withdrawing chamber. 'I'm not certain about the colour.'

'I think red suits you very well, my lady,' Annis answered in surprise, dropping the handkerchief she'd been embroidering. It was her second day at court and the fact that she was speaking to a former princess was still overwhelming. Part of her expected to wake up at any moment.

'Oh, I know that.' The girl tipped her head closer, laughter in her eyes. 'I only wanted an excuse to get you away from the others. Now tell me, what's his name?'

'My lady?' She gave a guilty start.

'The man you met in the avenue yesterday.' Lady Elizabeth gave her a pointed look. 'And don't pretend you didn't. I saw the look he gave you as he walked past and then I saw you go off in the same direction. It wasn't so hard to guess what was going on. I like you more and more, Mistress Annis. He's a member of my brother's household, is he not? I know I've seen him before.'

Annis threw a nervous look in Isolde's direction, though fortunately she was busy sorting through some skeins of thread. She *really* didn't want her half-sister finding out about her meeting with Ben, especially when it had proved to be so underwhelming. She couldn't understand why he'd even bothered gesturing to her if all he'd wanted was to tell her they *shouldn't* meet. He'd told her *that* on the road.

He'd been so severe, she'd felt like a naive fool for being excited about seeing him again. Obviously she'd misinterpreted the way he'd looked at her when they'd parted beside the river; the warmth she'd thought she'd seen in his eyes a mere product of her imagination. She'd thought they were friends at least, but obviously she'd been nothing more to him than someone to protect. As for their kiss, clearly it hadn't meant anything to him at all… Just as it shouldn't to her, she told herself sternly. She didn't need or want a husband, so what did it matter whether or not he liked her or if she *ever* saw him again? That was what her mother would have said. No, the feelings of Sir Bennett Thorne were of absolutely no concern to her. Their relationship, such as it had been, was over. She needed to put him out of her mind, once and for all.

'Don't worry, Isolde didn't notice where you went.' Lady Elizabeth followed the direction of her gaze. 'None of the others did, but I keep my eyes open, especially for handsome gentlemen, so tell me what's going on…' She gave Annis a sharp nudge with her elbow. 'That way you won't compel me to say anything.'

'He's just an acquaintance, my lady.'

'A courtier acquaintance you meet all alone in the knot garden?' Lady Elizabeth made a scornful sound. 'You'll have to do better than that.'

'Truly. There's nothing more to tell.' A sigh escaped Annis's lips. 'His name is Sir Bennet Thorne and he's from Draycote Manor. It's only a few miles from where

I grew up so, when he saw me, he wanted to make sure I was all right.'

All of which was true, sort of...

'Oh.' The Princess looked disappointed and then shrewd. 'But do you like him? And not just as an acquaintance?'

Annis hesitated, struggling to think of an honest answer. *Did* she like Ben as more than an acquaintance? She liked—correction, she *had* liked—being with him. She *had* liked him enough to kiss him, but maybe that was just because they'd spent so much time together, or maybe because she'd been curious about what it would be like to kiss him, and then let herself get carried away in the moment. Now that she thought about it, that was the most likely explanation... And the Lady Elizabeth was still looking at her, she realised, awaiting an answer.

'Not in that way, my lady. I've no wish to marry.'

'Why not?'

'Because my mother told me it takes away women's freedom and independence and turns them into property.' She bit her lip, belatedly remembering Ben's advice about sharing her opinions. 'Forgive me, my lady.'

'For what?' Lady Elizabeth tilted her head. 'I agree with everything you just said.'

'You do?'

'Completely. I also intend never to marry.' She gave her an arch look. 'Does that surprise you?'

'Yes! I mean, you're the daughter of a King.'

'So I'll have to marry someday? Probably. Although there have been lots of discussions about prospective betrothals already and they've all come to nothing. Sometimes life doesn't turn out the way people expect.' For a moment, the girl looked far older than her years. 'But I saw your face when you noticed your "acquaintance" yesterday and I think you *do* like him.'

'Maybe I did for a while,' Annis conceded. 'But he doesn't like me that way. He's still in love with his first wife and he sees it as his duty to look after me because we're neighbours, that's all.'

'Then he must be either blind or very foolish.' Lady Elizabeth embraced her suddenly. 'Poor Annis. On the other hand, if your mother was right, you're much better off without him.'

'Come with me.'

Annis looked up to find Isolde standing before her. Lady Elizabeth had left for her lessons and her ladies were enjoying some free time to read and play music or cards.

'Of course.' She put her book of Arthurian legends aside. 'Is something the matter?'

'I'm not certain yet. Apparently there's a man here to see me, a nobleman, with news from Somerset. His name is Oliver Hawksby.'

'Hawksby?' She lurched to her feet.

'Do you know him?'

'Yes. My father had a sister who married a Hawksby. Their eldest son was called Oliver. Sir Bennet asked me about him after the attack. He thought—' She paused, still unwilling to acknowledge the idea.

'What?'

She winced. 'He thought he might have been involved somehow. As my cousin and heir, he has a motive to want to get rid of me.'

'Interesting…' Isolde gave a small huff. 'You know you look like Mother when you do that.'

'What?' Annis felt a jolt of surprise. It was the first time Isolde had ever compared her to their mother.

'She used to frown like that when she was thinking.'

'Lots of people frown when they're thinking.'

'But you catch your bottom lip between your teeth just like she did.' Isolde stared at her for a long moment, her expression almost wistful, before she tossed her head and turned away. 'Come. He's waiting in the hall. Let's go and see what he has to tell me.'

'There he is,' Isolde whispered, gesturing for Annis to peer through a crack in the screen at the end of the hall. 'Are you certain you've never met him before?'

'Yes.' Annis pressed her eye to the screen and squinted. The man at the far end of the hall was dressed all in black with fair hair and a short beard... She gasped, remembering just in time to muffle the sound. 'But I *have* seen him! The morning we left Draycote Manor, a group of riders came after us. We hid in the woods, but I saw their faces. *He* was one of them.'

'Are you certain?'

'Completely.' She curled her hands into fists. 'From what I remember, the Hawksby estate is at least thirty miles away, but he was following us just after dawn. How could he have heard about the attack so soon unless he was involved?'

'We shouldn't jump to conclusions, although I admit that does sound suspicious. In any case, stay here until I call you.' Isolde stroked a hand across her throat as she stepped around the edge of the screen. 'Oliver Hawksby?' Her tone was aloof as she strode confidently across the hall. 'You wished to see me?'

'Lady Isolde Downing?' The man made a bow. 'Thank you for agreeing to meet with me.'

'You may have a few minutes, although this *is* most unusual.' Isolde moved to one side, allowing Annis a clear view of them both. 'I don't believe we've met before, sir.'

'No, my lady. Robert Flemming, your stepfather, was my uncle, my mother's brother.'

Annis stiffened. It seemed bizarre to hear her father referred to in that way, although she supposed it was true. Her father had been Isolde's stepfather, even if they'd never met, so far as she knew anyway. Isolde still hadn't told her anything about her or their mother's past.

'I know who Robert Flemming was.' Isolde's voice sounded even sharper than usual. 'What of it? I'm a busy woman.'

'Forgive me, my lady, but knowing of your family connection my mother suggested I ought to pay you a visit. Unfortunately, she's too old to make the journey herself.' He paused. 'I regret to inform you that your mother is dead. There was an attack on Cariscombe almost two weeks ago. From what I've been able to learn, a mob came to the house with torches.'

There was a long moment of silence. Annis stared hard at the man's expression, searching for traces of guilt, but to her surprise there were none, which meant he was either an excellent actor or genuinely sympathetic.

'I see.' Isolde's voice betrayed not the faintest hint of emotion. 'Do you know what was behind this attack? Or who?'

'I'm afraid not, my lady. The Justice of the Peace is investigating, but it's not yet clear who the ringleaders were.' He bowed his head. 'However, I'm afraid there's more bad news. It appears that your half-sister, Annis Flemming, was trapped in the house when it was set on fire. I'm deeply sorry to be the bearer of such ill tidings.'

'Not ill tidings for you, surely?' Isolde's tone was unwavering. 'With both my stepfather and half-sister deceased, you stand to inherit the Cariscombe estate, do you not?'

'What?' Hawksby's head jerked up again, his indrawn breath audible. 'No!'

'No?'

'That is…yes, but I assure you, the news brings me no joy.'

'I find that hard to believe. You'll be a rich man.'

His face flushed as he bristled. 'What exactly are you suggesting, my lady?'

'Nothing at all.' Isolde turned her head briefly, looking straight at the crack in the screen. 'Tell me, how did you find out about the attack on Cariscombe? Have you been to the house to see the damage for yourself?'

'Yes. As it happens, I saw it the very morning after the attack. There was a rumour that somebody was rousing a mob against your mother so I went to warn her. Unfortunately, I arrived too late.'

'To warn her?' Isolde's brows snapped together. 'I thought there was a rift in the family? My understanding was that your mother and my stepfather were estranged.'

'Sadly, they were.' He pulled his shoulders back. 'However, I don't believe in feuds or holding onto bad feeling. Family is family. I therefore felt an obligation to warn her. I only wish that I'd arrived in time.'

'How laudable of you to try.' Isolde's lips pursed. 'So you arrived at Cariscombe to find both my mother and half-sister dead?'

'I'm afraid so. A neighbour had sent men to collect your mother's body, but there was no sign of my cousin, so I can only presume she was inside the house. Now if you'll excuse me, my lady, my duty is discharged so I should go.'

'But not to Cariscombe.' Isolde's tone shifted finally, her expression turning from cynicism to exaggerated pleasantness. 'You may be pleased to discover that you were wrong about the death of my beloved half-sister. Here she is, alive and well. Annis!' She waved a hand, summoning her. 'Come and greet your cousin.'

Annis didn't hesitate, stepping out from behind the screen with her head high.

'Good day, cousin.' She took a few steps forward, though she didn't curtsey.

'Mistress Annis?' Hawksby's jaw dropped so far it was a wonder it didn't detach itself completely and clatter to the floor. 'I don't understand. How did you get here?'

'I rode.' She lifted her chin even higher, enjoying his obvious discomfort. Up close, he looked younger than she'd expected, though the shape of his eyes and brows reminded her of her father, too. That explained why she'd thought he looked familiar on the road.

'But that's impossible!'

'How can it be?' Isolde was all innocence. 'When here she is, clearly standing before you?'

'But...' Hawksby still looked confused. 'Are you certain this is her?'

'Are you suggesting I would not know my own sister?'

'My apologies.' He shook his head as if he were trying to clear it. 'This is wonderful news, of course. I'm just surprised.' He turned back to Annis. 'We thought, when we couldn't find you in the ruins, that you must have been trapped, though we searched the woods and followed the road, searching for you, just in case.'

'I know. I saw you.'

His jaw fell again. 'But then why didn't you call out? Why come all the way to London?'

'Who else would I turn to for safety but my own sister?' She met his gaze squarely. 'Besides, we'd never met before so I had no idea who you were. All I knew was that *someone*—' she put a heavy emphasis on the word '—had attacked my home and killed my mother.'

'You're right.' His voice faltered. 'You weren't to know who I was at the time. I should have thought of that. I'm just thankful to find you alive and well now.' He moved a few steps closer towards her. 'It's good to finally meet you, cousin, and, I can assure you, you're safe with me, too. In fact, I would be honoured to escort you back to Somerset, if you wish to return? My mother would be glad to welcome you into our household until Cariscombe can be restored. What could be more fitting than that? I've brought a dozen men for protection.'

'I think not,' Isolde interrupted, her tone imperious again. 'I have my sister's reputation to consider and she can hardly be riding about the country with an unmarried man, even a cousin. Besides, I think it unwise for her to return to Somerset at present, not until we know precisely who was behind the attack.'

'Of course, my lady, if that's what you wish.'

'It is.' Isolde looked even more regal than Lady Elizabeth herself. 'In the meantime, Annis will reside here at Hatfield House with me, her sister.' She arched an eyebrow, echoing his words. 'What could be more fitting than that?'

* * *

Isolde waited until Hawksby had gone before whirling back towards the screen, beckoning for Annis to follow her.

'What do you think?' As usual, Annis struggled to keep up as her half-sister marched briskly up the staircase.

'Peace!' Isolde shot a fierce look over her shoulder. 'We'll discuss it in private. I don't want us to be overheard.'

Annis bit her tongue, waiting until they reached their bedchamber before digging her heels in. '*Now* what do you think?'

'Just a moment.' Isolde stuck her head back out into the corridor, apparently checking for eavesdroppers.

'There's nobody there.'

'I know that now!' She shut the door firmly behind her. 'I think that when I mentioned the inheritance, he seemed genuinely shocked, and everything else he said made sense, about why he was there that morning and why he was following you. Honestly, I don't think he had anything to do with the attack.' She waved an arm back in the direction of the hall. 'Did that boy seem like a killer to you?'

'No.' Annis admitted, dropping down onto a bed. Hard as she tried, it was impossible to believe he could be behind it. 'But you practically just accused him!'

'Only because I wanted to see how he'd react.' Isolde sat down beside her. 'Annis, is it possible the attack on Cariscombe was just what it seemed? That the mob really did think our mother a witch and it had nothing to do with any inheritance? As horrible as it is, maybe it all comes down to rumour and ill-will and ale.'

'But there *were* no rumours, not that Sir Bennet's mother had heard anyway, although perhaps they just hadn't reached Draycote yet...' Annis frowned. 'But that doesn't explain the things Mother said to me or why she sent me away. She really seemed to think I might be in danger. Sir Bennet thought so too. And there was your message. He never told me what it was, but we presumed it was about my cousin.'

'No.' Isolde shook her head. 'I can see why Sir Bennet might have thought so. I was deliberately vague, but it was nothing to do with Oliver Hawksby.'

'Then who?'

'It doesn't matter now. All I'm saying is that maybe Mother panicked and overreacted. As for Sir Bennet, he probably thought it was his duty to do whatever she asked.'

'That sounds like him.' Annis compressed her lips for a moment. 'But if you're right, that means no one was chasing us when we left Draycote Manor. The men we saw were a rescue party.'

'Yes, if your cousin was telling the truth just now.'

'Then Sir Bennet and I rode all this way for nothing! Sleeping outside and eating berries!' She laughed, enveloped by a sudden warm glow of relief. 'Do you know what this means? Nobody's trying to kill me! I can go home!'

'I didn't say that.' Isolde held up a hand. 'I said *if* your cousin was telling the truth. There may still be something or somebody we're missing.'

'Who else would want to hurt me?'

'I don't know, but you can't go back to Cariscombe anyway. You told me it was badly damaged in the fire.'

'Not all of it.'

'I still don't like the idea of you living there alone. It wouldn't be fitting.'

'I don't care about what's fitting.'

'But *I* do and our mother sent you to me.' Isolde straightened her shoulders. 'That means she trusted me to do what's best for you.'

'*I'll* do what's best for me.' Annis pushed herself purposively to her feet. 'Cariscombe is mine. It's my home. I appreciate everything you've done, but I don't belong here. I definitely don't belong in any court. If I'm not in danger then I intend to go home and get justice for Mother.'

Isolde gave her a long look before nodding. 'Very well. It's your choice, but we'll have to arrange an escort for you. You can't just ride home by yourself.'

'I won't be.' She was already heading back to the door. 'I'll ask Sir Bennet to take me. He's leaving for Somerset tomorrow!'

Annis made her way back towards the staircase, seized with a new sense of purpose. She was going home! Just the thought of it made her feel ten times lighter. Hatfield House had been fascinating and eye-opening, and she was glad to have met Isolde, not to mention the Lady Elizabeth, but it wasn't home.

She stopped halfway along the corridor, struck with a tingling sensation on the back of her neck, as if somebody was watching her. Quickly, she threw a glance over her shoulder, but the space behind her was empty. Still... She hesitated, peering deeper into the shadows before shaking her head. Obviously, her cousin's visit had disturbed her more than she'd realised, making her imagination play tricks on her.

She turned back around, wondering where Ben might be at this time of day. In the Prince's rooms? But where were they? She had no idea, but she would ask someone. If she was leaving then her reputation didn't matter any more.

She stopped again at the top of the staircase, wondering how Ben would feel about accompanying her back to Cariscombe. Given how distant he'd been the last time they'd met, it occurred to her now that he might be irritated rather than pleased by the idea. Maybe he wouldn't want to escort her home. Maybe he'd be too afraid she might try to kiss him again. That idea was mortifying. And here she was, excited to see him again, as if she hadn't learnt her lesson in the knot garden! Well, maybe she didn't want to travel with him either. In fact, maybe she didn't even want to see him again...

There was a creak behind her, but this time she ignored it. She wasn't going to jump at every noise. She wasn't going to live her life in fear. She'd done that for the past two weeks and she refused to do it any longer. She was going to go home, find out who'd roused the mob, bring them to justice and then claim her life back. She would be the independent woman her mother had raised her to be! And she would start by going downstairs and finding somebody who wasn't Ben to escort her home. She had money, after all. She could buy guards if necessary.

She was two stairs down when she heard the tread of footsteps, fast ones, coming towards her. Unconsciously she moved aside, thinking that somebody needed to get past, a split second before a hand touched the small of her back and shoved.

She heard herself cry out as her feet lost touch with the step and she lurched forward, struggling to comprehend what was happening. She felt a moment of confusion, then panic and a sensation of weightlessness, before she was tumbling through the air, falling straight towards the hard flagstones below.

Chapter Twelve

Ben saw Lady Isolde approaching, her long skirts swishing purposively across the yard, as he emerged from the stables where he'd been making sure Emma and Berengaria were sufficiently recovered for their ride back to Somerset. He didn't know her well—in fact he could count the conversations they'd had on the fingers of one hand—but a single glance at her face made it obvious something was wrong. Her lips were compressed into a thin straight line and her usually haughty expression was agitated.

'What's happened?' He felt a sharp sense of foreboding, not bothering with a formal greeting as he accelerated his steps to meet hers. 'Is it Annis?'

'Yes.' She jerked her head, drawing him into the shadows at the side of the stables. 'She was found at the bottom of the staircase an hour ago.'

'Found?' His heart stopped. 'Is she…'

'She's alive, but we don't know how badly she's hurt. She hasn't woken up yet.'

'What happened?' His heart started again, though unsteadily. 'Did anyone see?'

'No. I was the one who found her. We'd been talking in my bedchamber, then she left and I followed a few minutes later. By the time I arrived at the staircase, she was just lying there.' Her brow tightened as she lowered her voice. 'Sir Bennet, you know what happened at Cariscombe. That means you're the only person I can trust to talk to about this. I'm afraid it wasn't an accident. Her cousin, Oliver Hawksby, came to visit me earlier.'

'Hawksby?' He stiffened.

'Yes. He thought she'd been trapped in the fire at Cariscombe. Then when he saw her alive he was…startled, to say the least, but I thought he was telling the truth. He *seemed* innocent. I even told Annis so. We thought she was safe so she was making plans to go home. She was coming to find you when…'

'When she was pushed.' He finished the sentence heavily.

'Yes. It's too much of a coincidence that she simply fell down the stairs so soon after his visit, but it doesn't make sense either. Surely he'd know that we'd suspect him. So I checked with the guards and they said that he left the house immediately after our meeting, which means either he sent an assassin or there's somebody else here who wishes her harm.'

'If there's an assassin, they'll be long gone.' Ben swore under his breath. 'And if it's someone else, we need to make sure they don't try again. Where is Annis now?'

'In my chamber.' Isolde clutched at his arm as he made to go past her. 'But you can't go there.'

'Try and stop me.'

'You can't. People will talk!'

'I don't care.' He yanked his arm away, striding back in the direction of the house.

'Sir Bennet!' She ran after him, but he didn't falter. There seemed to be noise all around him: blood rushing in his ears, the heavy pounding of his pulse and words, too—the cold ones he'd spoken to Annis the last time they'd met. He wished he could call back every one of them.

'If Annis was pushed then it means she's no safer here than she was at Cariscombe.' He hurled the words over his shoulder. 'I should have kept a better eye on her. And *you* shouldn't have left her alone.'

'Of course I haven't left her alone.' Lady Isolde snapped, hurrying to catch up. 'Richard Northam is tending to her injuries so I asked him to stay until I returned.'

'You left *Richard* as a guard?' Ben echoed, horrified. Richard was a good friend, but a strong wind was capable of blowing him over right now. Never mind that, when he was distracted with a patient, he wouldn't notice if an entire army was standing in the same room.

'I told him not to let anyone else in.'

'As if that will do any good...' Ben charged in through a side door, pausing briefly at the bottom of the staircase. 'Is this...'

'Yes.' Isolde nodded tersely.

'She fell all the way down?'

'I don't know, but judging by the way she was lying...' She lifted a shoulder. 'I suppose it's *possible* that she tripped?'

He gave her a sceptical look.

'I don't think so either.' She started up the staircase, leading him along the corridor to a narrow oak door. 'It's really not proper for you to be here. I only told you so you could help me, not make the situation any worse.'

'I know.' Ben drew his brows together. Lady Isolde was right, he ought to keep away for propriety's sake, but he couldn't *not* go to Annis. He had to see her, had to protect her, had to be there when she woke up. He couldn't think about anything else, let alone what anybody else thought.

'Has she shown any signs of waking yet?' Isolde spoke first when they entered the room, walking round to the far side of the bed.

'No, but she was muttering to herself a few moments ago.' Richard looked up from where he was wrapping a bandage around Annis's ankle. If he was surprised to see the pair of them together, he didn't show it. 'Nothing particularly comprehensible, except for a name.'

'Whose name?'

'His.' Richard jerked his head towards Ben. 'Curious, wouldn't you say?'

'You must have misheard.' Isolde snorted dismissively.

'How is she?' Ben's heart wrenched as he looked down at Annis's still, bloodless face. He had to fight the impulse to reach down and pull her into his arms. 'Did she break any limbs?'

'I don't think so, amazingly. There's a significant amount of bruising and she won't be able to walk on that ankle for a while, but she's been very fortunate.'

'You call *that* fortunate?'

'I do, given what could have happened. It's a long way down the staircase.'

'What can I do? Does she need anything? Medicine?'

'No.' Richard rubbed his hands together as he stood up. 'I've done as much as I can. All we can do now is wait and see. There may be some memory loss or confusion when she wakes. Come, my friend.' He gestured towards the door. 'Lady Isolde will send for us when she wakes.'

'No.' Bennet took the seat Richard had just vacated. 'I'm not leaving.'

'For pity's sake, you have to.' Isolde exchanged a sharp look with the physician. 'It's bad enough that you insisted on visiting her. If you stay, it could cause a scandal.'

'Better that than another attempt on her life.'

'*Another* attempt? So you think this was deliberate?' Richard looked pointedly at Isolde. 'You didn't tell me that.'

'There's a…chance she was pushed.' Isolde pursed her lips. 'Just a chance. We can't be certain until we speak to her.'

'We should still act as if we're certain.' Ben spoke authoritatively. 'There needs to be someone with her at all times and the door should be kept bolted. We can't risk an assassin getting inside.'

'Clearly there's been a lot more going on than anyone's told me,' Richard muttered. 'But why on earth would anyone want to hurt her?'

'Because she's an heiress. If she dies then somebody else inherits her father's fortune.'

'Somebody?'

'Her cousin, who just happened to visit this morning.'

'I still think it's too obvious,' Isolde interjected.

'Perhaps, but we need to inform the guards to be on the lookout in case Hawksby or any of his men return.'

'*No!*' For the first time, Lady Isolde sounded panicked. 'This stays between the three of us. As far as anyone else is concerned, it was an accident. If the King finds out what's happened, that there's been an assassin so close to his daughter, there'll be an investigation. They'll ask questions about who brought her here and who let her stay. It won't matter that Lady Elizabeth is safe, you and I could both be facing the Tower.' She met Ben's gaze squarely. 'I'm not just saying this for my own sake. If anything happens to us, who will be left to protect Annis?'

He clenched his jaw. 'You're right. In that case, we'll take turns to guard her.'

'But you can't—' Isolde started to protest some more, then jumped half a foot into the air as the door swung open and Cecilia burst in—Lady Lettice, as usual, at her heels.

'We just heard what happened!' Cecilia flung a hand to her chest as she looked at the bed. 'Is she all right?'

'It's hard to tell yet, but we think so.' Isolde nodded.

'Your half-sister appears to be accident prone. First she collapses and now this.' Lady Lettice looked down her nose scathingly. 'But this isn't a sick room and she's caused enough disruption. Let her recover elsewhere.'

'She can't be moved,' Richard protested. 'It could be dangerous.'

'That's not my problem. As far as I'm concerned, she's been nothing but trouble since she arrived. Put her in the hall.'

'We're not moving her anywhere.' Ben stood up and folded his arms. 'She hit her head.'

'What does this have to do with you?' Lady Lettice's eyes flashed angrily. 'You're in the Prince's household, are you not? What are you even doing here?'

'I'm a friend.'

'A friend? A *good* friend, I think?'

'Let it go, Lettice. Look at the poor girl.' Cecilia turned to Isolde. 'Of course she can't be moved. We'll find somewhere else to sleep.'

For a moment, it looked as though Lady Lettice was going to argue some more. Her mouth opened and closed several times before she threw one last venomous look around the room, then swung on her heel and stormed out.

'Well, that's done it. No matter what happens now,

Annis's reputation is ruined. Everyone at Hatfield House will know about your "friendship" by nightfall.' Isolde made a sound of frustration.

'If not sooner.' Richard lifted his eyes skyward. 'I'll come back later, Lady Isolde. In the meantime, I need a drink. Let me know if there's any change.' He paused in the doorway to lift an eyebrow at Ben. 'Good luck guarding your friend.'

Annis heard a soft click, like the latch of a door falling.

'Isolde?' She dragged her eyelids open. The room was dark except for a single candle flickering on a table beside her bed.

Her bed... She frowned. This wasn't her bed. The view was similar, but hers was usually crammed in a corner, and this one was placed in prime position, directly opposite the fireplace.

'She's gone for something to eat.' Ben's face swam into view. 'It's the first time she's left your side since yesterday, but she'll be back soon.'

'I don't understand.' Annis tried to focus on his face, but her vision was still blurry, never mind her thoughts. Why had Isolde been sitting with her since yesterday? What was she doing in bed? What was *Ben* doing there? Instinctively, she tried to sit up...

'Wait! Don't try to move.' He held a hand out but it was too late—a streak of lightning shot up her spine and burst like a firework behind her temples. 'Ow!' She cried out in pain, catching her breath as black dots danced before her eyes. 'What's happened to me?'

'You had a bad fall down the staircase. Here.' He put one hand on her shoulder and the other behind her head, helping her to lie down again.

'Oh.' She swallowed as his fingertips brushed lightly across her forehead. 'I thought that was just a bad dream.'

'Richard says you should try to stay still.'

'Richard?'

'The Prince's physician. He's taking care of you. Trust me, you're in good hands.'

She closed her eyes for a few seconds, waiting for the pain to recede. 'How did I fall?'

'Don't you remember?'

'No.'

'Well, don't worry about that now.'

'Everything hurts.' She opened her eyes again. She was too disoriented to work out what Ben was doing there, but despite her resolve not to see him again she was glad that he was. His presence made her feel safer. Though, now he was finally coming into focus, she could see how wretched he looked, too. Even more haggard than when they'd arrived at Hatfield House. Was that because of her?

'I know, but you're going to be all right. You're safe now, I promise.' His tone was reassuring. 'I won't let anything hurt you.'

'Thank you.' She closed her eyes again, his face the last thing she saw as she slipped back into unconsciousness.

Chapter Thirteen

The next time Annis woke, Ben was still sitting at her bedside, still looking haggard, but this time Isolde was beside him. Meanwhile, a grey-haired man with an impressively long beard stood on the other side of the bed, holding one of her wrists.

'How are you feeling?' To her surprise, her sister's expression was almost tender.

'Better.' She wriggled, testing each part of her body in turn. 'I'm just slightly afraid of moving.'

'Then don't. Lie still.' The man laid her wrist gently down on the bed. 'I'm Richard Northam, at your service, mistress. Now, can you tell me *your* name?'

'Of course.' She blinked, surprised by the question. 'Annis Flemming.'

'And do you know these people? And where you are?'

'Ye-es. They're Lady Isolde Downing and Sir Bennet Thorne and we're at Hatfield House near London.'

'Good. Now can you tell me, if I had twelve sweetmeats and lost half, how many would I have?'

'Six.' She narrowed her eyes. 'I'm not a child.'

'I know that.' He chuckled. 'However, in cases of head injuries, I need to make certain there's no hidden damage.

Now, I want you to think back to your childhood, as far as you can go. What's your earliest memory?'

'Earliest?' She sucked her bottom lip into her mouth, thinking. 'Walking in the orchard at Cariscombe with my parents. When I was very little, Father would hoist me onto his shoulders so I could pick apples for them. My mother would carry a basket.'

'What a charming picture.'

'Does this mean she's all right?' Isolde interrupted.

'I think so, but I still don't want her moved just yet. These bruises need time to heal.'

'Can she answer a few questions about what happened? It won't take long.'

'I can,' Annis answered for the physician.

'Very well, but only a few.'

'Good.' Isolde moved to sit on the edge of the bed. 'Do you remember what happened? Did you trip?'

'I don't know,' Annis answered tentatively. 'I remember walking along the corridor. I was going to look for... someone. Then I stopped at the top of the staircase and...'

'And?' It was Ben who spoke this time, his gaze very intent.

'Then I thought I heard footsteps.' She knitted her brow. 'They were moving quickly so I moved aside. Then I started to turn, to see who it was, but...' She gasped as fragments of memory came back to her. 'I felt something touch my back!'

'Something? Or a hand?'

'I don't know. Why? Do you think somebody pushed me?'

'We're still trying to work out what happened.' He gave her a reassuring look. 'You said you heard footsteps? Did you hear skirts rustling too?'

'I don't think so, but I wasn't paying a great deal of attention. I was thinking about going home to Cariscombe.'

'Did you glimpse anything suspicious at all?'

'No. That is… I thought I saw a shadow, but it wasn't distinct.' She swallowed, a chill running down her spine at the implication. 'Hawksby! But we agreed that he was innocent.' She looked wide-eyed at Isolde. 'You said—'

'I know what I said.' Her sister's tone was sharp again. 'But I spoke too soon.'

'Or maybe it was just an accident?' she protested. 'Maybe somebody was rushing and they didn't see me? Maybe they pushed me accidentally and then ran away because they were afraid of getting into trouble?'

'Perhaps.' Bennet looked doubtful.

'It *had* to be an accident,' she argued back, aware of a tight *knot* in her stomach now. 'This is Hatfield House! It's where the King's children live. That makes it one of the safest places in England, doesn't it?'

'Yes. Or it ought to be.' Isolde leaned backwards. 'Which is why you have to leave. As soon as possible.'

'What?' Annis sucked in a breath as Ben rose to his feet and moved across to the window.

'There's no need to look so offended.' Isolde clucked her tongue. 'You *wanted* to leave yesterday.'

'That's when we thought I wasn't in danger any more.'

'I know, but the blunt truth is that I can't protect you. If you're not safe here then you're not safe anywhere.'

'She can't travel back to Somerset just yet,' Richard protested. 'And if nowhere's safe, where is she supposed to go?'

'It's not a question of where.' Isolde caught Annis's eye and thrust her chin out, as if she were bracing herself for a fight. 'If Hawksby is so determined to get his hands on your fortune then there's only one way to stop him.'

'What?'

'You won't like it.'

'What?'

'Marriage. You need a protector. Until then, you're vulnerable.'

'No!' This time, Annis pushed through the pain, sitting bolt upright in bed.

'Yes! Once you marry, your possessions will belong to your husband and *his* heirs and there'll be no way for your cousin to inherit. Hawksby will lose any claim on your fortune, which means there'll be no reason for him to try and hurt you any more.'

'Don't you hear what you're saying?' Annis glowered. 'All of my possessions will belong to my husband! You say that like it's a good thing! Like I ought to be pleased!'

'Maybe in this case you should be. It's your life that's at risk.'

'Why can't we just accuse Hawksby of pushing me?'

'With what proof? He wasn't in the house when it happened, I checked, so we're only guessing that he sent somebody in to do his dirty work.' Isolde's expression wavered and then hardened again. 'This isn't about what you want, Annis, it's about what you need, which is to stay alive. For pity's sake, be sensible.'

'I *am* being sensible! If I marry, then I'll have to give up everything. My money, my independence, my very *self* if my husband wills it!'

'I know. And I'm sorry. But you need a husband.'

'Mother said—'

'Mother was *wrong*!' Isolde's eyes flashed. 'She thought

that she could keep you hidden away and safe from the world, but she couldn't, and neither can I. Nobody can. Fortunately, we already have options. William Dalrymple asked me about you the evening after you arrived.'

'*Who?*'

'You sat next to him at dinner that first day.'

Annis gasped in horror. 'He had a white beard!'

'Nonetheless…'

'He could be my father! And what about going back to Cariscombe and getting justice for Mother? How will I be able to do that if I'm married to some old man?'

'You won't be able to. You'll have to give up the idea of going back or getting justice.' Isolde's expression was implacable. 'Leave that up to the Justice of the Peace. I already told you, there's nothing we can do about it.'

'So you won't even try to do anything?'

'I'm keeping you safe. Mother would have wanted that more than you trying to avenge her.'

'I won't marry William Dalrymple!'

'You have no choice.'

'Yes, she does.' Ben turned away from the window abruptly. 'Me.'

'What?' Annis sucked in a breath.

'There's me,' he repeated. 'I know it's not ideal, but your sister's right. If an assassin can get in here then they can find you anywhere. If we had any kind of proof about who attacked you then it might be different, but we can't take the risk of them trying again. You could have been killed.'

'Only because I thought I was safe. I'll be on my guard next time.'

'And live the rest of your life looking over your shoulder?' He held onto her gaze for a long moment before turning to Isolde. 'Would you give us a few minutes alone together?'

'Of course.' Her half-sister looked between them speculatively. 'I'll wait outside the door.'

'And I'll go...somewhere.' Richard was already heading towards the door.

'Annis.' Ben took a seat beside the bed again. 'I'm sorry. I know that marriage isn't something you want, but it may be the only way to keep you safe.'

She frowned at him, remembering the way he'd behaved in the knot garden. She'd never wanted to marry, not after all her mother's warnings, but she'd always imagined that if she *were* to change her mind then it would be for love. The idea of marrying a man who didn't want her— worse, who was still in love with his first wife—simply as a means of protecting herself against some unknown assassin was horrifying.

'It's not just me. Neither of us want this,' she said pointedly. '*You* said you made a promise to yourself never to marry again.'

'I did,' he acknowledged, 'but it seems to me that keeping you alive is more important.'

'What if I ran away instead? I could go to France or Italy.'

'And do what?' He sounded infuriatingly reasonable. 'Even if you *could* run on your ankle at the moment, what would you live on?'

'I don't know, but I'd think of something.'

'I'm sure you would.' He gave a small smile and then sighed. 'Annis, if you leave the country then you might as well renounce your inheritance. Then Hawksby or whoever did this would have won anyway.'

She closed her eyes, the bruise on her head throbbing as she tried to find a way out of her dilemma. If she couldn't leave the country, and wouldn't marry William Dalrymple, then Ben was the only other choice. And at least if she married him, she could go back to Cariscombe, or close to it anyway. That was what she wanted most of all, wasn't it, to go home? Only not like this…

'Annis, the truth is, my being here in your room has already started rumours.' Ben hung his head. 'I'm sorry. I should have been more discreet.'

'I see.' She turned her face away. For a brief moment, she'd thought maybe he'd cared about her, but the truth was, he was just doing his duty again, because she was already compromised…

'You don't have to be noble.' She murmured. 'You don't have to protect me all the time.'

'I'm not just being noble. I wouldn't do it for Lady Lettice, for example.' His lips curved softly before his brow creased again. 'Annis, I can't offer you much as a husband, but maybe the fact that neither of us wants to marry makes this all right. We both know where we stand so neither of us will have any expectations of the other.'

'Expectations…' The word tasted bitter in her mouth. He was as good as telling her his heart wasn't involved. 'Very well, if I were to agree—*if*—what would it be like? Would we live together?'

'Yes, to begin with. I'd take you back to Draycote Manor. Hopefully the Justice of the Peace will have found some evidence against Hawksby by the time we arrive, but if not we'll investigate the attack on Cariscombe together. Then, when we've got justice for your mother and you're safe, I'd return here.'

'So you'd just leave me there with your mother and son?' She tensed at the thought of being a mother, even a step-mother. She had no experience with children. How would she know what to do?

'Only if you wanted to stay. I'm sure that my mother would like to get to know you, but I wouldn't expect any-thing. You could rebuild Cariscombe and return there, if that's what you want. I won't touch a farthing of your for-tune, I promise. You can be as independent as you wish.'

'How do I know you're not just saying all this now?' She tilted her head back suspiciously. 'If we marry then you'll be able to tell me what to do. I'll be dependent on you upholding your side of the bargain.'

'I would, I promise.' He looked straight at her, his eyes glowing with a new kind of intensity. 'You can trust me, Annis. I hoped that you'd know that much by now.'

'I do.' She dropped her gaze, feeling guilty for the accu-sation. 'It's just... I never expected to be in this position.'

'I know, but we get along, don't we?' He sat forward. 'Friendship is a reasonable basis for marriage, is it not?'

She looked away. Friendship *was* a reasonable basis—or it might have been if they'd never met in the knot garden! Because the horrible, depressing truth was that if it hadn't been for that, part of her might not have objected to this marriage. Part of her might even have been excited, but she *had* met him and he'd been emphatic about the fact that he didn't want to see her again! He'd made it clear how he felt about her and nothing could take that back, no matter how much he might look like he cared. Now she wasn't sure she *could* ever think of him as a friend again, let alone a husband. But what choice did she have? She could keep her pride or, potentially, her life.

'Very well.' She turned back to face him, forcing herself to look calm. 'In that case... I accept.'

'Good.' He held onto her gaze for a long moment before standing up. 'I'll send Isolde back in to sit with you and then I'll ride to Hampton Court at once.'

'Hampton Court? Why do you need to go there?'

'I need to ask the King permission for your hand. Then we'll marry and leave as soon as possible.' He stopped in the doorway, looking back over his shoulder. 'You don't have to worry, Annis. I promise you'll only have to stay at Draycote Manor until we're certain you're safe. After that, you can go wherever and do whatever you want. You have my word.'

She waited until he was gone before picking up the cup beside her bed and hurling it at the wall.

'Well?' Isolde came marching along the gallery as Ben closed the door behind him. He had the distinct impression that she'd spent the whole time pacing.

'She agreed.' He pressed his fingertips against his brow. It felt very tight all of a sudden. He could hardly believe that he'd just proposed, but he'd had no choice. Isolde was right, marriage was the only way to make Annis safe, no matter how she felt about it. And yet the appalled way she'd looked at him when he'd said the words had gone straight to his heart, reminding him all too vividly of Eleanor. Considering that she'd kissed him less than a week before, he'd hoped that perhaps Annis wouldn't completely loathe the idea, but she'd seemed utterly horrified. Obviously her kiss had been nothing more than a farewell gesture, and now he'd broken the promise he'd made to himself, exchanging an arranged marriage for a marriage of convenience. How was that any better? But at least he could put right one of his failings from his first marriage. He hadn't protected Eleanor when she'd needed him, but he *could* protect Annis.

'Thank goodness.' Isolde closed her eyes and then opened them again quickly. 'Why did you do that? You didn't have to offer for her.'

'I know.'

'Then why?' Her gaze sharpened. 'Do you want Cariscombe?'

His chin jerked as if she'd struck him. 'This has nothing to do with her fortune.'

'Forgive me, but she's my sister. This isn't your problem.'

'It became my problem the moment you gave me that message for your mother. If you object to me marrying Annis then just say so.'

'It's not that. It's not personal. I just don't trust men. *Any* men.' She looked him over. 'Although I admit, you seem better than most.'

'Careful.' He gave a brusque laugh. 'That almost sounds like a compliment.'

'But I still don't understand why you're doing this.' Isolde's gaze sharpened again. 'Because you compromised her?'

'In part, but mainly because you're right, she needs protection,' he answered, choosing his words with care. 'The truth is, after my first wife died, I promised myself I'd never marry again. I wasn't a very good husband to her and I can't offer Annis much better. I can't promise to make her happy, but I can promise to do everything in my power to keep her safe. Trust me, if there were any other way I'd leave her alone, but I don't want to see her get hurt. So I'll marry her, I'll help her find out who attacked

Cariscombe and then I'll give her the independence she wants. She'll be alive and safe, that's the main thing.' He gave her a pointed look. 'And she won't be bound to an old lecher like William Dalrymple.'

Chapter Fourteen

In some ways, Annis found her convalescence quite enjoyable. There was always somebody with her for safety, so she spent the time playing chess with Richard and talking with Isolde. Her half-sister wasn't exactly talkative, and she *still* hadn't told her about their mother's past, but little by little she was coming to seem more like a sister. Then, after three days, Richard pronounced her fit enough to rise from bed. Her bruises still hurt, but she felt strong enough to stand and move around a little, which meant, according to Isolde and her usual lack of sensitivity, that it was time for her to marry and be gone.

'I've made arrangements for us to go to a friend's house after the ceremony,' Ben answered when Richard expressed his concern about her travelling too far or too fast. 'It's only ten miles from Hatfield and they've assured me we can stay for as long as we need.'

'But will it be safe?' Isolde challenged him. 'We need to allow time for Hawksby to find out about this marriage. Until then, you'll need to stay on your guard.'

'Don't worry.' Ben set his jaw. 'I'll make it safe.'

'Good. Then we'll go ahead with the wedding early tomorrow morning. I've already spoken to Kat and she's agreed to release me from my duties for a few hours.'

'Don't I get a say in any of this?' Annis spoke up from where she was sitting on the edge of the bed, but nobody seemed interested in her opinion, least of all her future husband. He'd barely looked at her, let alone spoken with her, since he'd proposed.

'No,' Isolde answered curtly.

She leaned back on her elbows as they made plans around her. Apparently, it was too dangerous for Lady Elizabeth to attend the ceremony, and since Annis scarcely knew anybody else, and the Prince and his men were still away at court, there would be just the four of them in attendance. Then, afterwards, she and Ben would leave Hatfield House straight away. There would be no music, no dancing, no feast, no celebration at all. As mornings went, it would be almost uneventful, except for the fact that she would be married, and her identity irrevocably altered, by the end of it. She would have done what her mother had advised her never to do—her cherished independence would be lost for ever. The only good part was that she would be returning to Somerset shortly afterwards.

At last Ben and Richard left the room, leaving her alone with Isolde. Slowly, her half-sister barred the door and came to sit beside her in silence.

'You're going to look beautiful,' Isolde commented, gesturing at the gorgeous amber velvet gown Cecilia was lending her for the ceremony. It was finer than anything she'd ever worn before, its tight bodice ornamented with hundreds of tiny pearls and its long sleeves shot through with gold thread. Cecilia had suggested she wear her hair loose too, except for a simple gold coronet, to which they would attach a white silk veil.

'Mmm...' Annis answered noncommittally. Personally, she couldn't see any point in so much finery when the marriage was a mere formality. It wasn't like Ben would care what she wore; he probably wouldn't even notice. She knew it wasn't fair to resent him, not when he was trying to protect her, but she couldn't seem to help it.

'Annis?' Isolde's elbow nudged into her side. 'I said, you're going to look beautiful.'

'Thank you.' She tried to add a little enthusiasm this time.

'I have something for you, too.' Isolde handed her an old, faded portrait in a gilt frame. 'Call it a wedding gift.'

'Mother.' Annis caught her breath as she cradled the frame in her fingers. The painting inside was unmistakably of their mother—now that she'd spent some time with Isolde she could see more differences between them—only she was much younger, dressed like a queen in a crimson dress with gold trim. Meanwhile, her neck was positively dripping in jewels: rubies and emeralds and sapphires all vying for attention, with gold chains and a gilded headpiece. 'I don't understand.' She looked up in bewilderment. 'Why is she dressed like this?'

'You really don't know?' Isolde tilted her head to one side. 'She really told you nothing of her past?'

'No. All she ever told me was that she was born in Chester.'

'That's true. She lived there until she married my father when she was fifteen years old and he was fifty-two, and a widower.' Isolde paused. 'He was also the Earl of Newcastleton.'

'Earl?' Annis had to clench her fingers to stop herself from dropping the portrait in shock. 'But that means…she was a countess? I don't believe it.'

'Believe it or not, that's what she was. As famous for her beauty as she was for her low birth. She was the daughter of a silk merchant, but my father saw her in the marketplace one day and pursued her. His children by his first marriage objected, of course, but he married her anyway. Some people said she'd bewitched him. It caused a great scandal.'

'How romantic.'

'I doubt it.' Isolde snorted. 'I don't suppose she had much choice in the matter. They were married for ten years before he died.'

'I'm sorry.'

'I was only seven years old when it happened.' Isolde's voice wavered. 'But I remember it clearly. She came to the nursery and held me for two hours while I cried. Then the following day my half-brother Charles ordered her out of the house for ever.'

'That's awful!' Annis gasped with outrage. 'How could he get away with such a thing?'

'Very easily when she was a widow with no one of influence to support her. She was allowed to leave with the clothes on her back while he inherited everything else. She wasn't even permitted to attend the funeral, and there was nothing she could do about it, especially since…'

'Especially since what?' Annis braced herself as Isolde stopped talking abruptly. She had a feeling she wasn't going to like the next part.

'Especially since my father's death was so sudden. There were no warning signs before he collapsed. So when she protested about being sent away, Charles *suggested* that perhaps she'd had a hand in it. The threat was obvious.'

Annis felt a tremor of unease. *Sudden death…* Just like her own father's.

'She had no home to go back to in Chester,' Isolde went on. 'Her parents were already dead and she had no brothers or sisters, but fortunately there was one place she could go. Cariscombe. *Your* father had been a friend of my father's and was already besotted with her. So when she appealed to him for help, he offered to marry her.'

'Oh.' Annis felt cold. 'You mean, they weren't a love match either?'

'Not for her, not at first anyway.' Isolde's voice softened. 'Although from what she wrote to me, I believe she came to care for him. Remarrying so soon after my father's death caused another scandal, of course, but at least she was safe.'

'What about you? Why didn't you come to Cariscombe with her?'

'Because I wasn't allowed to.' Isolde's voice hardened again. 'Charles ordered her to leave me behind. I was raised in his household with his own children.'

'I see…' Annis winced at the note of remembered suffering in her half-sister's voice. 'Were they unkind to you?'

'I was an inconvenience.' Isolde sniffed. 'They kept me there because I shared their name and it would have brought shame on them to throw me out, too. But they had no love for me. It was lonely. Then, when I was old enough, Charles sent me to court.'

'To find a husband?'

'And give up my dowry? Ha! No, I was sent as a present to the King. To serve his household in whatever way he saw fit. So I was appointed to serve the Lady Mary and then Lady Elizabeth. I've been at Hatfield House ever since.'

'And you never saw our mother again?'

There was a momentary pause before Isolde answered. 'Just once. She came here in secret with your father. You won't remember because you were only a small child at the time. Then we found ways to send messages to each other. We couldn't risk it often. My half-brother is surprisingly well-informed about what happens at court, but we managed. She used to tell me all about you. She loved you a great deal.' A shadow of bitterness crept into her voice, before she clucked her tongue. 'I'm not saying that she didn't love me too, but it was different. So there you have it, that's who she was.'

'Oh!' Annis gave a startled jolt, stuck by a sudden idea. 'The message you sent with Sir Bennet, was it about your half-brother Charles?'

'Yes. It was a warning that he'd heard news of your father's death. I thought he might make life difficult for her.'

'But why a warning? Do you think he might have been involved in the attack?'

'No.' Isolde shook her head firmly. 'Though, I admit, I wondered about it when you first told me. He always had a mean streak, but if he'd wanted to hurt her then surely he would have done it twenty years ago.'

'Unless he hated her even more than you realised, but never dared act on it because of my father?' Annis suggested, chewing on her lip. 'It makes sense. When the mob came, she told me that trouble had been coming for her for a long time.'

'What do you mean?'

'That's what she said, that her past was catching up with her. I didn't understand what she meant at the time, and then Sir Bennet and I assumed it had something to do with Oliver Hawksby and the family feud. But maybe she was thinking of your half-brother?'

Isolde stared at her intently for a few seconds before

shaking her head again. 'I still don't think so. She might have assumed that because of my message, but it doesn't sound like Charles. Accusing her of witchcraft and rousing a mob is the sort of thing that draws attention, and that's the last thing he'd want. It might make people remember the connection between them. After all this time, he probably hopes that people have forgotten who my mother was.'

'So is *he* the reason she kept away from court? Why she hid me away from the world too?'

'In part.' Isolde's shoulders heaved. 'She knew how vindictive he could be so she probably thought it safer not to provoke him by being seen in public. He could easily have made life worse for me, or even influenced the King against your father if he'd wanted. But her experience of the world, of men in particular, wasn't good either. I think she became a recluse because she was scarred by her past and wanted to withdraw from the world, to protect you from it, too. Your father provided a safe haven.'

'That makes sense, although she could still have told me about you.'

'And would you have been content to stay at Cariscombe, knowing that you had a half-sister you could never see?' Isolde smiled sadly. 'She did what she thought was best. She wanted you to be safe and independent, to have a better life than she'd had. Or I had, for that matter.'

'I'm sorry.'

'Don't be. I've learnt to take care of myself.' Isolde's shoulder nudged almost imperceptibly against hers. 'Annis, I'm sorry you have to marry when you don't want to, but I have something else for you to wear, something I think might help you tomorrow…' She opened a box beside the bed and pulled out a large ruby on the end of a long gold chain. 'Mother gave it to me in secret on the day she left.' She draped it around Annis's neck, her eyes looking suspiciously moist before she turned away again. 'It's only on loan. I want it back straight after the ceremony.'

'Thank you.' Annis touched her fingertips to the pendant, feeling a lump swell in her own throat. Coming from Isolde, the gesture was as good as an embrace. 'What do you think she would have thought, seeing us together like this? Do you think she would have been pleased?'

'Yes.' Isolde paused briefly. 'As am I. It looks good on you.'

'Not as good as it would on you. I think you're even more beautiful than she was.'

'For all the good it does me.' Isolde rolled her eyes. 'Do you know what they say about beautiful women at court?'

'No. What?'

'That they hope they don't catch the eye of the King.'

'*Oh.*'

'Don't worry. He's too old and fat to do much about it these days.' Isolde's mouth twisted. 'But your new husband is a good man, remember that. He won't expect anything of you that you don't want. And don't tell me you don't like him a little. You were murmuring his name in your sleep after your accident.'

'Maybe I did like him once.' Annis felt her cheeks flush. 'I thought I did anyway, but that didn't mean I wanted to marry him! And *he's* only marrying *me* out of duty, because Mother entrusted me to him and now he feels responsible for me.'

'*Or* he wants to protect you, just like your father did our mother. Maybe there's hope the two of you might come to care for each other like they did?'

'I doubt it. He's in love with a ghost.'

'Ghost?' Isolde looked taken aback. 'What ghost?'

'Mistress Annis?' Kat opened the door at that moment. 'Lady Elizabeth wishes to speak with you.'

'Me?' Annis exchanged a swift, surprised look with Isolde before pushing herself to her feet, wobbling slightly on her sore ankle.

'Yes.' Lady Elizabeth swept into the room, her bright eyes sparkling. 'I wanted to see how you are.'

'Thank you, my lady. I'd curtsey, but...'

'But you have too many bruises from your accident.' The girl smiled. 'Don't you dare even try.' Her gaze shifted, moving pointedly between Isolde and Kat. 'You may leave us.'

'That might not be wise.' Kat sounded anxious.

'What I have to say will only take a few moments. Go!'

'Is something the matter, my lady?' Annis asked once they were alone.

'Not at all. I just came to wish you joy. Kat tells me you're marrying Sir Bennet and going back to Somerset in the morning.' She got straight to the point. 'Is that true?'

'Yes, my lady.'

'So I was right about the two of you?' To her surprise, Lady Elizabeth leaned forward, pressing a kiss to her cheek, then whispering in her ear, 'You know, I hear more than most people think. I'm very good at looking like I'm not listening, but I overhear all kinds of rumours.'

'You do?' She swallowed nervously.

'Yes. They called my mother an upstart and accused her of things too. There was no proof, but it was the word of a man against hers.' She pulled back again. 'So I know how it feels.'

Annis caught her breath, aware of her heart pounding very fast suddenly. 'Thank you, my lady.'

'The important thing is to not let them beat you. Do what you must to survive.' Lady Elizabeth winked. 'And don't go near any staircases for a while either.'

'Isolde thinks that once I'm married I'll be safe.'

'She might be right, but from what I've seen, men don't like to be thwarted, especially not by a woman. So keep your eyes open, be careful and, who knows, maybe we'll see each other again one day. Maybe there'll even be a place for you in my household.'

'I'd like that, my lady.' Annis smiled gratefully. 'Thank you.'

Bennet picked up his cup of wine and then set it down again. On the eve of his second wedding, he couldn't help but think back to his first. He'd only been eighteen years old back then, full of hope and excitement, looking forward to his wedding night, too. Now he was older and wiser and acutely aware of all the conflicting emotions whirling around his head, *especially* regarding the wedding night. He wanted nothing so much as to pick up the cup and drain it to the dregs, but he owed it to Annis not to have a headache in the morning. Besides, he needed to stay alert. He'd kept watch in a chair—hidden away in a corner of the corridor outside Isolde's bedchamber—every night since the 'accident', and he couldn't afford to let his guard down now.

Just like Eleanor, Annis hadn't smiled at him once since he'd asked her to marry him. So much for history not repeating itself. It already was, right before his eyes, which was why he was now avoiding looking at her. It was obvious that, if it wasn't for the danger she was in, she'd still be protesting about the very idea of marriage. So would he, to be fair, albeit for different reasons, which in a strange way made them perfectly suited. Since neither of them wanted a marriage, it would be a union in name only. *Without* a wedding night. Only it would be a great deal easier if he wasn't quite so attracted to her. He had a feeling that he was going to be spending even more time away from Somerset in the future, simply for his own sanity.

'There you are, my friend.' Richard came meandering along the corridor towards him. 'You know, Lady Isolde bars the door from the inside. Your bride-to-be is completely safe.'

'She won't be safe until we're married.' Ben contradicted him. 'And even then...we still don't know for certain that her cousin is behind all this.'

'No, but it seems a reasonable assumption. What possible other reason could there be for somebody to attack her?'

'I don't know. That's the problem.'

Richard quirked an eyebrow. 'Don't tell me you're having second thoughts about this marriage?'

'And third and fourth ones.' Ben pushed a hand through his hair and sighed. The thought of another bad marriage was almost more than he could bear. 'What if this is another terrible mistake? What if I make her as unhappy as I made Eleanor?'

'You know, I never met your first wife, but from everything you've told me, she sounds like a very different person to this lady.'

'She was.'

'So maybe you need to stop comparing them? In any case, you want to protect Annis, yes?'

'Yes.'

'Then this is the best way.' Richard smacked his arm before wandering away again. 'Now I'm going to bed. I have a wedding to attend in the morning.'

Chapter Fifteen

The journey away from Hatfield was a sharp contrast to the one they'd made towards it—across country and often in hiding—just over a week before. To Annis's great relief, the weather was significantly cooler for a start, and they were able to use highways again, accompanied by half a dozen guards that Ben appeared to have borrowed from somewhere. It *felt* safer, though she still found herself peering around the curtains of her horse-drawn litter at regular intervals, scouring the horizon for any signs of pursuit. There was never anyone there, but she still couldn't shake the eerie sensation of eyes watching her from a distance.

As for her other feelings, they were so confused that she'd given up trying to make sense of them. She and Ben were married, though the idea still seemed unreal to her. The ceremony had been short and strangely impersonal, over almost as soon as it had begun. They'd exchanged rings and said their vows, but they'd barely made eye contact the whole time. Then, afterwards, she'd changed out of her amber velvet into a plain green linen travelling dress, said goodbye to Isolde and Richard, and left Hatfield House before most of the residents had broken their fasts.

Now her new *husband* was riding beside her litter, though he made no attempt to engage her in conversation. That was another difference from their first journey together. The camaraderie they'd shared had been completely lost. So much for a marriage based on friendship. They were behaving more like strangers.

It was evening by the time they finally turned off the highway. Then they rode beneath a gatehouse that looked like a miniature castle in itself, complete with crenellations around the roof and a freshly painted blue and yellow coat of arms above the archway. This led towards a substantial timber-framed house, surrounded by half a dozen smaller stone buildings.

'Is this your friend's house?' Annis asked as their procession drew to a halt in the courtyard.

'Yes.' Ben drew rein and dismounted beside her. 'I met Roger when I first went to London to enter the King's service. I found the court overwhelming at first, but he took me under his wing and now he's like a second father to me. As for his wife, Juliet, she likes to mother everyone.' He extended a hand to help her out of the litter, his expression sympathetic. 'I know today's been a long day, but they say we can stay here for as long as we need.'

'That's kind.' She tensed as she put her gloved hand in his. Part of her still wanted to keep some distance between them, but, after a day spent lying in one position, her limbs felt numb and heavy. She was afraid she might fall if she didn't hold onto something.

'Come.' He tugged gently, leading her towards a massive front door that opened into a hall so vast it almost rivalled Hatfield's. There was linenfold panelling on two of the walls, while the others were draped with tapestries in vivid shades of red, green and gold depicting scenes of warrior knights doing battle. Whoever they were, Ben's friends were clearly important people.

'Ben!' A woman with a square-shaped face and dark curls escaping from beneath a yellow hood came rushing forward the moment they entered, arms outstretched. Judging by the lines on her brow she was at least twenty years older than he was, but the warmth of her smile made her seem younger. 'Welcome.'

'It's good to see you, Juliet.' Ben opened his own arms with a smile.

Annis watched them embrace with surprise. It was the first time she'd seen Ben smile since they'd arrived at Hatfield House, she realised, the first time the muscles of his face had relaxed even slightly. It made him look younger too.

'Where's Roger?' Ben looked around.

'Here.' A man with grey hair emerged from behind a screen. 'My wife was too excited by your arrival to wait for me.'

'Pshaw.' The woman rolled her eyes. 'It's not my fault I can move faster than you.'

'Ben.' The man grasped his shoulder. 'It's been too long.'

'It has, but I warn you, I might be imposing on your hospitality for a while.' Ben stepped backwards, extending an arm out towards Annis. 'Allow me to present my wife. Annis, these are my friends Roger and Juliet Markham.'

'Annis.' The woman beamed at her. 'I'm delighted to meet you. I couldn't believe it when Ben wrote to say he was bringing his new wife to visit us. I never thought I'd see the day. When were you married?'

'Just this morning, my lady.' Annis dipped into a curtsey, her lips curving despite the awkwardness of the situation. After the tense atmosphere of Hatfield House, it was a relief to see a pair of cheerful faces.

'This morning?' The woman clasped a hand to her throat. 'But surely you haven't come all the way from London today?'

'I'm afraid so,' Ben answered for her. 'It was necessary, but I'll explain why later.'

'Well, no wonder you look so exhausted.' Juliet reached for Annis's hands, clutching them between hers. 'You must go to bed at once. Your chamber is all ready and I'll have some food sent up.'

'Thank you, my lady.' Annis exhaled gratefully. 'That sounds wonderful.'

'It's this way.' Juliet led her towards the screen, slanting a significant look at Ben on her way past. 'I'll be back soon.'

'In other words, there was no choice.' Bennet leaned back in his chair as he finished his story.

'Not for her, no, but for you…' Juliet looked disappointed. 'She wasn't your responsibility.'

'I was the one who took her to London.'

'Which was already more than most men would have done. You didn't have to marry her as well.'

'So you think I should have just left her to the mercy of whoever killed her mother?' He put his cup down more heavily than he'd intended, splashing wine over the table.

'Of course not.' Juliet tutted at the mess. 'You did the honourable thing, as always, but sometimes you're too noble for your own good. When you introduced us like that, and the way you looked at her…'

'What way?' He frowned.

'Like this.' She turned a doting gaze towards her husband.

'I did not look at her like that.'

'Well, it was something similar.' She sighed. 'I thought it was a love match, that's all.'

'Like yours, you mean?' Ben looked between the two of them. 'Not many people are so lucky.'

'No, but you're young. You had time to fall in love. There was no need to do this. You could have protected her in different ways.'

'I don't think so.' He frowned into his cup again.

'There's just one thing I don't understand…' Roger finally spoke. 'If you were only married this morning, then why are you still down here drinking with us when you could be upstairs in bed with your pretty new wife?'

'Haven't you been listening? Because the poor girl fell down a staircase less than a week ago and she was clearly exhausted when she arrived.' Juliet batted his arm before turning back towards Ben. 'You must stay for as long as she needs to recuperate.'

'Thank you.' He inclined his head. 'I'm grateful, but you should know, there may still be a risk from whoever attacked her.'

'I thought you said that marrying her made her safe?'

'Hopefully, but it's early days. Until we can be certain that word of our marriage is out, we still ought to be careful. It could be dangerous for you too.'

'Pshaw. We're not afraid.' Juliet waved a hand dismissively. 'I still say this whole situation is a shame though.'

'But it's done. We're married. I only hope…' Ben stopped, clenching his jaw tight.

'What?'

'I only hope I can make her happier than I did Eleanor.'

'Pah. You have to stop blaming yourself for Eleanor's

behaviour. Nobody could have made her happy and she took her unhappiness out on you. With any luck, you and this one are better suited.'

'*This one?*' Ben lifted an eyebrow. 'How much wine have you drunk?'

'Possibly a little more than I should have.' She chuckled. 'Annie, was it?'

'*Annis.*'

'Well, danger or not, I insist on you staying. The two of you need some time to get used to each other as husband and wife before you go back to Draycote. A mother-in-law *and* a stepson is a lot for a new wife to take in. Besides, marriage of convenience or not, maybe there's still a chance for you to fall in love.'

'Juliet…'

'Don't Juliet me.' She reached across the table, placing a hand on his arm. 'Ben, I know you were deeply hurt by Eleanor, but you deserve to love and be loved, no matter how she made you feel.'

He hesitated, looking down at her hand. 'It's just hard to forget the way she used to look at me. Like I was some kind of ogre.'

'Of all the men I've ever met, you're the least like an ogre, my friend.' Roger laughed. 'Except in appearance, obviously. Besides, some women like an ogre in their beds.'

'Hush.' Juliet gave him a shove.

Ben laughed, aware of a tension in his chest at the thought. 'What if it all goes wrong again?'

'Maybe it will. Or maybe it won't.' Juliet squeezed his arm. 'But if you don't even try then you'll be letting Eleanor destroy your future as well as your past. If you have a chance to be happy with Annis then seize it.'

Ben drew his brows together. He and Annis had got along well enough before they'd reached Hatfield House. Maybe they could again. What if he treated their stay with Roger and Juliet as a kind of honeymoon? What if he made an effort the way he had in the early days of his first marriage, before it had become obvious that nothing would make Eleanor happy? *Was* there a chance their marriage of convenience could grow into something more? Or would he simply be asking to be rejected again?

'You might be right,' he conceded. 'I'm not promising anything, but I'll think about it.'

'Then it's agreed.' Juliet clapped her hands. 'You'll stay and I'll tell her all of your good points.'

'That might actually be useful.' He laughed. 'Thank you.'

Ben crept into their bedchamber a little while later, closing the door softly behind him. It was completely dark, except for the fire, which cast flickering orange patterns on the walls. It was enough for him to make out the shape of Annis lying in bed, her back turned towards him. Some instinct told him she wasn't asleep, though since she didn't turn to greet him, she obviously wanted him to believe that she was. He chose to act convinced. The last thing he wanted to do was disappoint another wife on their wedding night.

Slowly, he removed his clothes, slid under the blankets and rolled his shoulders, trying to get comfortable without disturbing her, but—despite the feather-filled mattress—it was impossible. He'd come upstairs feeling as bone tired as he'd ever been in his life, and yet suddenly every part of him was wide awake. Despite the arm's length between them,

Annis was still far too close for comfort. He could feel the heat of her body across the bed, a tantalising warmth that was provoking a series of unhelpful images in his mind. He couldn't help but wonder what it would be like to draw her towards him, to slide his arms around her and pull her beneath him, on top of him, to feel that warmth pressed against his own skin. He would never touch her, not without her permission, but apparently his imagination didn't know that. And his imagination was far too vivid for its own good. He felt intensely aware of everything about her, of every soft breath and gentle inhalation. At this rate, he'd be lucky to get more than a couple of minutes of sleep.

'Your friends are very pleasant.' Her voice made him jump.

'Yes, they are.' He cleared his throat, making a monumental effort to sound like he hadn't just been thinking about her naked body. 'I thought you'd be asleep by now.'

'I was for a while.' She rolled over to face him, resting a hand beneath her cheek. 'Only so much has happened recently, my mind won't let me. It feels like it's spinning.'

'Mine too.' He met her gaze and gulped. This position was even more intimate. Her warm breath was actually skimming his face, making his blood stir in a way that was definitely *not* going to help him sleep.

'You looked beautiful this morning.' He said the words quickly. They were the first ones that came into his head, though the thought had been on his mind all day. His first sight of her had taken his breath away. 'At our wedding, I mean. I should have told you so at the time.'

Surprise flickered in her eyes. 'Thank you. Cecilia lent me the gown.'

'It suited you.'

She gave a small smile, pressing her lips together as if she were trying to think of something else to say. 'How long will we be staying here?'

'Just until you feel better.' He paused, watching her for her reaction. 'Although Juliet thinks it might be useful for us to have some time together before you see my mother again and meet George.'

'Oh...yes, maybe.' To his relief, she sounded thoughtful rather than alarmed. 'How will your mother react to us being married, do you think?'

'She'll probably be shocked at first, but after that I think she'll be pleased. She's been telling me I ought to marry again for the past two years.'

'Because of your son?'

'Yes. Now she's getting older, she's finding it hard to keep up with him. I've known for a while I ought to do something, but I wasn't sure what, especially since she refuses to hire a maid to look after him.' He winced as he realised how the words sounded. 'Not that I expect you to do it either. I promised you your independence and I meant it. George is my responsibility.' He was struck with a familiar stab of guilt mixed with heartache. 'I want to be a good father to him, I only wish I knew how. The truth is, I hardly know him. I've no idea how to talk to him.'

'Then you ought to learn.'

He quirked an eyebrow. 'Just like that?'

'Just like that.' She held onto his gaze, her own undaunted. 'You said he's only five so there's still plenty of time. It's what your wife would have wanted, isn't it?'

He froze. There it was again, the question of what Eleanor might or might not have wanted from him. He had no idea how to answer that. 'Probably.'

'Well then.' She rolled onto her back as if the question were settled.

He lay beside her, turning his own gaze towards the ceiling. Now that they were both obviously awake, his nerves felt more alive than ever, as if every inch of his skin were tingling. He was simultaneously buzzing and more frustrated than he'd ever been in his entire life. Tension seemed to spark and crackle in the small space between them. Was he imagining it or could she feel it too? Briefly, he considered holding a hand out towards her. Would she take it?

Then again, maybe she couldn't sleep because she was anxious about sharing a bed with him. Now they were married, maybe she needed reassurance that his intentions truly were honourable. In which case, touching her would be the absolute worst thing he could do.

'Annis?' He broke the silence again.

'Yes?' There seemed to be a nervous catch in her voice this time.

'Goodnight.'

Chapter Sixteen

'Forgive me for saying so, my dear, but you don't seem very happy,' Juliet commented as she and Annis walked in the garden the following afternoon, enveloped by the potent scents of honeysuckle and trailing roses.

'I'm sorry.' Annis gave her an apologetic look. Juliet had suggested they go for a walk to get to know each other. Some fresh air had struck her as a very good idea, especially since Ben was out with Roger, inspecting a new windmill his friend was building close by. 'Your garden is beautiful and I'm glad to be here. It's just that I feel so…' she lifted her shoulders, searching for the right word '…lost.'

'Lost?'

'Yes. My parents raised me to be mistress of my own life, but ever since my father died it's like I've lost all control over everything. I wanted to confront the mob, but my mother sent me away. I wanted to stay at Cariscombe and find out who was behind the attack, but Ben insisted on taking me to London. I wanted to come home again, and somebody pushed me down a staircase. I *still* wanted to come home, but everyone told me I had to get married for my own safety… I've done more and seen more in the past month than I have in the whole rest of my life and I feel like

I'm struggling to catch up. I'm afraid if it goes on I'll lose touch with who I am completely.'

'I'm sorry.' Juliet put an arm around her shoulders sympathetically. 'Ben told us you didn't wish to marry, but he's a good man. Honourable too.'

'I know,' Annis agreed. 'I dread to think what would have happened to me without his help. It's just…strange.'

'I understand. Marriage is a big adjustment for any woman.'

'Will you tell me about Ben's first wife?' she asked. Since she was alone with Juliet, it occurred to her that this was a perfect opportunity to learn more about her husband. 'What was she like?'

'Hasn't he told you?' Juliet stopped to pluck a weed from the gravel at their feet.

'No. Every time I mention her he changes the subject.'

'Ah. Well, that makes sense, I suppose. She was very beautiful. Tall and slender with golden hair, large blue eyes like a doe and…' Juliet stopped and made a face. 'My apologies, that's not what a new wife wishes to hear, is it?'

'Not really,' Annis admitted. 'But I asked, and I prefer the truth.'

'Well then, the truth is that she was also as miserable as she was beautiful. I only met her on a handful of occasions, but I've never known a person so discontented. When she was at court she wanted to be at home, and when she was at home she wanted to be at court. Nothing ever seemed to satisfy her.'

'Really?' Annis regarded the other woman in surprise. There was a hard, slightly bitter edge to her voice, as if she hadn't liked Eleanor at all. 'That must have been hard for Ben, especially when he cared for her so deeply.'

'Ye-es.' Juliet gave her a strange look. 'He did everything

he could to make her happy, but it was an impossible task. If he'd offered her the moon, she would only have sighed and told him it wasn't big or bright enough.'

'Oh...' Annis looked away again, feeling a deep pang of sympathy for her husband. Juliet's words painted a very different image of Eleanor to the one she'd built up in her mind. How horrible it must have been for Ben to love someone who hadn't loved him back. The idea made her uneasy, as if her brain were trying to warn her of something.

'That's why I wouldn't want him to be hurt again.' Juliet gave her a meaningful look.

'Hurt?' Annis frowned. 'I've no intention of hurting him. I doubt I could.'

'You might be surprised.' Juliet led her into a rose-covered arbour and sat down on a stone bench. 'By the way, I've arranged a special banquet for tonight in honour of the two of you.'

'Oh, that's really not necessary.'

'Yes, it is. A marriage ought to be celebrated properly, no matter what the reason behind it. Now tell me, what news of court?'

'Um...' Annis gave her a dubious look. 'Ben told me I shouldn't talk about such things. He says it's dangerous.'

'Ordinarily I'd agree, but I'm a friend, not a spy.' Juliet tipped her head closer. 'And I won't tell him you told me, I promise. Come, there must be some news of the King at least?'

'Well... I didn't see him, but they say he's happy with his sixth wife.'

'I'm sure *he* is. Poor Katherine.'

'Why "poor"?' Annis wrinkled her brow in confusion. 'Surely being Queen is a great honour?'

'Maybe it was twenty years ago, but if you'd seen the King recently, you'd understand what I mean.' Juliet snorted and gave an exaggerated shudder. 'Let's just hope her role is more that of a nurse than a wife. Imagine sharing a bed with a man like that…'

'What do you mean?'

'I'm talking about what passes between a man and a woman in the marital bedchamber. In *bed*.' Juliet gave her a sidelong look. 'You don't know? No, maybe you don't. Well, there's plenty of time. You were only married yesterday, after all.'

'But Ben and I slept in the same bed last night,' Annis protested.

'Ye-es, but *only* slept.'

'What else would we do there?'

'A great deal!' Juliet looked away with a laugh before turning her head back sharply again. 'Do you really not know? Has nobody told you?'

'Told me *what*?'

'Oh, dear, if I'd had daughters instead of three sons, this might have been easier. Somebody really ought to have told you. I'm talking about consummating the marriage.'

'Consummating?' Annis repeated the word quizzically. She didn't even know what it meant.

'*Joining.* As in joining your bodies together.' Juliet craned her neck, peering up and down the garden path, before making an exasperated sound and shuffling closer. 'Oh, very well. It seems we have a lot to discuss.'

'What have you two been talking about?' Ben smiled a greeting as he strode to meet Annis and Juliet on the terrace. Roger was still at the mill, deep in conversation with his team of builders, but he'd returned early and noticed them sitting in the arbour on his way back from the stables. He'd been about to join them when they'd stood up and started walking back towards the house. Now he noticed a strange, slightly dazed look on Annis's face. Her skin was flushed and she appeared to be having trouble meeting his eyes. Juliet, meanwhile, looked far *too* bright and cheerful, like a woman trying to hide something.

'Oh, nothing in particular,' Juliet answered breezily, *definitely* trying to hide something. 'How was your ride?'

'Very enjoyable. It's a beautiful day, is it not?' He directed the question to Annis.

'Yes.' Her gaze connected briefly with his, flashing with some fierce emotion, before sliding away again. 'Most pleasant.'

'Can I fetch you something to drink? You look hot.'

'It's the sun,' she answered quickly. 'Or perhaps I've walked a little too fast on my ankle. Excuse me. I need to...' She twirled her hand in the air as if she were trying to think of an excuse to get away. 'Lie down.'

'Are you feeling unwell? Do you need me to help you upstairs?'

'No!' She sounded positively alarmed by the idea. 'That is, no thank you. I can manage very well on my own.'

'As you wish.' He bowed, beginning to feel distinctly uneasy. 'I'll see you later.'

'Have a good rest, my dear.' Juliet gave what looked like a conspiratorial smile as Annis darted through the door to the hall.

'*What* have you said to her?' Ben whirled around the moment she was out of sight.

'What on earth do you mean?' Juliet immediately adopted an overly innocent expression. 'We've just been talking, that's all.'

'That is *not* all. What did you talk about?'

'That would be our business.' She put her hands on her hips. 'Although if you must know, I've been trying to help, and, honestly, you ought to be thanking me instead of glaring at me.'

'Thanking you?'

'Yes! It's about time somebody told her the facts.'

'The facts? What facts? Juliet, what are you talking about?'

'About marriage!'

'What?'

'The poor girl had no idea what I was talking about at first.' Juliet's expression turned accusing. 'I know you said you married in haste, but, from what I can tell, nobody's prepared her at all. Nobody's even mentioned what happens in the marriage bed, least of all her husband.'

'I thought...' He put a hand to his head, his unease turning into a very definite sense of panic. What *had* he thought? In all honesty, he *hadn't*. There hadn't seemed any need to think about it, since their marriage was supposed to be one in name only, but he supposed if he *had* thought about it then he would have assumed that she'd already known. Although...isolated as she'd been at Cariscombe, and considering how little time she'd had to prepare for their wedding, *how* would she have?

'I didn't think there was any need.' He was aware of how weak the words sounded.

'Of course there's a need!' Juliet looked outraged.

'No, there isn't. This isn't going to be that kind of marriage.'

'What?'

'I told you yesterday, I married her to protect her from her cousin, that's all.'

'So you're not... You have no intention of... Oh.' Juliet's face seemed to wrestle with several competing ideas at once. 'Well, she still had a right to know.'

'You're right. I just wished you'd talked to me first.' He pushed a hand through his hair. 'How much have you told her?'

'Enough for her to know you haven't consummated anything yet.'

He groaned aloud. No wonder Annis had been looking at him oddly. No wonder she'd run away too. She'd been worried enough that marriage would mean giving up her fortune and independence. Now she was probably afraid it would mean giving up her body too. She was probably cowering in their room in horror.

'Where are you going?' Juliet called after him as he made for the door.

'To speak to my wife!'

'Annis!' He caught up with her halfway up the stairwell. 'We need to talk.'

'No, we don't.' She threw a swift look over her shoulder and then accelerated her steps, almost running along the gallery to their bedchamber, despite her sore ankle.

'Yes, we do.' He rammed his foot between the door and its frame as she tried to close it behind her, following her inside. 'About what Juliet told you... I'm sorry. She was trying to help but—'

'I know she was trying to help!' Annis whirled about in the centre of the room and glared at him, her face flaming anew. 'And you don't have to apologise for her. I'm grateful to *her*! At least *she's* been honest with me!'

'I've been honest with you.'

'Ha!' She flung her head back. 'You never told me any of that!'

'There hasn't been time. We were only married yesterday.'

'But you proposed to me five days ago! That gave you plenty of opportunity to tell me.'

'You were still recovering from your accident.'

'I wasn't too injured to listen! You *should* have told me. *Somebody* ought to have told me before the wedding, but nobody mentioned a single word about the marriage bed. It's embarrassing that I didn't know! I'm not a child!'

'I know, I'm sorry.' He took a step towards her, opening his hands out in a placatory gesture. 'It was remiss of me, but I just assumed somebody else had discussed it with you.'

'Who? My mother never had a chance!'

'Your sister perhaps?'

'She's unwed!'

'Yes, but at court…' He stopped. Now probably wasn't the time to start discussing the ethics of the court. 'You're right. The truth is, it never occurred to me to talk about it because I promised you a marriage based on friendship and I meant it. Even if I had thought about it, I wouldn't have wanted to alarm you.' He winced. Somehow all his words were coming out wrong; he had no idea if he was making things better or worse. 'I mean, I wouldn't have wanted you to think I expected anything of you.' He cleared his throat awkwardly. 'What I'm trying to say is, you don't have to be worried. We don't have to do that…*it.*'

She jerked her head backwards. 'Because you don't you want to do it with me?'

'What? No! That's ridiculous.' He could barely express just how ridiculous it was when he'd lain awake for most of the previous night, his whole body yearning to touch her. 'But we agreed this was a marriage of convenience, to protect you and your fortune. I thought that was what you wanted.'

'Urgh!' She threw her hands up, her voice rising with emotion. 'Stop talking about protecting me! It's all you ever say. It's like being married to my own personal bodyguard! And our marriage doesn't even count. Juliet says it's not valid unless it's consummated.'

He tensed, resolving to have a few more words with Juliet later. 'Did she?'

'Yes. She said the wedding could be dissolved if anyone ever found out. Then Oliver Hawksby would still be my heir and all your talk of protection would mean nothing.'

'It *could* be dissolved, yes...' he spoke carefully '...but who's going to know whether it's consummated or not? Juliet might like to talk, but she's also trustworthy. She won't tell anyone.'

'Maybe not, but for me to be completely safe then we'd have to consummate the marriage at least once, just in case.'

'In theory...yes.' He slid a finger beneath his collar, beginning to feel several degrees too hot.

She thrust her chin into the air. 'Then it would seem like the sensible thing to do, wouldn't it?'

'*Sensible.*' He echoed the word heavily. Put like that, she made it sound as appealing as a prison sentence.

'And I admit, I'm curious.' Her gaze dipped before she

lifted it again defiantly, looking him square in the eye. 'The question is, what do *you* want?'

'This isn't about me.'

'Of course it is.' She made an exasperated sound. 'This marriage involves both of us, doesn't it? So I want to know. What do you want? And *don't* just say to protect me. Tell me honestly. Do you want to do it or not?'

Ben swallowed, aware of his entire body going suddenly rigid. What he wanted was to carry her to the bed and consummate their marriage right there and then. At length and repeatedly, if possible. It might be a huge mistake, it would definitely change everything between them, but he couldn't get his brain to focus on that right now. Never in his wildest dreams had he expected her to suggest what she seemed to be suggesting...

'Ben?' She was looking at him very intently.

'I'm not sure you understand what you're saying.' He felt as though he'd just been hit on the head with a hammer. 'You should take some time to think.'

'There you go, treating me like a child again!' She swung away, turning her face to the wall.

'Annis.' His nerves leapt as he came to stand behind her. 'I don't think of you as a child, trust me.'

'No?'

'No.' He moved closer, breathing in the scent of her hair as his chin brushed against the back of her hood. If he lowered his head and leaned forward he could press his lips against the side of her throat, touch his tongue to the shell of her ear...

'Well then?' She half turned her face back towards him. 'What do you want?'

'I want to.' He paused, still needing to be sure he wasn't

imagining things. 'So… You're saying that you *also* want
to consummate our marriage?'

'Yes, unless…' There was a slight quaver in her voice
before she controlled it. 'Unless it would make you feel like
you were betraying the memory of your wife.'

'It wouldn't,' he answered quickly. 'But are you certain
you feel well enough?'

'My bruises have mostly healed.'

'Right.' He drew in a deep breath and then let it out again
slowly. This wasn't what he'd intended. He'd intended to
keep well away from her, but if this was what she wanted,
he certainly wasn't going to say no. Frankly, he doubted
he'd be able to if he tried. 'Very well then. We'll do it. Tonight after Juliet's banquet.'

'Tonight?' Her voice sounded several notes higher
pitched all of a sudden. 'I mean…good. If we're both in
agreement, that's all there is to say.' She coughed heavily.
'Now I think I'd like to be alone for a little while.'

'Of course.' He nodded, stepping back towards the door.
He had no idea what else to say either. Only he felt oddly
like singing.

Annis waited until Ben had gone before walking across
the room to the window and pressing her forehead against
the glass. Her skin wasn't simply flushed—it was positively
burning up. She'd been shocked enough by the things Juliet had told her, but her conversation with Ben had just
pushed her over the edge into fever territory. The words
coming out of her mouth seemed to have belonged to someone else. She'd just told him that she wanted to consummate their marriage! And he'd told her that he wanted to
as well! And they were going to do it tonight!

She didn't know whether to be excited, terrified or both.

How had it happened? When she'd left Juliet, she'd been filled with mortification and anger and hurt. It was bad enough that she'd had to give up her independence and fortune for marriage, but for Ben *not* to have told her something so important made her furious! As if the fog around her hadn't been thick enough, he'd deliberately kept her in ignorance, too! And that was all on top of the searing sense of rejection she'd felt! It was like the knot garden all over again, only a hundred *thousand* times worse!

She'd had no intention of confronting him, not until she'd had a chance to think anyway, but when he'd come after her she'd been too angry to stop herself. She'd asked what he wanted because it had seemed like the only way of finding out the truth, and then, somehow, when he'd said that he wanted to consummate their marriage, she'd heard herself agreeing. Because it *was* the sensible thing to do to make their marriage secure, and because she *was* curious, but also because it was the truth. She did want to, even if she didn't entirely understand why.

She moved backwards, fanning her face with her hand as she studied her reflection in the glass, firmly ordering herself to be calm. She might have been completely naive an hour ago, but after telling Ben not to treat her like a child, she wasn't going to act like some nervous girl now. She was going to take charge of her own life again and be a confident married woman!

Somehow.

She walked over to where her new chest sat at the foot of the bed and lifted the lid. Thanks to Isolde, there were several new gowns inside—practical travelling clothes and day dresses mostly—although there was one gown suitable for a special occasion, a gift from Lady Elizabeth herself. All she needed was a little help to get it on and prepare herself for the banquet.

And she knew just who to ask.

Ben sat at a table in the hall, surrounded by the noise and bustle of Roger's extended family and retainers, wondering what was taking Annis and Juliet so long. The afternoon had already felt like the longest in his entire life—his patience was stretched almost to breaking point. He wasn't particularly hungry either, but the sooner this banquet was over with, the sooner he and Annis could retire to bed. Now the idea of consummating their marriage was out in the open, he felt like a dog in heat. Nightfall could hardly come quickly enough. She just had to come down to dinner first.

He'd caught only one brief glimpse of her since their conversation. She'd come downstairs shortly afterwards, given him a quick nod as if nothing of significance had happened, then drawn Juliet aside to ask her something. He'd been too far away to hear what, but the other woman's face had lit up in a way that probably ought to have worried him.

'Are you all right?' Roger asked, interrupting his brooding.

'Hmm?' He jerked his head around. 'Yes, perfectly.'

'Only you've been staring at that door for a good quarter of an hour now.' His friend chuckled. 'You're going to bore a hole through the wood if you're not careful. Are you missing your new bride?'

'Something like that.'

'Personally, I'm impatient for the food, although Juliet tells me she's arranged some entertainment too.'

Ben groaned inwardly. Entertainment sounded like

something that would make the evening last even longer. Given Juliet's lack of tact, she'd probably arranged for the minstrels to sing love poetry to them.

'Ah.' Roger gestured across the room. 'Here they are, at last.'

He lifted his head just in time to see Juliet sweep into the hall, Annis on her arm. And not just Annis, but Annis dressed in an emerald-green gown that brought out the red lights in her hair and clung to her hips in a way that made him want to start drooling. His heart stuttered at the sight.

'Husband.' Juliet smiled as they approached.

'It's about time.' Roger gestured towards their chairs. 'Come, wife, you promised me beef.'

'All you think about is your stomach.' Juliet rolled her eyes. 'Give Ben a chance to greet his wife first. She looks very fine, does she not, Ben?'

'She does.' He stood and met Annis's gaze, his body clenching with desire. 'You look perfect.'

'Thank you.' She slid her tongue along the seam of her lips, moistening them as if she were nervous.

'That's what I said…' Juliet looked distinctly smug. 'Now let's eat.'

Chapter Seventeen

Annis paced restlessly back and forth in front of her bed-chamber fireplace, dressed in a thin linen night-rail, hoping that movement might help to calm her taut nerves. Juliet had laid on a lavish feast of roast beef, rabbit pie and fried boar, not to mention date fritters, jellied fruit and a large sugar sculpture of a sailing ship—meant to symbolise her and Ben's future journey through life together—all to the accompaniment of half a dozen minstrels in the gallery. But she'd been too distracted to enjoy herself properly, retiring upstairs as soon as could be considered polite, which had still been three tortuously long hours. Ben had stood and bowed over her hand as she'd made her excuses, murmuring into her ear that he'd follow shortly, and somehow she'd managed to bow calmly in response, despite the flare of excitement in her chest. Then she'd walked away from the table, aware of his gaze on her back the whole time. The feeling had excited her even more.

Unfortunately, it must have been half an hour since she'd left and he *still* hadn't come to join her.

She stopped pacing and glared at the door, wondering if she ought to just climb into bed and forget the whole thing. She didn't know how much longer she could pretend a confidence she didn't feel. Maybe the whole idea was a mistake better forgotten.

She was halfway to the bed when there was a faint knock and the door finally opened.

'I'm sorry I took so long.' Ben entered, wearing an apologetic expression. 'The more Roger drinks, the more talkative he gets. Eventually, Juliet had to order him to let me go.'

'Oh. I see. I was just…' Annis let her voice trail away, unable to think of any way to finish the sentence when her inner organs were distracting her by all jumping up and down at once. Instead, she held her arms out to her sides, filling her cheeks with air before letting it out slowly. 'So what should I do?'

'There's no *should*.' Ben glanced briefly at the bed before removing his doublet and casting it aside, coming to stand in front of her. 'I don't want you to do anything you don't want to do.'

'I know, but…' She swallowed, very aware of the heat emanating from beneath his shirt, making her pulse accelerate so fast that she had a horrible feeling she might actually be shaking. 'I'm not sure where to start.'

'In that case, I have an idea.'

She caught her breath as he lowered his head and skimmed his lips softly against hers. They felt warm and reassuring. Meanwhile his hands curved around her shoulders, drawing her closer towards him until their hips were almost, but not quite, touching.

'Ben…' She murmured his name, aware of a tight feeling low down in her abdomen and between her legs.

'Mmm?' He pulled his head back slightly.

'That feels…nice.'

'Good.' She felt him smile against her mouth before he moved his lips away, trailing them across her cheek, then her ear, then nuzzling them against her neck as he buried his face in her hair. Instinctively, she tipped her head back, sliding her fingers around his back and hooking them beneath his belt, holding herself upright as her knees trembled beneath her. She wasn't entirely sure what was happening to her body, but she knew that she liked it, and apparently Ben did too. He gave a low moan in the back of his throat and claimed her mouth again, sliding his tongue past her lips as she pushed herself up on her toes.

She let herself relax, sinking into the moment as he bent down, wrapped an arm around the back of her legs and lifted her off her feet.

'Ben?' she whimpered as he carried her across the room and laid her down on the bed, trying to hold onto him as he drew his arms away and took a step back.

'I need to undress too,' he explained, gazing down at her as he tugged his shirt over his head, then reached down to his breeches.

Annis inhaled sharply. For a moment, she felt as though she was back at the river again, telling herself to avert her eyes. Only this time she was completely unable to look anywhere other than at Ben. Fascinated, she pushed herself up on her elbows as he removed his underclothes and stood completely naked before her. In the candlelight, his skin looked shiny, the smoothness of his chest broken only by a sprinkling of dark hair.

'May I?' He indicated the bed.

She nodded and wriggled sideways, shivering as he lay down beside her.

'Are you cold?' He reached for the coverlet.

'No.' She caught at his hand. Her body felt as though it was covered with goosebumps, but cold had nothing to do with it. She was so hot she felt as though she were coming down with a fever.

'Ah.' He pressed a row of kisses along her collarbone and then moved on top of her, sliding his legs carefully between hers. 'Annis, you should know that it might hurt to begin with.'

'I know. Juliet told me.'

'She seems to have told you a lot.' He smiled. 'Remind me to thank her the next time I see her.'

She smiled back as she lifted a hand to his chest and slid her fingers across his skin, exploring every contour. He felt hard and soft at the same time, ridged with muscle and sinew. Slowly, she swept her hand downwards and heard him suck in a breath. Somehow the sound made her feel even hotter. Impulsively, she lifted her head, touching her tongue to the dip at the base of his throat and then blowing gently.

'Annis.' He groaned and shifted sideways, taking the weight of his body on one arm as he slid his other hand between them and touched her in her most private area.

'Ben!' she exclaimed in shock, stiffening.

'Do you want me to stop?' He held onto her gaze, his own dark and questioning.

'No, but...' She found herself panting. 'What are you doing?'

'It's hard to explain. Let me show you?'

She nodded tentatively, and then his lips claimed hers again while his fingers started to move in slow circles, teasing her gently until she couldn't stop herself from squirming beneath him. Without thinking, she started to move too, arching her back and pushing herself upwards, aware of a feeling of dampness, of heat building around and inside her, causing a tight throbbing sensation in her stomach.

'Why are you stopping?' she protested as he drew his fingers away, after what felt like only a few moments, using them to untie the laces at the top of her night-rail instead.

'Does that mean you like it?' He grinned, though his voice sounded rough.

'I do.' She blushed at the admission.

'Then I'll do it again. Later. Right now, I want to see you.' He drew her night-rail over her head. 'I want to feel you against me.'

She gasped as the air touched her skin, then gasped again as he caught one of her breasts in his mouth, sending a tremor of feeling straight to her core.

'You're so beautiful.' He lifted his head again. 'Just promise me one thing.'

'What?' She tried to focus, only so many new sensations were swirling inside her she was beginning to feel light-headed.

'If you want me to stop, or if I do anything you don't like…tell me.'

'I promise.' She nodded as he lowered himself over her. The tight sensation in her stomach was so strong she could hardly stand it any more. Then he was parting her legs, pressing against her and… She gulped, feeling the pressure of his manhood between her thighs. And, according to Juliet, he wanted to put that inside her? It didn't seem possible. She tensed, wondering if she were making a dreadful mistake after all. There was no way this could work. He was too big and she was too tight. All she could feel was a hot stinging sensation as he pushed, just a little, and then pulled away again.

'Ben?' She felt a pang of disappointment. Obviously he was thinking the same thing she was, though she was faintly offended that he'd given up so easily. No sooner had the thought entered her mind, however, than he caught at her hands, pinning them above her head, as he did the same thing again—entering her and then almost withdrawing, over and over, thrusting deeper and deeper, a little more each time, until he was completely sheathed inside her.

'Ah!' she cried out, but the stinging sensation was already easing, transforming into something else.

'Annis?' He sounded as if he were in pain too. 'Are you...'

'Yes.' She panted. 'It's all right. Go on.'

He started to move again, slowly and carefully to begin with, then faster and harder as the tightness receded and she began to relax. Without realising, she found herself copying his movements, pushing and pulling away in a matching rhythm, aware of a delicious friction building between them. The throbbing sensation deep in her belly seemed to be getting stronger and fiercer and then, incredibly—almost impossibly—stronger again. Instinctively, she wrapped her legs around him and closed her eyes, dazed with sensation. They were both slick with sweat now, groaning and panting and gasping, as if they'd somehow become one body with one aim. It was like nothing she'd ever felt before, simultaneously too much and yet not enough. She wanted it to stop and she wanted it to keep building and she wanted to hold on to the moment and she wanted to know where it was leading and she wanted...

Her thoughts fell silent as something quivered and then

burst inside her. She clutched hold of Ben, a cry of both pleasure and pain bursting from her lips as her whole body convulsed and seemed to break apart. Somehow the movement caused him to jolt and then stiffen in response—for one horrible moment she thought she'd done something terribly wrong. Then he gave a long shudder, murmuring something she couldn't understand, before heaving a sigh and collapsing on top of her.

Annis opened her eyes a little while later, surprised to discover that she'd fallen asleep. She was still lying on her back, but Ben's body was pinning her to the bed, his head resting between her breasts. It was no surprise that she'd woken up. She was beginning to have trouble breathing.

'Ben?' She lifted her hands to his shoulders, whispering his name as she tried to push him away.

'Mmm?' He sounded sleepy.

'You're crushing me.'

'Oh.' He lifted his head quickly, staring at her with a dazed, faintly dreamy expression for a few seconds, before seeming to come back to himself.

'Sorry. Are you all right?' He shifted to one side, his expression genuinely worried. 'How do you feel?'

She touched her tongue to her lips, uncertain about how to answer. On the one hand, she felt relaxed and drowsy, her curiosity well and truly satiated. Meanwhile, her body was still tingling with new sensations—the part that wasn't numb from him lying on top of her anyway—and there was an ache between her legs telling her that she hadn't dreamt the whole thing, which was a relief. Now that their marriage was consummated, she didn't have to fear her cousin's attempts to steal her inheritance any more. That danger was past.

And yet… She squirmed as an uncomfortable thought pushed its way to the forefront of her mind, bringing with it a wave of mortification. Her emotions had been so tangled before, it only now occurred to her that maybe Ben had been lying when he'd said he wanted to consummate their marriage. Especially since he'd always been so definite about *never* remarrying. Maybe that was why he'd stayed downstairs for so long that evening, because he'd been berating Juliet for telling her what consummation meant? Maybe deep down he'd been hoping she might never find out, so that he'd never have to bed her. Maybe he'd been thinking of his first wife the whole time!

She screwed her eyes shut as her thoughts spiralled. Had Ben only agreed to placate her? Or, worse, out of a sense of duty? Had she seen what she'd wanted to see in his eyes? In which case, what must he think of her now? Of the shameless way that she'd responded? She had a feeling she'd actually whimpered at one point!

How did she feel? She *didn't* feel like a confident woman taking control of her own life any more. She felt like someone who'd given up yet another part of herself, who was even more married than she'd been before, who thought she'd found a way out of the fog, only to feel more confused than ever. She felt like a fool.

'Annis?' Ben pushed himself up on one elbow, a note of alarm in his voice now.

'I'm well,' she answered quickly. 'Just tired.'

'Are you certain?' He laid an arm gently across her stomach. 'You're not having any regrets?'

'No. Why? Are you?'

'None.'

She felt her panic ease slightly. He sounded as if he were telling the truth. Maybe she was worrying about nothing. Maybe he really had wanted to do it, and his arm felt so warm and comforting, she wanted to curl up into it...unless he was *still* trying to placate her?

Swiftly, she rolled away onto her side, feeling him draw his arm back as she curled herself into a tight ball. 'Good. Well, that's over and done with. We're officially married. Good night.'

There was a moment of silence before she felt him lie down again.

Chapter Eighteen

'Thank you for your hospitality.' Ben embraced Juliet and Roger on the steps of their house. After four days, it was time for him and Annis to leave while the weather was still good enough for travel. 'I'm indebted to you.'

'Don't be silly. You're welcome to stay anytime.' Juliet leaned forward to kiss his cheek. 'But are you certain Annis is recovered enough for the journey?'

'So she tells me.' He glanced over his shoulder at his wife. She'd already said her farewells and was waiting in the litter, though she looked away the moment she caught his eye.

'How are things between the two of you?' Juliet sounded concerned. 'I thought you were beginning to warm to each other the other evening, but, if anything, you're even more awkward now than when you arrived.'

'I know.' His heart wrenched at the words. Consummating their marriage had been an even greater mistake than he'd feared. He'd thought they'd both known what they were doing. She'd told him that she was curious and that she wanted to make their marriage legally valid, while he…well, in all honesty, those reasons had been enough for him. But he supposed he'd also hoped that going to bed together would bring them closer, which it had at the time. Briefly. It had been even better than he'd dared to imagine, and she'd seemed to enjoy herself, too. Yet afterwards she'd withdrawn from him just as Eleanor had, as if she regretted letting him touch her at all. They'd barely looked at each other, let alone spoken since, and the worst part was that every time they accidentally locked gazes their night together was all he could think about. He wanted her now more than ever. Unfortunately, once appeared to be more than enough for her.

It was just as he'd feared. His second marriage was following the same pattern as his first, only this time the rejection hurt even more.

'Whatever's happened between you, don't give up. Talk to her.' Juliet patted his shoulder sympathetically. 'Find out what the matter is.'

'I know what the matter is.' He gave her a heavy look. 'She doesn't want to be married to me.'

They took the rest of the journey slowly and steadily, stopping at the houses of Ben's friends and acquaintances on the way, though never staying anywhere else for more than one night. They were both polite and attentive to each other, but Annis felt the divide between them deepening every day. There were a few occasions when she looked in his direction only to get the distinct impression that he'd just looked away, but neither of them broached the subject of their night together and she made a point of going to bed early so that she was always asleep, or pretending to be, by the time he came to join her. Not that he slept in the same bed anyway, preferring to stretch himself out in a chair or even on the floor by the fireplace instead. If anyone found their behaviour odd for newlyweds, nobody commented, at least not in her hearing.

Meanwhile the days themselves were excruciating. She was so lost in the fog now that she felt utterly powerless, with no idea which way to turn. Alone in her litter, swaying back and forth along dusty roads that seemed to go on for ever, she had far too much time alone with her own thoughts and when her mind wandered, she found herself reminiscing about their night together, remembering the feeling of Ben's hands on her body and his lips on her skin… The only way to bear it without screaming was by reminding herself that every mile was a mile closer to Cariscombe. Home would set everything right and make her feel like herself again. It had to.

Finally, after seven interminable days, they turned onto the track through the woods that led to Draycote Manor. Annis felt her muscles tense, afraid that the house might bring back memories of the attack, and yet, as they turned a corner and it came into view, she struggled to recognise anything familiar. Of course it had been dark when she'd fled there, and she'd been too frightened to notice a great deal, but still—if she hadn't been told it was the same place she would never have believed it.

She heaved a sigh of relief, looking up at the building. It was impressive, three times the size and a couple of centuries more modern than Cariscombe, with a steeply pitched tile roof and at least a dozen chimneys. The bottom two floors also appeared to be made of brick, while the top was a combination of wood and plaster, painted in black and white with several overlapping gables, each with its own glass window.

She stole a glance at Bennet, riding beside the litter just as he'd done for the entire journey. She was nervous enough about their arrival, but his jaw was clenched so tight she was amazed she couldn't hear his teeth grinding together. Was he nervous about presenting her to his family and servants, she wondered, or was it because he was anxious about spending time with his son again? Maybe it was a combination of both. It was impossible to guess what kind of reception awaited them, although it seemed they wouldn't have to wait long for the answer. There was already a figure waiting outside the front door, somebody she *did* remember— her new mother-in-law, Lady Joan. It struck her that Juliet might have had a point, after all.

'Mother.' Ben dismounted at once, embracing his mother on the doorstep.

'Ben.' She folded her arms around him. 'I'm so glad you came back. I was afraid you wouldn't have time before having to resume your duties at court.'

'So was I.' He gestured towards Annis as she climbed out of the litter. 'And as you can see, I'm not alone.'

'Annis.' His mother inclined her head with a quizzical expression. 'This is a surprise. It's good to see you too.'

'And you, Lady Joan.' She curtsied politely. 'I hope you're well?'

'I am, only I thought the plan was for you to stay in London?'

'It was, but our plans changed.' Ben's voice sounded sharp suddenly. Apparently he didn't believe in prevaricating either. 'Annis and I are married.'

'What?' Lady Joan gave a startled jolt, her eyes darting between them. *'Married?'*

'Yes. I'll explain everything later, but right now we're tired and we—' He stopped as a small boy peered around the edge of Lady Joan's skirts. He had curly fair hair and large, blue eyes—opened so wide they seemed to take up half of his face.

'Hello, George.' Ben cleared his throat. 'Do you remember me?'

The boy nodded, though he didn't speak.

'Bid your father good day, George.' Lady Joan wrapped an arm around the boy's shoulders, nudging him gently forward.

'Good day, Father.' The boy's voice was small and frightened.

There was an awkward silence while father and son stared at each other, neither of them seeming to know what to do next.

'Hello, George.' Annis crouched down impulsively, putting her face on a level with the boy's. 'I'm pleased to meet you. My name is Annis.'

'Hello.' The boy regarded her suspiciously. 'Are you my new mother?'

'Um…' Annis twisted her head to look at Bennet, but his face was studiously blank. 'I'm your father's new wife so I suppose I'm your stepmother, but you don't have to call me that if you don't want to. I'd be happy just to be your friend.' She held a hand out and smiled. 'This looks like a very nice house, but it's *so* big, I'm sure I'll get lost unless some kind person shows me around.'

'Maybe you could give Annis a tour while I speak to your grandmother?' Ben suggested.

The little boy looked from her to his father and then back again, slowly extending his own hand.

'Thank you.' Annis took it triumphantly. 'Let's go.'

'Have you kept an eye on Cariscombe, as I asked?' Bennet asked his mother the moment they entered the solar.

'It's good to see you too.' Lady Joan folded her arms. 'I thought you were only escorting her to London.'

'That was the original plan.'

'Because if you'd wanted to marry her, you could just have done it here and saved yourself a journey.'

'I know.' He closed the door behind them with a sigh. 'Honestly, I had no intention of marrying her when we left, but in the end there was no choice. It wasn't safe for her to remain unmarried.'

'What do you mean?'

'I mean that I thought she'd be safe at Hatfield House, but there was an attack on her life while we were there. We can't prove who was behind it, but, as far as I can see, her cousin is the only person with a motive. As long as Annis remained unmarried, he was next in line for her fortune.'

'Well, I can't say it's not a shock.' His mother dropped into a chair with a thud. 'But it's what I've been telling you to do, I suppose. Although she's not the bride I would have chosen for you.'

'I already married somebody you chose for me, remember?'

'Harumph.' His mother pinched her lips together. 'At least she seems to have made a good start with George.'

'Unlike me, you mean?' Ben clenched his jaw. Naturally his mother assumed that Annis was there to stay, to be a new mother to George, too, and he didn't have the energy to tell her otherwise at that moment... 'Forgive me, Mother, I don't mean to be discourteous.' He rubbed a hand over his face, softening his voice to a gentler tone. 'How are you?'

'Even older and achier than the last time you saw me.'

'Then I'm doubly sorry for being brusque. It's just been a long few weeks. A nerve-racking journey, too.'

'How so? If you've made Annis safe by marrying her, what are you worried about?'

'I'm not certain. There's just something about all this that doesn't make sense. Her cousin might want her fortune, but to murder her mother in cold blood, try to burn down her home and then have her pushed down a flight of stairs in the house of the King's heirs...' He shook his head. 'It all seems a little extreme. What if there's more behind this than just greed? What if I'm missing something?' He lifted an eyebrow. 'Has the Justice of the Peace discovered anything?'

'No. The man's next to useless. He claims one of the local villages must be behind the attack, but he has no idea which one, since he has no evidence and no witnesses. *I*, however, have discovered something.' She looked smug. 'Do you remember asking if there were any rumours about Mistress Flemming?'

'Yes.'

'Well, it seems there were, only they hadn't reached here before the attack happened.'

'What kind of rumours?'

'Ones that suggested she had a hand in her husband's death. *And* her first husband's. That's why so many of their servants left just beforehand.'

Ben sat up straighter. 'So you think the mob might have been local people, after all?'

'No. That's the strange part. I sent a couple of our maids to the village to ask questions. They have family there so I thought they might get more honest answers, but they say nobody in the village has any idea about what happened. They were all as shocked as we were.'

'Maybe because they were hiding their guilt?'

'I don't think so. Somebody would have said something.

But there *were* stories of a man, a merchant, who passed through the area about a week before the attack, saying things about Mistress Flemming, claiming she was dangerous. That would explain the gossip. It struck me as the kind of thing a person might do if they wanted to get people away from Cariscombe, people who might try to defend her against a mob, for example, with the added benefit of implicating them afterwards...'

'Which also points to somebody from outside the area. Although, unfortunately, it still doesn't bring us any closer to proving that Hawksby was behind it. Urgh.' He leaned forward, draping his forearms over his knees. 'I feel like I've been looking over my shoulder for weeks.'

'You look like it too. When was the last time you slept properly?'

'I don't know. Sometime in the spring maybe.'

'Then you need to go to bed right this moment.' His mother pushed herself back to her feet. 'I'll look after Annis.'

'No. We've just arrived. I need to show her round.'

'George is doing it. You'll be no use to her or anyone else if you're asleep on your feet.'

Ben hesitated, glancing at the ceiling. The thought of his own bed was extremely tempting. 'Keep guards close by?'

'If you really think it's necessary.'

'I do.'

'Then I will. I promise.'

'Maybe just a couple of hours then.' His feet were already moving. 'Thank you, Mother.'

It had taken a substantial amount of determined chatter before George began mumbling a few words in response to

Annis's questions. Not many, but enough for her to think he wasn't totally averse to her presence. He'd led her through the porch into a great hall that had looked vaguely familiar, though thankfully not enough to evoke my unpleasant memories, then through a parlour into a dining room, off which was another smaller parlour and a study, then out through the back of the house to the kitchens, larder, pastry room, bakehouse and brewhouse, then back inside and up a square, corner staircase to the bedchambers on the first floor.

'This is my room.' He showed her into a generously sized chamber with a bed in one corner, a collection of several oak chests of assorted sizes, and a desk and chair set underneath a window.

'It's very nice.' Annis looked around, smiling enthusiastically.

'I have some toys too.' George gestured towards one of the smaller chests. 'I can show you if you like?'

'I'd like that very much.' She sat down on the floor while he opened the chest, lifted out a heap of wooden animals and deposited them all in her lap.

'Oh, these are lovely.' Annis picked up a wooden carving in the shape of a bear. 'I used to have ones just like them when I was younger.'

'Really?' George's small face registered interest. 'What happened to them?'

'When I grew too old for them, my mother stored them away in a chest in her solar. Hopefully they're still there.'

She compressed her lips, disturbed by the thought. *Were* her toys still at Cariscombe? Did her mother's solar even still exist? Ben had said they'd managed to put out the fire on the night of the attack and saved half the building, but which half? And had it been closed up afterwards?

She hoped so. She hated the thought of people raiding the rooms and rifling through her family's possessions. She'd have to ask Lady Joan the next time she saw her...

Fortunately, the idea had barely entered her head before that lady appeared in the doorway, her expression as severe as ever.

'How are the two of you getting along?'

'Very well.' Annis began lining the wooden animals up on the floor. 'George was very thorough. I think I've seen everything.'

'Good boy.' Lady Joan's face creased into a smile. 'In that case, George, perhaps you could run along to the kitchens and find something to eat? Annis and I need to talk.'

'Is something the matter?' She tilted her head as the boy ran away.

'No. I just came to tell you that Ben's gone to get some rest.' The old woman lowered herself onto the side of the bed. 'Also, to tell you that we buried your mother.'

'Oh.' Her throat closed up so tightly she found it difficult to speak.

'I don't think I ever got a chance to tell you how sorry I am about what happened, but I am.'

'Thank you.' Somehow she croaked the words out. 'How is Cariscombe? Is any of it still habitable, do you think?'

'I doubt it. Why?'

'I just wondered.' She swallowed, turning her face to the window. If that were the case, the sooner she started making plans to rebuild the better. That way, once all this was over, she'd have somewhere else to go. 'I'd like to see for myself.'

'Now?' Lady Joan made a startled sound. 'Surely you don't want to leave again so quickly?'

'No, but now I'm so close, I feel like it's calling to me...'

'It's impossible, I'm afraid. For now anyway. My son would have my head if I let you go while he was asleep.' She paused, her expression thoughtful. 'But perhaps there's another way. Come with me.'

She waved a hand, indicating for Annis to follow her out into the gallery, then up a narrow staircase and through a door onto a small, walled balcony over one of the gables.

'There it is.' Lady Joan pointed into the distance. 'Cariscombe. You can just see it through the trees.'

'Oh.' Annis leaned forward over the wall, feeling a sharp pang in her chest at the sight. From this distance, it was hard to tell the extent of the damage, but at least one turret was still standing. 'Is it closed up to stop looting?'

'No. There was no need.'

'What do you mean?'

'There were...' Lady Joan sounded reticent suddenly. 'Stories in the village.'

'What kind of stories?'

'About a ghost.' She made a face. 'They say a woman haunts the ruins.'

'They think that Cariscombe is *haunted*?' Annis whirled about, her voice louder and angrier than she'd intended, but just the idea made her blood run cold. 'First people call my mother a witch and now a ghost?'

'Peace.' Lady Joan put a hand on her arm. 'I haven't said anything to anyone else, but I wonder if there's a simpler explanation. People think there's a ghost because there have been sightings of a woman—maybe there *is* somebody living there, amid the ruins.' She gave Annis a pointed glance. 'You said that your mother had a loyal attendant, did she not?'

Annis caught her breath. 'Margery?'

'I remember you asking Ben about her after the attack and him saying she was nowhere to be found.' Lady Joan lifted her shoulders. 'Maybe this is her.'

Annis clenched her fists, feeling a sudden surge of hope and purpose, as if a path were opening up through the fog that surrounded her. 'In that case, I *definitely* have to go. She saw the attack. If she's still alive then she might know who did this. She might have proof. She might be a witness to who killed my mother.'

Chapter Nineteen

'Good morning.' Annis was perched, fully dressed, on the edge of the bed when Bennet stirred and opened his eyes.

'Morning?'

He lifted his head and looked around the room. They'd travelled so much over the past month that he needed a few seconds to remind himself where he was. Not that he particularly cared at this moment. Just the sight of his wife sitting beside him was enough to make his heart leap and a warm glow spread through his chest.

'How long have I been asleep?'

'Since yesterday afternoon.'

'What?' He pushed himself up on his elbows. 'What time is it now?'

'Almost noon.'

'I'm sorry. I didn't mean to abandon you on your first night.'

'Well…' She lifted her eyes to the ceiling. 'I *did* think about waking you for dinner yesterday evening, but you were so deeply asleep, I decided against it. *Then* I thought about waking you for breakfast, but again, you looked so peaceful.' A slow smile spread across her lips. 'I'm only here now because it's almost midday and I need you for something. Do you think you've slept long enough?'

'I think I can probably manage to get up.'

'Good. Here.' She went over to a table and came back with a cup of ale. She was dressed in one of the fashionable new gowns her sister had given her—blue velvet with lace around the square neckline and three-quarter-length sleeves, but she'd dispensed with a hood and left her hair loose so that it bounced around her shoulders as she walked. 'You must be thirsty.'

'Parched. Thank you.' He took the cup, pleased that they were talking in more than brief sentences again. That was progress. Now he just had to keep her talking... 'So, how are you finding Draycote?'

'It's nice. Everyone is being very kind.' She met his gaze briefly before looking away again. 'I'm not certain your mother approves of me, but she talks as if she expects me to stay permanently. She tried giving me the household keys this morning. I had to tell her I wasn't ready to take over from her just yet.'

'Ah. I haven't had a chance to explain our arrangement to her.' He winced at the lie. 'Actually, I have, but I put it off. She's not going to be happy. But I'll do it. Soon.' He paused. 'Did you sleep...'

'There.' She gestured to the other side of the bed.

'Sorry. I intended to give instructions for you to have your own room.'

'It's all right. I was so exhausted I could have slept anywhere.'

Even next to him...

He took a long mouthful of ale at the implication.

'So what is it you need me for?' His voice sounded gruffer than he'd intended.

'Two things. The first can wait. The second can't.' She

sat down on the edge of the bed again. 'I need you to come and watch some archery. George wants to show you how much he's progressed since you were last here.'

'George wants to show *me*?' He lifted an eyebrow sceptically.

'All right, he wants to show me, but I'm sure he'll appreciate a bigger audience.'

'I wouldn't be so certain of that.' He put the cup aside and dropped his head back down onto his pillow.

'Ben...' To his surprise, Annis touched a hand to his chest. 'I know you're exhausted, and I know that's because you've been so busy protecting me for the past few weeks, but this is important. You might find it hurtful that he's so shy around you, but he's just a child. It's not personal. He needs some time, that's all.' She pursed her lips. 'He's a nice boy.'

'I know.' He drew in a long breath and then let it slowly out again. 'But if he doesn't want me here then the best thing I can do is leave him alone.'

'That's absurd.' She made a scornful sound.

'What?'

'He's a child and you're his father. Of course he wants you here, even if he doesn't show it. All children want love and affection, especially from their parents. I might not have much experience with children, but I know that much.' She sounded almost angry. 'Have you ever considered that you're making him more unhappy by not being a part of his life? Or that this is just as hard for him as it is for you? All he knows is that you come home occasionally, act distantly around him and then leave again. It's no wonder he's so shy with you. How do you expect him to react?'

'Annis—'

'*You're* the adult so you need to be the one to fix this. Give him some attention and be patient. Let him know that you care.' She knitted her brow. 'You *do* care, don't you?'

'Of course I care.'

'Then prove it. Stop thinking about how *you* feel and think about *his* feelings instead. Make an effort. It's not too late to build a relationship with him.'

Ben pushed himself upright, feeling faintly stunned by her words. Was she right? Was he making the situation even worse, transferring all of his old feelings about Eleanor onto his son, simply assuming that George didn't want him there, when the opposite might be true? Had *he* been the one pushing his son away rather than the other way round? He was aware of a lump in his throat as something shifted inside him. 'You're right. I thought…' Impulsively, he reached for her hand. 'It doesn't matter. I'll make more of an effort.'

'Good.' She dropped her gaze to his fingers, her cheeks flushing slightly. 'So you'll come and watch him?'

'I'll come. Just give me ten minutes to get dressed.'

'Ten minutes.' She nodded and stood up, drawing her fingers away slowly. 'We'll be waiting on the lawn.'

'Well done.' Ben applauded as George hit the outer rim of the target five times in a row. 'You're better than I was at your age.'

'Truly?' His son looked back at him in surprise, his pleasure at the compliment overcoming his shyness. 'Grandmother says you're one of the best archers in the whole of England. She says you teach the Prince.'

'I do, but it took a lot of practice for me to become so good, whereas you appear to be a natural. May I?' Ben crouched down and reached for his bow, examining the wood as George handed it over. 'However, I think it's time you had a bigger and better bow to practise with.'

'Yes please!' George's face lit up.

'I'll see what I can find. I must have something more suitable for your skills. If not, we'll make a new bow. Together, if you like?'

'Thank you, Father. And will you teach me like you teach the Prince?'

'Of course.'

'Well now.' Lady Joan's voice had a husky catch in it as she held a hand out to George. 'That's enough archery for today. I think it's time for your lessons.'

'Urgh. Do I have to?'

'Yes. You can practise again later if you want.'

'That went well, I think.' Annis gave Ben an arch look as Lady Joan and George walked back to the house.

'I think so, too,' Ben agreed, waving as his son looked back over his shoulder. 'He's said more words to me today than he has for the past five years.'

'You were very good with him.'

'I did what you said. I stopped thinking about how I felt and thought about his feelings instead.' He drew in a deep, satisfying breath. His chest felt lighter, as if a heavy weight he hadn't known was there had finally been hoisted away. For the first time in all the years he'd been coming back to Draycote to visit, he'd felt as though his son had actually wanted to spend time with him. The morning had given him a glimpse of what his life there could be like, if only he could find a way to put aside his guilt over Eleanor.

He blinked at the idea. It occurred to him now that, for once, he'd barely thought about her since he'd arrived.

Maybe because he'd been too tired, even to feel guilt. Or maybe because there was something different about this visit—or *someone*.

'Thank you for the advice.' He smiled at Annis, seized with a deep sense of gratitude and an accompanying surge of desire. With a cloud of russet waves blowing around her shoulders in the light summer breeze, she looked as much of a hoyden as she had the first time he'd set eyes on her. They seemed to finally have regained some of their earlier camaraderie, too. Maybe things had simply moved too fast and she'd needed some time to herself after they'd consummated the marriage? Maybe there was still hope for them. He hoped so. He ached to kiss her again. He wondered how she would react if he leaned forward, right there and then, and pressed his lips against hers. Would she recoil or kiss him back? He wished he knew.

'You're welcome.' She returned the smile. 'Although if you want to thank me properly, there's something you could do for me in return.'

'Anything.' He took a step closer, his body tightening as he caught the scent of rose water in her hair.

'Take me to Cariscombe.'

He stopped abruptly and stepped back again, disappointed. Now the change in her behaviour made sense. Of course she wasn't trying to reconcile with him. She was thinking of Cariscombe, thinking of the independent life she would lead once it was safe to go back, the life she wanted to lead without him, the one he'd promised her.

'That's not a good idea, not yet.'

'I know we still have to be careful, but...'

'But you think going to the exact place Hawksby would expect you to go is a wise thing to do?'

'No, but you said we would keep investigating. *And* you said I shouldn't have to live my life in fear.'

'I'd still rather speak to the Justice of the Peace first. He thinks the villagers were responsible for the attack, but he might have inadvertently discovered something useful, something that proves Hawksby was behind it. I'd rather he was under lock and key before we let down our guard.'

'So would I, but I *need* to go back to Cariscombe.' Her eyes widened imploringly. 'I need to see where they killed my mother. I want to mourn her. And...' She hesitated before continuing. 'I want to find the ghost.'

'What?' He clamped his brows together.

'Your mother says people think there's a ghost. They've seen a woman amidst the ruins and assumed it's my mother, but what if it's Margery? What if she survived the attack and she's been there the whole time?'

'It's possible, I suppose.'

'And if she *has* been there then she might have some evidence, but she doesn't know who she can trust to share it with.' She put a hand on his wrist, her tone urgent. 'But she'll trust me.'

'Annis...'

'Please. It's worth the risk to find out what she knows. Besides, I hate the thought that she's been alone all this time.'

Ben hesitated. Her fingers on his wrist were warm and distracting. Somehow they made it impossible to refuse. 'Very well. I don't like the idea, but if it means so much to you...'

'It does.' She nodded quickly.

'But you'll need to wear a disguise again.'

'You mean, be Thomas again?' She grinned.

'Yes.' He nodded, pushing an image of her in breeches firmly out of his mind. 'But not today. Tomorrow. Early.'

'Tomorrow at dawn,' she repeated, tightening her grip on his wrist. 'Thank you.'

Chapter Twenty

It was a glorious morning, the kind that gladdened the heart and fed the soul with its beauty. The tops of the sycamore trees lining the road to Cariscombe were gilded with sunshine and the air was fresh and crystal clear, filled with the sound of birdsong and buzzing insects.

Annis rode alongside Ben, dressed in boys' clothing again, feeling her nerves twist and tighten as they approached. Doing something constructive made her feel better than she had in days, as if she were regaining some control over her life. Though she knew she had to prepare herself, not just for the sight of Cariscombe in ruins, but for possible disappointment. There was a good chance the stories of a ghost were just fanciful, people's imaginations running riot, and Margery was already dead.

She drew rein half a furlong from the house. She'd kept her gaze on the ground as they rode, but now she took a deep breath, lifted her head and looked.

Half of the house, the side that held the hall and kitchens, was just as she remembered. The other was a blackened, crumbling heap of stone. Her own bedchamber was gone. There was only a gaping hole in the wall where her door had once been. It was going to take longer to rebuild than she'd imagined.

'Oh.' She heard the cry pass her lips, though she wasn't aware of making any sound.

'Are you all right?' Bennet edged his horse closer.

'No.' She pressed her lips together hard. 'I mean, I knew there was a fire, but somehow I didn't quite believe it.'

'I'm sorry.'

She nodded, swallowing the lump in her throat. She needed to be strong for her next question. 'Where did you find her?'

He didn't ask who she meant. Instead, he nudged his horse forward a few more paces and dismounted, gesturing for his men to spread out. 'Over here.' He led her towards the front door.

'Right here?' She looked down at the ground. It seemed her mother hadn't got very far before she was stabbed, but there were no tell-tale marks or any sign of blood to indicate where she'd fallen. The spot looked ordinary, mundane, as if nothing of any importance could ever have happened there.

She sank down and placed her hands flat on the ground, trying to sense something of her mother, but there was nothing.

'I think part of me was hoping it was all a mistake and she'd still be waiting here for me.' She looked up again as Ben crouched in front of her. 'But she's really gone, isn't she?'

'I'm afraid so.'

'I miss her.' She flung her head back, looking up at the cloudless blue sky for a few seconds before bellowing at the top of her lungs.

'Margery!'

There was no answer.

'Margery?' she called again, removing her hat and climbing back to her feet this time.

'Annis.' Bennet gave her a warning look.

'She might not recognise me in these clothes.' The wind whipped a lock of hair across her face as she turned round on the spot, peering into the trees. *'Margery!'*

Still no answer.

'If she were here, she'd come and see me, wouldn't she?' She twisted back towards Ben, aware of the desperation in her own voice. 'She wouldn't hide from me.'

'I don't know.'

'Maybe it was just a rumour, after all. Maybe she's...' She let her shoulders slump forward, unable to finish the sentence. 'I've seen enough. Take me back to Draycote Manor.'

'Here.' He placed her hat gently back on her head, resting his hand on her shoulder for a long moment before leading her back to the horses.

She threw one last lingering look over her shoulder at Cariscombe before riding away.

'You know, my mother likes you,' Bennet commented as they rode back through the woods.

'Really?' Annis snorted. Clearly he was trying to make her feel better, but he might have said something a little bit more believable.

'Yes.' He laughed at her sceptical expression. 'I admit it might not be obvious, but I can tell.'

'What would she be like if she *didn't* like me?'

'A few more days and she'll give you a compliment, just wait and see.'

'I can't wait.' She gave him a sidelong smile, then hauled

on her reins as a figure in a long grey cloak emerged out of the trees, stepping into the road ahead of them suddenly.

'Hold!' Bennet moved his horse in front of her, drawing his sword as the figure lifted their hands and drew back their hood. The face beneath was pale and haggard-looking, but there was no doubt of their identity.

'Margery!' Annis jumped down from her horse before anyone could stop her, rushing forward and flinging herself headlong into the other woman's arms. So much had happened, it felt like years since the last time she'd seen her.

'Annis.' Margery staggered slightly before embracing her back, her voice cracking with emotion. 'Thank goodness you're alive.'

'You too. I was afraid to hope.' Annis pulled her head back. 'But what happened? How did you escape from the mob?'

'I didn't. I never confronted them.' Margery's face took on a guilty expression. 'Your mother was more cunning than I realised. She asked me to go upstairs to watch and make certain you crossed the lawn safely. I suspected something, but not...' She paused, her lips twisting as if it were hard to go on. 'She must have gone straight outside the moment I was gone. I heard the mob shouting, but by the time I ran back downstairs, she was already lying on the ground. I tried to save her, but it was too late.'

'You didn't do anything wrong.' Annis clasped her hands. 'You did what she wanted. You survived.'

'I failed her. If I'd been there, I would have fought.'

'And what then? They would probably have killed you too,' Annis answered vehemently. 'Did you see who—'

'No,' Margery interrupted her. 'The room was at the back of the house, and by the time I reached her, the mob was already dispersing, except for a couple of them who decided to torch the house on their way.'

'Oh.' Annis swallowed her disappointment. 'But have you really been here since it happened? People think you're a ghost!'

'I know.' Margery chuckled. 'I usually hide in the tunnel whenever I hear horses approaching, but I also have a shelter in the forest that gives me a good view of the house. I suppose some people glimpsed me through the trees. I don't know who was responsible for the attack, but if they come back I'll be waiting and watching for them. I'm not going anywhere until I find out who did this.' Her focus shifted. 'But thank goodness you're all right. Did Sir Bennet do what your mother asked?'

'Yes. He took me to London in secret.'

'Ah…' Margery's eyes darted past her to where Ben was standing a few feet away, frowning into the undergrowth as if he expected an assassin to leap out at any moment. 'Then you've met Isolde?'

'Yes.' Annis blinked in surprise. 'You knew about Isolde?'

'Of course I knew.' Margery tutted. 'I knew your mother for most of her life, since she was five years old, long before she ever met the Earl of Newcastleton.'

'Really? I thought…' Annis pressed her brows together. Actually, she'd never thought about how long Margery had known her mother. She'd always just taken her presence for granted.

'I was born in Chester too,' Margery explained. 'I went to work as a maid in your grandparents' house, your mother's parents' house, that is, when I was a child, just a few years older than your mother. She and I became close so, when she married, she asked to take me with her. I stayed with her ever since. I was at her side when both you and your sister were born.' Her eyes turned misty. 'It would have pleased your mother to know that you'd finally found each other. She always wished it were possible for the two of you to meet.'

'I'm glad of it too, but...' Annis hesitated. This probably wasn't the time or the place for questions, only she couldn't seem to help herself. 'Isolde told me some things about my parents, too. She said that my mother only married my father because she had nowhere else to go after her stepson threw her out.'

'It wasn't quite like that.' Margery clucked her tongue. 'Your mother met your father while she was still married to the earl. She knew that he was a good man, and trustworthy too, so when the earl died she went to him for help. That's when he offered to marry her.'

'But was it just for protection?' Annis's gaze drifted back towards Ben.

'Not *just*. Personally, I think she already liked him, and he her, although she would never have betrayed her marriage vows to the earl.'

'And one other thing...' Annis took a deep breath, flinching inwardly as she said the words. 'Isolde said that her own father died suddenly too.'

'Ah.' Margery's look seemed very knowing. 'Like *your* father, you mean?'

'Yes.' Annis dropped her gaze, feeling guilty just for asking the question. 'I don't believe my mother was involved. I don't believe what they said about her either, but...'

'But it's natural to ask questions.' Margery nodded slowly. 'The truth is, the old earl's death wasn't sudden. He was sick for a long time, from some kind of wasting illness.

Your mother nursed him for months. Isolde was only a child in the nursery so she didn't see much, and your mother didn't tell her because she didn't want to upset her, but trust me, there was nothing sudden about it. I was there.'

'I'm sorry. I shouldn't have asked.'

'No. It's better to know. As for your father, I think it was his heart. I don't suppose we'll ever know for sure, but I do know that he and your mother loved each other. She used to say that she'd found the last good man. Whatever killed him, it had nothing to do with her.'

'Thank you. I never truly thought it did, but this past month has been so confusing.' Annis closed her eyes briefly. 'Margery, do you think Mother knew who was behind the attack? She seemed so scared after father died, like she knew something was going to happen.'

'She said so to me too, but she didn't know what. And I…' Her voice wavered. 'Truth be told, I thought she was overreacting. After she married the earl, she became such a hated figure. She knew what people called her—an upstart, a seductress, all kinds of names, although she'd never even wanted to marry him. She only did what her parents told her to do. She knew she had enemies, just for having dared to rise above her station, and she felt hounded—hated. Later, she found happiness with your father, but she never quite recovered from that feeling of enmity. It made her prone to irrational fears. That's why she didn't like to leave Cariscombe, or take you anywhere either. As the years went by it got worse. It might not have been the right thing to do, but it was what she needed.'

'But why did she never tell me about her past? I would have understood.'

'She intended to tell you one day. Only it was hard for

her to talk about that part of her life. So she kept putting it off. Then, when your father died, she was too distraught. Afraid too, yes, but she hardly knew of what—or who. Everyone, maybe.'

'Has anyone been here, anyone at all since the attack?'

'Yes. Sir Bennet's men arrived first. They came here that first night and moved her body, then again the next day to take her away. I hoped that meant you'd reached Draycote Manor safely. Then another group of men came the morning after it happened. They seemed to be looking for you, calling your name as if they thought you might be hiding in the woods.'

'What did they look like?'

'The one in charge was young, barely a man.'

'With a pale beard?'

'Yes. Do you know him?'

'That's my cousin, Oliver Hawksby.'

'Hawksby? The one who stands to inherit?' Margery's brows snapped together.

'Yes. Sir Bennet thinks he's the only person with a motive for all this, but I don't understand how my own cousin could be so callous. What caused the rift between our families in the first place?'

'It was your parents' marriage. Your father's family didn't approve and his sister was particularly vocal on the subject. She called your mother some names your father could never forget.'

'That explains it then. Hawksby must hate us too.' Annis sighed. Somehow she'd been hoping it was all a big mistake, but this confirmed everything she and Ben had suspected. All they needed was proof. 'We think the attack on my mother was meant to be an attack on both of us.'

'Then you're still in danger.' Margery looked alarmed.

'I was. Somebody pushed me down a staircase in London, though thankfully I wasn't too badly injured. It took me a few days to recover, that's all.'

'But they might try again.' Margery clutched at her arms. 'You shouldn't have come back here.'

'It's all right now. The danger's past, or at least, we think it is.' She took a deep breath and gestured towards Ben, still standing a discreet distance away. 'The fact is, Sir Bennet and I…' She swallowed, feeling acutely self-conscious all of a sudden. 'We're married.'

'Married?' Margery cast an outraged look in Ben's direction. 'Your mother sent you to him for protection, not so that he could get his hands on your fortune! Marriage was the last thing she wanted for you!'

'It's not like that,' Annis protested, offended on Ben's behalf. 'He did as she asked and took me to London, but after I was pushed down the stairs he offered to marry me for my own protection. This way, Hawksby isn't my heir any more.'

'I see.' Margery's tone softened slightly. 'Is he treating you well?'

'Yes.' Annis dropped her gaze, her skin warming as she remembered what had passed between them at Roger and Juliet's house. 'He says I can be as independent as I wish. He's not after my fortune. He says I can rebuild Cariscombe and come home, just as soon as we prove Hawksby was behind this.'

'Good.'

'In the meantime, why don't you come back to Draycote Manor with us? You must be in need of a good meal and a comfortable bed.'

'No.' Margery lifted her chin. 'I told you, I'm not going anywhere until I discover the truth. Whoever did this will give themselves away eventually, I'm certain of it.'

'Then I'll send you some food. Is there anything else you need? Blankets, clothing?'

'A little wine wouldn't go amiss.'

'I'll send you a barrel.' Annis grinned, embracing her one last time. 'We'll find a way to prove this was Hawksby, I know we will.'

Chapter Twenty-One

'George was very pleased with the new bow you gave him,' Lady Joan commented as their plates were cleared after a dinner of venison porridge and roast pheasant. It was the third time she'd made the same observation since they'd sat down.

'I'm glad.' Ben smiled, exchanging a swift, amused glance with Annis. 'I enjoyed taking him for a ride this afternoon, as well. He's much more confident on his pony now than he was on my last visit.'

'I thought so too. Do you have any plans for tomorrow?' Lady Joan's gaze slid towards Annis. 'With George, I mean?'

'Actually there's something else I need to do, but don't worry, there'll be plenty of time for archery lessons.'

'Well then, it's been a long day and I'm tired.' She pushed her chair away from the dining table. 'I'll see you both in the morning. Sleep well.'

'Good night, Mother.' Ben rose from his own seat, making a bow as she went past.

'She seems happy.' Annis smiled as the door closed. For the first time since their marriage, she wasn't nervous about spending time alone with Ben. Despite the emotional upheaval of visiting Cariscombe, she realised she was actually enjoying her time at Draycote Manor. Helping him to build a relationship with his son made their marriage feel a little less one-sided, as if there were more to it than simply his desire to protect her.

'She is.' He sat down with a pensive expression. 'What about you? I know this morning was difficult for you. How are you feeling now?'

'It was difficult,' she acknowledged. 'But I'm glad we found Margery, even if we didn't find any more clues.'

'About that… I've had an idea, but I wanted to discuss it with you before I decide what to do. It means I'll be away for a couple of days.'

'Away where?'

'First I want to speak with the Justice of the Peace. Then I think it's time I paid a visit to the Earl of Newcastleton. His estate isn't so far away.'

'What?' She jolted in her seat. 'But I thought we decided he wasn't involved in the attack.'

'We did, but I want to be completely certain. Then, unless I discover anything new, I'll go to Taunton and speak with your cousin. I can't think of another way to move things forward. We have no clues and no witnesses.'

'If you're going to confront Hawksby then I'm coming.'

'No.' He shook his head firmly. 'It's too dangerous. I don't want you taking any risks.'

'He's my cousin!'

'I know, but if he's the man we think he is then he's also ruthless. There's no telling what a man like that might do.' He held onto her gaze. 'Please, stay here and promise me you won't do anything foolish. I'll be gone for three days at most.'

Annis folded her arms. 'If there's no telling what he might do then that means it could be dangerous for you, too.'

'I won't go alone. I'll take some men with me, but it'll be easier if I'm not worried about you.'

'What will you say to Hawksby?'

'First I'll see if any of his men can be bribed to say anything. Then, if that doesn't work, I'll confront him directly. I want to look him in the eye when I ask him about Cariscombe. I'll tell him I know he was there the morning after the attack, and I know he was at Hatfield House just before you fell down the stairs. That might be enough to make him reveal something.'

'Very well.' She gritted her teeth and sighed. 'I suppose I can be good for a few days, but I don't like it and neither will your mother.'

'I know. I'm not happy about the idea of leaving George again so soon either, especially now I seem to making some progress with him, but at least this way I can be sure your cousin knows about our marriage. That will make Draycote safer for everyone. Besides—' he leaned back in his chair again '—the sooner we end this, the sooner you can rebuild Cariscombe and go home.'

'And you can go back to Hatfield.'

They fell silent, the words hanging in the air between them. That was what they both wanted, after all, Annis thought: separate, independent lives, to be married and yet not married. She just wished they could put aside the awkwardness between them and establish some kind of understanding, maybe even learn to be friends, especially since it seemed that Cariscombe was going to take longer to rebuild than she'd anticipated. But the only way to do that was to be honest and tell each other exactly how they felt about their marriage, which also meant addressing the one subject they'd never properly discussed—the subject hanging on the wall behind him...

'Is that your first wife?' She asked the question before she could lose her nerve, pointing towards a painting of a woman with the largest, bluest eyes she'd ever seen.

'Yes.' His face tensed. 'That's Eleanor. Forgive me, I should have had it taken down and moved.'

'You don't have to.'

'But I should. You're my wife now.'

'That doesn't mean you should hide her away, not for my sake. I know our marriage is...different.' She let her gaze roam over the woman's perfectly symmetrical, delicate features. 'You must have so many memories of her in this house.' She coughed. 'What I'm trying to say is that I understand if it makes it hard for you to be back here. I know that you loved her very deeply.'

'What?' His head jerked back as if she'd just picked up her goblet and hurled the contents across the table at him. 'Who told you that?'

'No one.' She blinked, startled by the sudden hard note in his voice. 'I just thought, because you never seem comfortable talking about her, and the way you look when you do, as if you're heartbroken... I just...assumed.'

'Annis...' His voice sounded different, almost pained, as if the words themselves were scouring his throat. 'What I felt for Eleanor wasn't love. It was pity.'

'Pity?' She was aware of her jaw hanging open, but she couldn't seem to close it, staring at him in shock while thoughts and emotions swirled inside her head so fast she felt dizzy. He *hadn't* loved his first wife. She really oughtn't to be pleased about that, and she wasn't; she felt sorry for the other woman. But, at the same time, the fact that he wasn't pining for somebody else made her feel as if a weight had just been lifted from her heart. She drew her tongue along the seam of her lips, trying to loosen them. 'Why? I mean…what happened?'

'We weren't suited.' He hung his head, staring down at the table. 'Even before the wedding, I had a feeling that something was wrong, but there was nothing either of us could do. It had all been arranged, so we went through with it.' He grimaced. 'It wasn't long before I realised what a terrible mistake we'd made. As did she, probably. I tried to love her, but she was never happy. I don't know whether that was her nature or whether she didn't like me, or whether she just didn't want to be married, but it was hopeless. Then George was born. The first moment I saw him, it was like my heart doubled in size, but Eleanor looked at me like she hated me. We never shared a bed again. We rarely even touched. No matter what I did, I couldn't make her happy. In the end, it made both of us miserable. So I left. It broke my heart, but it was the only thing I could think of to do for her.'

'How sad.' Annis looked back at the painting. Now she looked closer, there was a definite melancholic quality about the eyes. 'What did your mother think about you leaving?'

'She had opinions. Then about three years after George was born, the sweating sickness came. When I got word that Eleanor was sick, I rode day and night, but it was too late to reach her. She was already gone.' He rubbed a hand over his face. 'And I felt so guilty.'

'Why? It wasn't your fault. It wasn't anybody's.'

'I know, but it was bad enough that I couldn't make her happy. The least I could have done was protected her.'

'Protected her…' She echoed the words. 'Is that why you're so concerned with protecting me?'

'I suppose I thought maybe it would make up for that failure somehow.' He looked vaguely apologetic. 'But that wasn't the only reason I felt guilty about Eleanor.'

'What else?'

'I felt guilty because part of me…' He paused, a muscle clenching and unclenching in his jaw. 'You have to understand, I would never have wanted anything bad to happen to her. I truly pitied her for being unhappy and I would have protected her with my life. But once the shock of her funeral had passed and I realised that her being gone meant that I could come home, I felt…just for a moment…relieved.'

'Oh.' Annis didn't know what else to say. He was sharing the deepest, darkest secret of his soul. Words didn't seem quite enough.

'Until then, I hadn't realised how much I'd resented her for making me leave everything and everyone I loved.' He said the words with a groan. 'Then I felt even more wretched. I should have been grieving for her—instead I felt bitter and angry.'

'You couldn't help your feelings.' Annis stood up and moved round the table, sitting down beside him and placing a hand over his. 'You were relieved about being able to come home, not about what happened to her.'

'I know, but that didn't make me feel any less guilty. So I left again, I had to, and I made a promise to myself never to come back, not to live here permanently. I couldn't stay and be happy here after that. It would have felt wrong.'

'And you've been punishing yourself all this time?' She squeezed his hand. 'Ben, if you tried your hardest with Eleanor then it wasn't your fault she was unhappy. And it wasn't your fault that you couldn't protect her from the sweating sickness either. The reason you feel guilty is because you're a good man, but you don't need to punish yourself any longer. This *can* be your home again. You just have to forgive yourself.'

'You sound like Richard and Juliet.'

'Then maybe you should start listening...' She drew her brows together as a new thought occurred to her. 'Is this why you promised yourself never to marry again?'

'Yes. I knew I couldn't offer anyone else a normal home life afterwards, and the thought of making somebody else unhappy, or of another woman looking at me the way she used to...' His eyes flickered with shadows of pain. 'I couldn't bear to go through that again.'

'So you were afraid of the situation repeating itself, but you proposed to me anyway?' She gazed at him in confusion. 'Why? You could have abandoned me to William Dalrymple.'

'I told you, I didn't want anything to happen to you, William Dalrymple included.' He hesitated briefly, his dark gaze intensifying. 'And if I'm completely honest, maybe the fact you needed my help was just the excuse I wanted to break my promise to myself and be with you. Maybe, deep down, I was hoping that things would be different this time.'

'You mean, you *wanted* to be with me?' She jolted so sharply that her chair jerked backwards, scraping across the floor.

'Yes.'

'And you *wanted* to marry me?' She felt vaguely stunned, her breath so shaky it was an effort to speak clearly.

'Yes.'

She felt a sharp stab of guilt. 'So when I said I didn't want to marry you...'

'I can't say it didn't hurt, but I understood. You wanted to keep your independence.'

'I did—*do*—but that wasn't the main reason I objected so much.' She shook her head, her pulse accelerating the longer she spoke. 'I thought you didn't like me, especially not like that! I thought I was just a duty to you. I thought I was competing with a ghost!'

'A ghost?' He frowned. 'Trust me, Annis, you're not competing with anyone.'

'But when we met in the knot garden at Hatfield, you were so standoffish. I was so pleased to see you and you acted like you never wanted to see me again.'

'It wasn't because I didn't like you. It was all I could do not to kiss you that day. Annis, I liked you from the first moment I saw you, but I thought it was better for both of us to part ways. I didn't want to make you unhappy.'

'But you already have!'

'What?' He looked horrified.

'I thought you only consummated our marriage out of duty!'

'Duty?' He stared at her incredulously. 'There was nothing dutiful about it, I assure you, but I was afraid you regretted it afterwards.'

'I was embarrassed.'

'You shouldn't have been.' Slowly, he lifted a hand to the side of her neck, sliding his fingers into her hair. 'It was perfect.'

'I thought so too.' She felt her cheeks flush, heat blooming beneath her skin as everything she'd thought about him—about *them*—began to shift in her mind. It seemed so obvious now that she'd been denying her feelings for him, just as he'd been hiding his from her.

'I'm sorry.' He stroked his thumb across her jaw. 'I never meant to make you unhappy.'

'You're making up for it now.' She slid her tongue along her lips, trying to think clearly, but his thumb was very distracting. 'So all this time…we both liked each other and didn't know it?'

'Apparently.' He laughed. 'I would have bedded you every night if I could have.'

'*Every* night?' She felt a sharp tugging sensation in her stomach.

'At least.'

'In that case…' She looked towards the door and then rose to her feet, shivering with anticipation at the look in his eyes. They were black orbs, swollen and glittering with desire. 'Maybe it's time for us to retire upstairs too?'

Chapter Twenty-Two

'Wait.' Ben caught one of her hands, pulling Annis backwards into his lap. Their bedchamber seemed like a hundred miles away suddenly.

'What—' She gave a startled squeak, then a low moan as his lips touched the side of her neck, tilting her head back until it was resting against his shoulder.

'Am I dreaming?' He murmured the words against her skin, skimming his hands over her hips and then sliding them upwards over her stomach.

'I don't think so.' She moaned again. 'Unless I am too.'

'If we are, I don't want to wake up.'

'Won't the maids be coming to clear the room soon?' Her voice was ragged in his ear.

'Not until we leave.' He lifted his hands to cup her breasts. 'We don't have to go anywhere.'

'But surely you don't mean…' She twisted her head to look at him, her eyes widening in comprehension. 'In here?'

'We've wasted enough time with misunderstandings.' He shifted his legs slightly, pushing up towards her. 'I don't think I can wait any longer.'

Her lips curved in a smile. 'Me neither.'

'Good.' He stood up, lifting her with him and then turning her round in his arms. 'Because you have no idea how much I want you. It's been torture, sleeping in the same room as you every night. All I could think about was how it felt last time.'

'I know. I've barely slept a wink for days.'

'Some nights, I thought I might burn a hole through the mattress.'

She gave a delighted laugh and coiled her arms around his neck, drawing him closer while he slid his tongue inside her mouth, seeking hers. She surrendered it eagerly, each of them licking and tasting the other, as he lowered her carefully onto the table, pushing the plates and cutlery aside in the process.

'This needs to come off.' He pulled the hem of her gown up and then tugged at the ribbons of her bodice, parting them as she tore his shirt loose from his breeches and drew it over his head.

'What about your mother?' She gasped suddenly.

'My mother?' He froze in alarm.

'What if she comes back downstairs again?'

'Good point.' He took a deep breath. 'If I let go of you for a few seconds, do you promise not to move a muscle?'

'I promise.'

'There.' He picked up a chair and shoved it against the door. 'That should do it.'

'Thank you.' She smiled, perching on the edge of the table as she pulled her gown away from her shoulders, letting it fall slowly open to her waist.

'Annis...' He made a guttural sound as he gathered her back into his arms.

'Ben...' she whispered in return, wrapping her ankles

around his hips as he reached for the fastenings of his breeches, moving so that he could stand between her legs.

'Are you absolutely certain?' It actually pained him to say the words, but he had to ask.

'Yes.'

He didn't wait to be told again, pushing inside her with one thrust. She cried out, just as she had the first time, but this time it was more a groan of pleasure. Quickly, he slid a hand beneath her, trying to protect her skin from the hard wood of the table, but then she pushed herself against him and it was all he could do to think straight. This time their lovemaking was fierce and urgent, the sound of their cries mingling and building as they clung to each other.

'Wait.' He clamped his hands over her hips abruptly. 'I'll finish too soon.'

She flung her head back in protest and he couldn't resist moving again, thrusting even deeper and harder as she bucked against him. The feeling was more intense, several hundred times more intense, than anything he'd ever felt before. They were both sweating and panting. She was wet and tight and he could feel her muscles already beginning to clamp around him. He gritted his teeth, forcing himself to wait until he felt her shudder before letting himself go as well.

'Ben...' Annis murmured after a few minutes of combined panting, lifting her hands to his shoulders as she pressed her forehead against his, her voice dazed. 'That was even better than last time.'

'I know.'

'Juliet never told me you could do it on a table.' She giggled.

'Good.' He laughed too and then pulled back, looking

at the destruction they'd wreaked upon the dining room. There was cutlery all over the floor. 'I should probably clear some of this up.'

'So that nobody guesses what we've been doing in here, you mean?'

'I think we might have made too much noise for that.'

'Oh, dear.' She clamped a hand over her mouth, her smile both wicked and irresistible. 'I suppose I was a bit loud.'

'We both were.' He caught at her waist, hauling her back against him.

'Ben?' She gave him a startled look and then glanced downwards. 'Surely you're not...'

'That depends.' He nuzzled the side of her neck. 'What would you say if I was?'

'Well...' She found his lips again, pushing herself up on tiptoes to adjust the angle between them in a way that aroused him even more. 'I suppose I *could* be persuaded.'

'Good.' He grinned. 'Because I really didn't want to beg. Only this time, perhaps we should find a softer surface?'

'That sounds like a wonderful idea.'

They made a token effort to tidy the room before pulling the chair away from the door and running hand in hand towards the staircase.

It occurred to him afterwards that he'd completely forgotten Eleanor's portrait was still there.

Annis blinked her way back to consciousness, vaguely aware that she was alone. There was still a dint in the mattress where Ben had slept, his body wrapped around hers all night. It felt warm to the touch, as if he'd only recently left, but there was no sign of him. Meanwhile, the shutters across the windows had been opened, letting daylight wash into the room and over the floorboards. It looked like another beautiful golden morning.

She sat up, tucking the coverlet beneath her armpits just as the door opened and Ben entered, though to her dismay he was already dressed for travelling. After their heart-to-heart the previous evening, she'd completely forgotten about his plans.

'You're awake.' His lips curved at the sight of her.

'Only just.' She smiled shyly in return. 'I didn't hear you get up.'

'That was my intention.' He leaned over the edge of the bed, pressing his lips against hers while he skimmed the back of one hand lightly across her cheekbone. 'I just came to say goodbye.'

'Already?' She frowned. 'Are you certain this is a good idea?'

'I think it's our best chance of discovering the truth. My men are already waiting outside.'

'Do you promise you'll be careful?'

'Absolutely.'

'Just three days?'

'I'll come back as soon as I can.' He reached for one of her hands, toying gently with her fingers. 'And then when I'm back, maybe we can start making plans?'

'Plans?' She blinked, still feeling sleepy. 'For what?'

'For us. I've been thinking about what you said, about forgiving myself and coming home to be a real father to George. I want to. I'll have to return to London and ask the King's permission to leave my position, but seeing as he's in favour of marriage and family life these days, I don't think he'll have any objection. It's time to put the past behind me and make Draycote Manor a proper home again.'

'That's good.'

'And I'd like you to stay here too.' He lifted her hand to his mouth, his lips lingering over her knuckles. 'I want this to be more than a marriage of convenience. I want it to be real. I swear I'll do everything I can to make you happy. Ask me for the Crown Jewels and I'll fetch them for you.' He dipped his gaze. 'I know it's soon, but, after last night, I wanted you to know how I feel. I love you, Annis.'

'Oh.' She swallowed, her heart pounding so hard it seemed to be tearing itself apart in her chest. One half was elated. The other half was filled with a panic so intense she wanted to dive under her pillow and hide. She'd only just allowed herself to acknowledge that she had feelings for Ben, but did she love him in return? She didn't know. She hadn't had a chance to consider it, let alone to look any further ahead.

As much as she liked Draycote Manor, the thought of staying there for ever and not returning to Cariscombe caused a cold sweat to break out on her palms and the back of her neck. It would mean giving up the very last piece of herself, abandoning everything her mother had taught her. If she stayed, she would never be an independent, free woman, mistress of her own home and fortune. She would be a wife and mother at Draycote Manor. What would her mother say if she were still alive to see it? Her mother who'd suffered so much at the hands of men. It was bad enough that she still hadn't got justice for her. How could she betray her legacy too?

'I don't know what to say.' She could feel the panic growing, overwhelming any other emotion.

'Say that you'll think about it?'

'No.' She yanked her hand away, shifting across the bed away from him. 'I can't stay here. I want to go home. I *love* my home. I told you that from the start. And you promised I could go back. You can't ask me to give it up now!'

'I know. I didn't mean that you *had* to stay. It would be your decision, I just hoped…' He stood up. 'Of course. Forgive me, I shouldn't have said anything.' He bowed stiffly before turning towards the door. 'I'd better go. Take care, Annis.'

Ben made his way down the staircase and out of the front door of Draycote Manor with a leaden feeling in his chest, like an anchor dragging him down. Annis's reaction to his question hadn't been quite what he'd hoped for, not by a long way. He'd thought that she cared about him too, but whatever she felt, it obviously wasn't enough. He wanted to build a life together, but her resolve to return to Cariscombe was stronger than ever. He'd offered her his heart and she'd handed it right back with a horrified no, thank you.

How could he have been so foolish, swept up in his own enthusiasm, thinking that things would be different this time? Annis might care for him more than Eleanor ever had, but their marriage was still one of convenience, not love. His dream of a happy, loving home life with his wife and son…that was as far out of reach as ever. She had her own dream and he wasn't a part of it.

He took his palfrey's reins from a groom and mounted, staring back at the house for a long moment. He would be back soon, hopefully in three days if the weather stayed fine and he rode hard. He hoped, though he didn't necessarily expect, to have answers when he returned. All he could do was make sure that Hawksby knew Annis was married and had friends at court. That would make her safe, even if he couldn't necessarily get justice for her mother.

He signalled to his men and then kicked his heels, spurring his mount away, trying to outride his melancholy. He'd do what he'd intended at the start. He'd protect Annis. Then once she was safe he'd leave her behind, go back to Hatfield House and forget about love for ever. Eleanor had been right about him. He wasn't fit for marriage or fatherhood. From now on, his heart would be firmly closed, not just to Annis, but to everyone.

Chapter Twenty-Three

Two days.

Annis sat at the desk in George's chamber, feigning a cheerful demeanour as she played cards with her new step-son. It had been two days since Ben had left, though each one had felt like a week. It hadn't helped that she'd been trapped inside, unable to go anywhere, but she'd made a promise. Considering her last conversation with Ben, keeping it seemed like the least she could do.

'My lady?' A maid appeared in the doorway, jolting her back to the present. 'Lady Joan asks that you come down to the hall. She says it's important.'

'Is it Sir Bennet?' Annis leapt to her feet in excitement. 'Is he back early?'

'I'm afraid not, my lady.'

'Oh… Very well.' Annis bit back a swell of disappointment, making a funny face at George as she left. 'I'd better not keep your grandmother waiting.'

She hurried out of the room and down the staircase, glad of some distraction at least. Ironically, she'd been glad of the separation from Ben at first, since it had given her an opportunity to study her feelings, and it hadn't taken her long to realise the truth. Of course she cared about him! Of course she wanted to stay with him too! And she didn't have to sacrifice any part of herself to do it. Cariscombe was a part of her identity, but it wasn't *her*, and not going back didn't mean she would be giving up on herself or her mother's legacy. Her mother had warned her against marriage, yes, but she'd also raised her to be an independent woman who made her own choices, and this was what she chose. She would *be* herself, only with Ben.

Unfortunately, she'd been too panicked to see any of that at first, to understand how much her words must have hurt him. He'd told her about his fear of rejection and she'd rejected him the very next morning, compounding the hurt already inflicted by his first wife. Her heart ached at the thought. The moment she saw him, she was going to fling herself into his arms and tell him how much she truly cared for him...

She reached the bottom of the staircase and headed towards the sound of voices in the hall. Apparently Lady Joan had company.

'Ah, there you are, Annis.' Her new mother-in-law greeted her with a strained-looking smile. 'Thank you for coming so quickly. We have some guests, one of whom I believe you've already met?'

Annis turned her head and came to an abrupt halt, struck with such a surge of loathing it was all she could do not to turn on her heel and leave again. Either that or start throwing things. Oliver Hawksby was standing before her, holding the arm of an older woman with white hair, stooped shoulders and eyes the exact same colour as her own—and her father's.

'*Aunt?*' She gasped, anger turning to amazement.

'Yes. Please forgive the intrusion.' The old woman hobbled forward, taking her hands and clasping them in a surprisingly tight grip. 'I'm your aunt Isabella. Your father was my younger brother.'

'Oh…' Annis looked down at their hands uneasily. The woman might be her blood relative, but according to Margery she'd also insulted her mother. 'This is a surprise.'

'I told my mother about our meeting in London,' Oliver Hawksby explained, his voice tight as he caught her eye, as if he knew how she felt about him. 'Then we heard of your marriage to Sir Bennet and wanted to offer our congratulations.'

'I decided our family quarrel had gone on for far too long, and considering recent events… I wish it had never happened. We went to see Cariscombe before coming here and it broke my heart to see it in such a state. Your father and I were very close as children.' Her aunt's voice wavered. 'If you can forgive me, I'd like us to move on.'

Annis exchanged a swift glance with Lady Joan, still hesitating. The offer seemed too good to be true. Surely if it were so easy to set a feud aside, her father would have done it years ago? 'But I thought you didn't approve of my mother?'

She gave a jolt, taken aback by the sudden look of hatred on the other woman's face, though it was there and gone so quickly she wondered if she'd imagined it. In truth, she must have. Surely this small, stooped old woman could never have looked so frightening…

'I think that might have had something to do with it.' Oliver Hawksby stepped forward. 'Though in truth, I was never quite sure what happened. However, if we can set it aside…' He gave a conciliatory smile. 'May I call you cousin?'

Annis stiffened, a prickle of unease snaking down her

spine, though she kept her smile in place. A little old lady she might be able to accept, but this man…he was still their chief suspect for the attack.

'Cousin.' She narrowed her eyes at the word. 'This is most ironic. My husband is away, visiting you in Taunton.'

'Sir Bennet?' He looked confused. 'Why would he be visiting us?'

She hesitated, wondering how honest to be. Ben had said he would be blunt, so why shouldn't she do the same? 'He wanted to discuss the attack on Cariscombe. We're still searching for who was behind it.'

'So I understand, but what does that have to do with me?'

'You were at Cariscombe very soon afterwards, the morning after it happened, in fact. At Hatfield House, you told Isolde it was because you'd heard rumours that my mother might be in danger.' She looked him straight in the eye. 'I'd like to know who you heard those rumours from.'

'That would have been me.' His mother answered before he could. 'I make a point of keeping abreast of any news from Cariscombe. I heard there was malicious gossip about your mother so I told Oliver.'

'I see.' Annis frowned. 'But who told you these rumours?'

'Perhaps we might discuss the matter further after dinner.' Her aunt laid a hand on her arm again. 'Forgive me, but it's been a long journey and I'm weary.'

'My apologies, it can wait.' She turned to Lady Joan enquiringly. 'Dinner?'

'Yes. I invited your aunt and cousin to dine with us this evening.' Her new mother-in-law looked awkward. 'And then of course they must stay for the night.'

Annis stared back at her with a mixture of surprise and horror. It was one thing to offer a meal, but a bedchamber? After everything Ben had said? But she could hardly protest in front of them.

'Unless it's inconvenient, that is?' Her aunt looked up at her through watery eyes, her fingernails digging into her wrists.

'Of course not.' Annis smiled tightly. 'We'd be honoured if you would stay.'

'Thank you, cousin.' Oliver bowed his head, though not before she noticed a pleased look in his eyes.

'*Why* did you invite them to stay?' Annis waylaid Lady Joan in the upstairs gallery ten minutes later, pulling her into an empty bedchamber while her cousin and aunt drank wine by the fireside. 'What were you thinking? Ben said we ought to be careful.'

'What else could I do?' Lady Joan protested. 'They're your family and they've been travelling. Honour demands that we offer them shelter.'

'*Honour?*' Annis almost spat the word. 'That man is probably responsible for the attack on my mother! What honour did he show then?'

'We still don't know for certain he was involved.' Lady Joan clucked her tongue. 'He's just a boy.'

'It still wasn't your place to invite them! I'm the lady of the house now.'

For a moment, she thought that Lady Joan was about to argue, before her chin dipped and she looked away. 'You're right. I should have consulted with you. Old habits die hard, but it won't happen again.'

'Thank you.' Annis chewed the inside of her cheek, still shaken. 'We can't withdraw the offer now, but we'll have to be extremely careful. George should sleep in your bedchamber tonight and make sure you keep the door bolted. I also want men posted in the gallery and hall. I don't care how suspicious it makes us look.'

Lady Joan's expression shifted to one of alarm. 'But surely you don't think he would try anything here?'

'I don't know what to think, but I won't be caught by surprise again. I'm not taking any chances, especially with George in the house.'

'I had no idea...' Lady Joan started towards the door. 'I'll go and fetch him now. I won't let him out of my sight.'

Annis's shoulders sagged as she went to stand beside a window that looked out towards the woods. The sky outside was already darkening, casting an inky veil over the land. If Ben had gone to visit the Earl of Newcastleton before carrying on to Taunton then he would have taken a different route to the Hawksbys, which meant it was unlikely he would have passed them on the road. He would have arrived at their house to find it empty, but at least that meant he wouldn't be far behind. Only, considering the encroaching darkness, the possibility of him returning tonight seemed unlikely.

She felt a tug on her consciousness, an image of a noose flashing into her mind. It was the same noose she'd envisioned on the day the mob had come for her mother, encircling the house and everyone inside it.

Quickly, she pushed the image from her mind, wrapping her arms around herself for comfort. She wished they were Ben's arms instead, but surely it wouldn't be long before he returned. Then they would confront her cousin together. She just hoped she survived until then.

Chapter Twenty-Four

Bennet galloped along the forest road, his men on either side of him, the rhythmic thump of their hoof beats loud in the still morning air. He'd hoped they would reach Draycote the night before, but darkness had finally forced them to stop and make camp; as much as he'd wanted to ride on, he couldn't risk his men's safety. Now they were only a few miles away, but he couldn't shake a persistent sense of foreboding, as if he needed to get home as quickly as possible.

His journey had been both a success and a complete waste of time. The Justice of the Peace had talked a great deal, though he appeared to know less about the attack than Ben did, while the Earl of Newcastleton had deigned to give him an audience, but had been even more unpleasant than Isolde had described: rude, haughty and in no mood to be reminded about the existence of his 'common' stepmother. He'd launched into a vicious tirade on her character, one that had only abated once Ben had told him about the mob and their accusations. Then the earl's obvious horror, not at the attack itself, but at the possibility of people remembering his own connection to Cariscombe, had been so convincing that Ben had departed soon afterwards, convinced he'd played no part in it. Which had only left Hawksby, who, a servant had informed him on his arrival in Taunton, was away visiting a relative—words that had made him ride home faster than ever.

At last, he rounded the final bend in the road and there was Draycote Manor, looking perfectly solid and serene. The tightness in his chest eased slightly. Somehow he'd been afraid it would look like Cariscombe.

Looking up, he saw a figure on the narrow walkway above the east gable window, their long hair glowing scarlet in the morning sunshine, billowing like a flag welcoming him home. *Annis*.

The despondency he'd felt at their parting had eased over the past couple of days. The long ride had given him plenty of time to think—to realise how unfair and self-centred he'd been, so carried away with his own vision of a future together that he hadn't stopped to consider how much he would be asking her to give up. It was only natural that she'd been upset. Hadn't she told him how much she wanted to return to Cariscombe? It had been the very condition she'd placed on agreeing to go to Hatfield with him in the first place! Of course she wanted her home. He of all people ought to be able to understand that.

He'd asked for too much, too quickly, and the first thing he needed to do when he got back was tell her so. He could only hope that she'd forgive him and give him another chance to take things slower, but even if she didn't he wasn't going to run away again, not from his feelings *or* from Draycote. Annis was right, it was time to put aside his guilt over Eleanor and stop punishing himself. He would stay and be a good father and good son and, hopefully, one day, a good husband too. He'd wait for Annis, for ever if he had to, but in the meantime he'd keep his word and let her go, no matter how much it hurt.

His heart thumped with relief as she lifted a hand and waved. That looked promising. It didn't seem like the action of a person who wanted nothing more to do with him. Maybe there was still hope... That was when he noticed the other person standing behind her. His mother? No. The figure was small and hunched. The surreptitious way they were moving struck him as odd too, as if they were trying to creep up on Annis unawares, and there was something in their hand, something that glittered in the sunshine. His blood ran cold at the sight, and his wife was too busy waving at him to notice.

'Annis!' he called out, but it was too late. The figure behind her was already closing in, lifting their hands towards her throat.

Annis leaned forward over the low wall that ran around the edge of the balcony, relief flooding through her as Ben galloped up the road towards the house. He was home, *almost* home anyway. Now they could confront Oliver Hawksby, discover what had happened at Cariscombe once and for all, and then...she smiled...then they would do what he'd wanted and discuss their future together.

She stopped waving as his expression changed abruptly, turning to one of alarm. What was the matter? She frowned, feeling the hairs on the back of her neck stand on end. And now he was gesturing too, pointing to something behind her...

She turned just as a blade swept through the air, missing her throat by an inch.

Panic surged through her as she gave a startled scream and reacted instinctively, grabbing her assailant's wrist and twisting hard until she heard the knife fall to the ground with a clatter. Unfortunately, instead of running away, she looked up to see who it was, giving her aunt an opportunity to grasp the back of her neck and smash her forehead against the stone wall.

'Ah!' Pain shot through her skull, making her stagger so hard she had to grab the sides of the wall to stop herself from toppling from the roof. After watching Oliver and his men leave the house and go to the stables, she'd thought that she was safe on the balcony. She'd even counted the number of his retainers to be sure, but now she realised she'd been paying attention to the wrong Hawksby. The old woman had seemed so frail the previous evening, she'd even had to be carried upstairs to a bedchamber, but it had obviously all been an act. She'd dangerously misjudged the old woman's strength—the strength of her hatred too.

Pain brought with it a sudden, stark clarity, making her gasp with horror and sudden, terrible understanding. None of this had ever been about her inheritance. It was deeper and darker than that. It was hatred, pure and simple and terrifying.

'You arranged the attack on Cariscombe?' She pushed the words past her lips, though her tongue felt thick in her mouth and the world seemed to be spinning around her. 'You killed my mother?'

'Yes!' The answer was almost gleeful, a venomous rasp. 'It wasn't hard. Some men will do anything for money.'

'Including your son?'

'Pah! He had nothing to do with it and didn't know my plans. I only sent him there because, that way, if either you or your mother had survived, he would have brought you to me, thinking I'd protect you.'

'But why?' Annis could taste blood in her mouth now. 'Why hate us so much?'

'Because of what your mother did to my brother! She bewitched him, just like she did her first husband.'

'She didn't do anything! My parents loved each other.'

'He was a fool. Soiling our family name with her and then *you*! When I heard he was dead, I knew it was time to put things right. Oliver should be the owner of Cariscombe, not you!'

'You won't get away with this. You'll be punished!' Annis tried to fling herself backwards, but the pain in her head was too disorienting. Meanwhile, the old woman's hands were surprisingly strong, pushing between her shoulder blades, forcing her surely but steadily over the edge of the wall.

'Help!' she cried out, clawing her fingertips against the stone, but it was too smooth. She couldn't get a purchase and she could already feel her body tilting precariously over the edge of the wall. The ground was looming ahead of her and there was nothing she could do to stop herself from falling, nobody to rescue her, unless… She caught her breath as she caught a glimpse of movement out of the corner of her eye. A shadow seemed to be detaching itself from one of the chimneys and was moving towards them.

'You should be begging me for mercy.' Her aunt hissed in her ear.

'I'm not the one attacking my own flesh and blood, *aunt*!'

'Don't you dare call me that!'

The shadow moved so fast, it was a blur, launching itself towards the old woman. Quickly, Annis pressed her knees against the wall, bracing herself as it collided with both of them. And then the pressure against her back was gone. She could hear sounds of a struggle as she pulled herself upright and saw...

'No!' Annis flung herself forward as the two women toppled together over the side of the wall, catching hold of Margery's arm as she grasped at the parapet. From below, she heard a hoarse scream followed by a hollow thud, but she didn't look, keeping her eyes fixed on those of her old nurse as she held desperately onto her wrists.

'Let me go!' Margery called up to her. 'I'm too heavy. We'll both fall.'

'Then we'll both fall.' Annis gritted her teeth, holding on with every ounce of her strength. 'I'm not letting you go.'

'You have to!'

'No!' She screamed with a combination of pain and desperation. To her horror, she could feel Margery slipping away, and there was nothing else she could do. Her muscles were burning, her arms felt as though they were being wrenched from her shoulders and she could feel her toes lifting up from the floor. A few more seconds and Margery was right, they would both go over.

And then another pair of hands reached over the wall beside her, grabbing hold of Margery's shoulders and heaving her back onto the roof as if she weighed nothing more than a bag of flour.

'Annis?' Ben spun around, catching her as she collapsed into a breathless heap. 'Are you injured? Did she hurt you? I saw a knife.'

'It missed.' She coiled her arms around his neck and pressed her face into his chest as he laid his cheek against the top of her head, his heart hammering so hard she could feel it through his tunic.

From her rescuer...

...To her husband?

When a braying mob attacks her home in the night, heiress Annis Flemming seeks shelter with her enigmatic neighbor Sir Bennet Thorne. With her life at risk, Ben escorts her to safety at Henry VIII's Hatfield House. Though they grow closer on the journey, Annis's distrust of men makes her wary, and Ben still grieves for his late wife. But when they realize the threat has followed them, there's only one means of true protection—marriage!

CATEGORY: **HISTORICAL**

$7.99 U.S./$8.99 CAN.

ISBN-13: 978-1-335-59616-1

50799

9 781335 596161

Your romantic escape to the past.

HARLEQUIN
HISTORICAL

harlequin.com

'Thank goodness.' His voice was rough.

'How did you get up here so quickly?'

'There was no other choice.' He was holding her so tight, it almost hurt. 'I thought I was going to lose you. I've never run so fast in my life.'

'It was her all along. My aunt. She was the one behind everything. Oliver really thought he was there to help.' She closed her eyes, overcome with emotion for a moment.

'It's all right. We're all right. It's all over now.'

'But what were you doing here?' She turned towards Margery. 'I thought you said you wouldn't leave Cariscombe?'

'I didn't intend to, but she and her son came to visit yesterday before they came here. I watched them through the trees and saw her face. I've never seen such a malevolent look. That's when I knew she was the one responsible. So, when they carried on here, I followed and kept out of sight. People rarely notice old women, let alone pay any attention to them. I had a feeling that something terrible might happen.'

'So you followed her up here?'

'Yes, although she was faster up the stairs than I expected. I arrived just after you knocked the knife from her hand.' A faintly guilty expression passed over her face. 'Maybe I should have intervened sooner, but I wanted to hear her confess.'

'You what?' Ben sounded angry. 'You mean you just stood and listened while she tried to push Annis over the wall?'

'It wasn't for long.'

'The main thing is that I'm all right.' Annis wrapped her arms tighter around Ben when he looked like arguing some more.

'Mmm…' He frowned. 'Come on, we need to clean your injury.'

'What injury?' Annis touched a hand to her forehead, surprised to find it came away bloody. Was it her blood? She supposed it had to be. And why were her limbs shaking?

'Ben…' She lifted a hand to his shoulder to stop herself from tumbling sideways, catching a glimpse of her aunt's knife on the ground as she did so. A memory of the blade swiping through the air close to her face flashed into her mind before she promptly fainted.

'Ow!' Annis yelped, opening her eyes with a jolt to find herself lying down in bed, and Ben leaning over her, smoothing a damp cloth across her forehead.

'Sorry, but I need to clean the wound. There.' He pulled the cloth away. 'Now don't try and move just yet. You've had a bad fright and you need some rest.'

'Later.' She ignored him, heaving herself up to a sitting position. 'I want to know what's happening first.'

'It's all being dealt with.'

'What about Oliver?'

He grimaced. 'He's downstairs, in shock. He and his men were in the stables when it happened so thankfully none of them were witnesses to his mother's death. But as you'd expect, he's very upset.'

'What have you told him?'

'So far, just that she fell.' He spread his hands out. 'It's up to you what else we say.'

'You should tell him the truth.' Margery's voice came from a corner of the room, her tone blunt. 'He ought to know what his mother was capable of and that he has a man who murdered your mother and tried to murder you in his household, loyal to his mother and not to him, whom he will need to weed out and bring to justice.'

'I feel that telling him about his mother's actions will only make his grief worse, but I suppose we don't really have a choice.' Annis sighed heavily. 'In the end, though, he's my cousin—if he doesn't hate me too much after this then maybe we really can put this feud behind us. It would be nice to have some family.'

'If that's what you want.' Ben laced their fingers together. 'In that case, I will tell him the truth, and warn him that his retainers should be thoroughly investigated, but I'll go gently on him.'

'Thank you. And, Margery?' Annis called again as her old nurse started towards the door. 'Now that we know what happened, you don't have to live in the woods any more. You could stay here with me.'

'You mean, serve you as I served your mother?' The old nurse stopped in the doorway and sighed. 'Well, I suppose she would have wanted me to take care of you.'

'I think that was a yes.' Ben lifted an eyebrow. 'Now I'd better go down and speak to Oliver in private. After that, I think he'll want to leave as soon as possible. Will you get some rest?'

'I'll try. And then maybe we can continue our talk from the other morning?'

He opened his lips to reply, his gaze turning sombre, just as George came running into the room.

'You're back!' He flung himself against his father's legs.

'I am.' Ben crouched down, enveloping him in a hug.

'Are you staying this time?'

'For as long as you want me, but right now I have a job for

you. An important one. I have to go downstairs and speak to someone. Will you look after Annis for me?'

'Of course.' George leapt up onto the bed beside her. 'Good boy.'

'It was my fault.'

'What do you mean?' Ben stood beside his mother in the shadow of the porch as a devastated but grimly determined Oliver and his men rode away. Her expression was tense, her brows drawn so tight they met together in the centre of her forehead.

'I said they could stay here last night. I shouldn't have done that.'

'No, you shouldn't have.' He put a hand on her shoulder. 'But in a way, I'm glad that you did. At least now we know who our enemy was.'

'It's just so horrible. How could anybody hate so much? To send a mob in cold blood?' His mother shook her head. 'But at least it's almost all over now.'

He nodded silently, turning his face in the direction of Cariscombe. Whatever dark clouds had hung over the house were finally dissipating, letting the sunlight shine through again. Now that they finally knew the truth, and Oliver was tying up that last loose end, he and Annis could stop looking over their shoulders and start living again. They could move on, either apart or together, depending on what she wanted.

'I like her.' His mother sounded as if she were saying the words under protest.

'Annis?' He twisted his head in surprise. 'So do I.'

'She's stubborn and opinionated.'

'I thought you just said you liked her?'

'I do. I mean those things in a good way. They show she has spirit. She'll be good for you and George.'

'*If* she stays. The truth is, I don't know if she will, I promised her she could live wherever she wished.'

'Ah.' To his surprise, his mother didn't comment.

'But I'll be here, no matter what happens. This is my home.'

'Well, if she's shown you that, I like her even more.'

Chapter Twenty-Five

Annis pulled gently on her reins, coming to a halt beside the sycamore tree where she and Ben had first met just one short month before, her gaze fixed on the ruins ahead. It was the day after they'd discovered the truth about her aunt. She'd felt an instinctive urge to come back to the start, to make certain the fog around her had cleared completely.

'There it is…' she murmured, gazing at Cariscombe in the distance. 'It's not a shock any more, but it's still shocking to see it like this, if that makes sense?'

'Completely.' Ben stopped beside her. 'It's your home. You love it here. I should never have asked you to give it up.'

'I do love it.' She wrenched her gaze away to look at him instead. 'Thank you for understanding.'

'I told you, Annis, I love you. That won't change whether we live together or apart. I want to find a way to make this marriage work, but it's up to you. I want you to do what you want.'

'What *I* want…' she repeated, considering the words. 'I thought I knew what I wanted. My mother raised me to be mistress of this place on my own. She thought she was giving me a better life that way. So when you asked me to stay with you the other morning, I panicked. I felt like I'd be letting her down if I just gave up on that.'

'I know. I was wrong to rush you.'

'But I was also wrong to react the way I did. I'm sorry if it brought back bad memories for you. I didn't mean to hurt you like that.' She slid her feet out of the stirrups and dismounted. 'And I realised something while you were away. It doesn't matter where I live. I can still be the woman my mother raised me to be. So what I want is to stay at Draycote Manor, with you.'

'Are you certain?' He dismounted too, coming to stand beside her.

'Yes.' She lifted an eyebrow. 'Unless you want me to leave now that nobody's trying to kill me?'

'Never.' He reached for her hand. 'I just want you to be happy.'

'I already am.' She wrapped her fingers around his, squeezing gently. 'I think, in the end, that's what my mother wanted most of all. So it's time for me to let Cariscombe go. My father always said the building had outlived its time. It was a refuge for my mother, but I don't want to hide from the world like she did. I want to remember it as it was. My parents too. When I think of them, I want to think of them here, walking in the orchard.' She smiled coyly. 'Besides, we can still visit. We can bring our own children here one day.'

'Our own children?' He gave an audible intake of breath. 'Does that mean what I think it means?'

'That I want a real marriage too?' She nodded. 'As for what makes me happy, I'm looking at him.'

'Good.' He lifted her fingers to his lips. 'Because you should know that I consider your happiness my primary duty in life from now on.'

'Are you certain you won't miss life at Hatfield House?'

'I'll miss the Prince and Richard, but they'll manage without me.' His gaze slipped past her shoulder. 'You know, this spot looks familiar.'

'Why do you think I stopped here? It's where we first met.' She laughed and pulled him towards one of the sycamores. 'This was always the best one for climbing. Trust me, I spent years testing them all.'

'I think I fell in love with you that first day.'

She turned around, pressing herself back against the trunk. 'Didn't I threaten to attack you with a stick?'

'Yes, but you didn't.'

'Did I look *very* frightening?'

'You looked like nobody I'd ever met before. You still do.' He leaned forward, capturing her lips in a long, deep kiss. 'I love you, Annis.'

'I know,' she answered when they finally broke apart, touching her nose to his with a happy smile. 'I love you too.'

* * * * *

*If you loved this story,
you're sure to love more of
Jenni Fletcher's Historical romances*

A Marriage Made in Secret
"The Christmas Runaway"
in Snow-Kissed Proposals
The Highlander's Tactical Marriage
Cinderella's Deal with the Colonel

*Why not pick up her
Regency Belles of Bath miniseries?*

An Unconventional Countess
Unexpectedly Wed to the Officer
The Duke's Runaway Bride
The Shopgirl's Forbidden Love

HARLEQUIN
Reader Service

Enjoyed your book?

Try the perfect subscription for Romance readers and get more great books like this delivered right to your door.

See why over 10+ million readers have tried Harlequin Reader Service.

Start with a Free Welcome Collection with free books and a gift—valued over $20.

Choose any series in print or ebook. See website for details and order today:

TryReaderService.com/subscriptions